THE FALL OF ANGELS TRILOGY

Branded

Forsaken

Vindicated

Afterlife: the Novelette Companion to Vindicated

Also by Keary Taylor

THE EDEN TRILOGY

The Bane

The Human

The Eve

The Raid (an Eden short story)

The Ashes (an Eden prequel)

What I Didn't Say

THE McCAIN SAGA

Ever After Drake

Moments of Julian

Depths of Lake

Playing it Kale

For my beautiful little family.

"'For such a falling short, and for no crime,
We all are lost, and suffer only this:
Hopeless, we live forever in desire.'
When I heard this, great sorrow seized my heart,
For I saw men of great distinction there
Hovering in Limbo at the edge of Hell."

-Dante, Inferno

CHAPTER ONE

JESSICA

She stared back at me, her eyes wide with searching, looking for the answers to the question she didn't even know how to form. Her skin glowed in a way that seemed almost unnatural. It was almost as if there were a million tiny fireflies glowing from within. Her skin was so flawless it was unnerving.

I searched my face, looking for something. What was it that was so different? My eyes were the same hazel; the shape of my face wasn't any different. But why did my own reflection terrify me so much? I felt like I didn't even know myself anymore. Who was that person in the mirror? That wasn't the same Jessica I'd seen just a few months previous.

I'd changed so much in the last four months. I'd gone from my normal, ordinary self, to a skeleton with sunken eyes, to this thing that was nearly radiant.

What was happening to me?

"Jessica?"

Alex's voice jarred me from my tangled thoughts.

I glanced once more at my reflection in the mirror, swallowing hard. "Yeah?" I called as I pulled my tank top over my head, glancing over my shoulder briefly at the wings that spanned my back. I stepped out of my bathroom, looking for Alex.

"Have you seen my green T-shirt?" he called from his bedroom.

"Second drawer down," I said as I stepped into his room. I froze as I did.

I hated the way my heart leapt into my throat, the way I felt paralyzed in fear. It was hard not to recall everything the wings sprouting out of Alex's back implicated though. The memory of every trial, every brand pressed into my neck, the gleam of Cole's black eyes flashed through my head. But this was Alex. I had no reason to ever be afraid of him.

"Oh yeah," he said as he pulled it out of the drawer. "Thanks."

He turned toward me, the wings suddenly gone, and pulled the shirt over his head. A smile pulled at his lips as his eyes finally met mine. I hoped the traces of fear were gone from my face. I'd vowed Alex would never know the fright that could be invoked in me at the sight of the wings. "Morning," he said in a low voice as he pulled me to him, wrapping his arms around my waist.

"Morning," I said with a smile back. My lips found his and my blood felt as if it had turned electric and my body hummed. "Oh, no," I said as I shook my head and pulled away. "I have to get going. I'm running late. You're way too distracting."

Alex gave a sly smile but backed away a step. He grabbed his leather wristband and snapped it on before he put his phone and wallet into the pocket of his khaki shorts.

"So, you're going to frost the cake now and have it ready by the time we get back this afternoon, right?" I asked as I walked out of the room and started up the stairs. Alex followed behind me.

"Yep," he answered. "Lime green and hot pink, right?"

"Yes sir," I said as I grabbed my purse off of the hook by the front door. "We'll be back at two."

"I'll be ready," he said with a smile. He pressed a quick kiss to my lips as I opened the door that led to the garage. "Love you."

"I love you too," I said, feeling my insides quiver. Before I let myself become any later, I stepped out the door and closed it behind me.

I slipped into the GTO and tossed my purse into the passenger seat. I carefully backed out and pulled onto the road.

It had been nearly four months since Alex had made the trade that had saved my life. We'd seen no sign of Cole since he'd left that awful night. Life almost seemed normal. Besides the fact that Alex was now an angel and besides the fact that I couldn't figure out what was different about me. It was almost like things hadn't changed. Like the whole impossible thing had never happened.

Some things hadn't changed. That was the problem though.

I pushed that thought away and just focused on the road before me. The sun glared on my windshield, the day already warming in the July air. Summer was here in full force, and I loved it. It had always been my favorite season.

I pulled into the parking lot of the athletic center and joined the small crowd that walked into the building. Emily's class was growing quickly. While there had only been six or so of us in the beginning, we were pushing over twenty now. Emily was gaining a reputation for being the best yoga instructor in the area.

"Hey," I greeted her as I helped her pull the bin of mats out of the storage room.

"Hey," she said, her voice almost sad sounding.

"You okay?" I asked her, hauling the bin out.

"Yeah," she said, forcing a smile and giving a little nod.

I knew she was lying to me but didn't get a chance to push it further as class got underway. We started with a set of breathing exercises.

Emily had been different lately. She was normally one of the most upbeat people I knew and could nearly blind you with her smile. But lately she seemed almost…hollow. Fake. Something was wrong, but she wouldn't talk. All I could ever get was, "I'm fine. I'm just feeling a little off today." But she'd been *off* for the last month or so.

We fell into the normal routine of building flexibility and endurance. The class moved in unison, moving in a wave of ups and downs of fluid movement. I slowly moved myself toward another female student. I whispered to her, hiding my face from Emily with my unruly hair. The other girl smiled and whispered to the guy next to her. I watched as my words spread around the room, all without Emily noticing a thing.

As the class started coming to a close someone switched the lights off. We lay on our backs, eyes closed, palms facing the ceiling, each supposedly concentrating on our breathing.

"Happy birthday to you," someone started singing. Other voices instantly joined in. "Happy birthday to you!" more voices chimed in, including my own. "Happy birthday, dear Emily!" By now the entire room was singing as we lay in the dark. "Happy birthday to you!"

I heard Emily chuckle, a real sounding one. "Jessica," she said with a growl.

"Happy birthday, Emily," I said through the dark.

"Thanks everyone," she said with a chuckle. "Class dismissed."

Everyone got up and the mats and blocks were

quickly put away. I stayed behind, helping to put everything back in its place.

"So you remembered, huh?" she teased as we dragged the bins back into the storage room.

"Of course," I laughed. "What kind of a best friend would I be if I forgot your birthday?"

"Thanks," she said with a slight sigh as we walked back into the main room. "You're about the only one that would remember it, or have reason to remember it."

"Hey," I said, my voice sympathetic but stern. "You can't think like that. What good is it going to do?"

She gave me a sad smile before closing the gap between us and giving me a tight hug. "Thanks, Jessica."

"Now come on," I said as she let me go and we started toward the door. "We need to get some shopping done. Forget showering."

Emily chuckled. "Great. Now I'll *really* repel the men."

I just shook my head and dragged her into the GTO.

The mall was busy with people just like us, girls just hanging out and going shopping. Yet none of these other girls had brands in the back of their necks and wings raised into the flesh of their skin like we did. For that reason alone, Emily would forever be my best friend. She was the only one who could understand the horror that had been most of my existence.

Emily dragged me into her favorite store and started rummaging through the shoes. If there was one thing that could bring Emily out of a bad mood, it was shopping. I started looking through them too, pausing on a pair of bright red stilettos, a sly smile coming to my face as I wondered what Alex would think of them.

"So there's this guy at my work I think you should ask out," I said as we moved from one stack of shoes to the next. "I think you two would really get along well."

"The one that was ogling you when I picked you up last week?" she asked as she pulled the lid off of a box. "I'm not so sure I want to try and compete for someone's attention. Just look at you, no wonder he was drooling all over you."

"What?" I said, taken aback. "Look at nothing. I'm about as ordinary looking as it gets."

"You did *not* just call yourself ordinary looking," Emily said as she gave me a look like I was stupid. When I didn't respond she rolled her eyes and grabbed me by the shoulders. She wheeled me to a floor length mirror and made me look at myself.

"Seriously, how could you ever call yourself plain looking?" Emily demanded as she folded her arms across her chest. "Ever since the whole Cole incident and you nearly dying thing, I can hardly look at you. You look more like *them* than us anymore."

"Them?" I asked, my brow furrowing.

"Alex and Cole," she said as she raised her eyebrows, again questioning my intelligence. "Do you seriously not see it?"

"I don't know what you're talking about," I said as I looked back at myself in the mirror. Of course I was lying, but it was too terrifying to admit the truth to myself.

"Something's different about you, Jessica," she said as she looked around to make sure no one was listening. If they had been she probably would have told them off for eavesdropping. That was Emily. "I don't know what it is, but you're even more different than we were before."

I didn't want to admit it, but she was right. There was something different. Even with everything Emily had gone through, I felt different from even her. I didn't feel like I fit in anywhere, except with Alex. He was home; he was everything that was right with my world.

"Whatever you say," I said as I turned from the mirror. Emily just shook her head and went back to her shopping. I swallowed hard, my stomach twisted into tight knots.

We came out of the store with Emily having nearly maxed out her credit card and too many bags. Emily had a bad spending habit for the amount of money she actually brought in.

"So I've been thinking, maybe I should ask that guy…"

I didn't hear the rest of what Emily said as I looked ahead and saw a guy glance at me and duck into a store. My heart leapt into my throat as dark eyes peered at me from under a fringe dark shaggy hair. My knees nearly buckled.

"Are you okay?" Emily said as she touched my arm.

"No," I said as I took deliberate steps toward the store. "No, it can't be him."

"What are you talking about?" Emily said as she hurried to catch up with me.

"He is *not* coming back here," I said through clenched teeth as I stepped through the doors of the store. A figure in a nice white shirt hugged the back of the store, facing away from me. The collar stood up enough it covered the mark that I knew would be there.

Anger surged in my system as I weaved through the clothing racks toward him. I didn't know where this surge of confidence and anger had come from but I didn't care.

"What are you doing here?!" I demanded as I grabbed his shoulder and turned him toward me. The face that glared at me in confusion was nowhere close to the one I had expected to find.

"What the…?" the guy demanded as he glared at me.

"Sorry," I said as I shook my head and took a step back. "I thought you were someone else."

The guys face relaxed and a small smile tugged on his face. "I can be whoever you want me to be," he said arrogantly.

I just rolled my eyes at him and turned to walk out of the store. A confused and slightly annoyed looking Emily followed me out.

"You want to explain to me what the heck that was about?" she demanded, following me as I headed toward the doors.

"Not really," I sighed as I stepped outside and took a deep breath. It was a relief to be outdoors. I felt like the walls and all the people it contained were pressing in on me.

"You thought it was Cole, didn't you?" she demanded as she indicated for me to sit next to her on a bench.

"Fine! Yeah, I thought it was Cole."

"And just what did you plan on doing if it was him?"

"I don't know!" I spat. "Back off."

It caught Emily off guard to hear me speak so harshly. I never talked like that. "Sorry," she said quieter. "I didn't mean to jump on your back for no reason. I've just been, I don't know."

I knew what she meant. It was actually kind of

nice to hear her acknowledge it. Her normally sunshiny personality had taken a damper. And she occasionally snapped like she did just now. I hadn't pressed her on the issue, figuring if she wanted to tell me she would. Emily usually wasn't one to hold things back.

"It's okay," I said as I sat next to her. A few teenagers walked out the doors, laughing and making fun of one of the guys in the group for liking another of the girls. "Sorry I snapped at you."

We were quiet for a moment before Emily spoke up. "Can I ask you something? You don't have to tell me if you don't want. I know it's kind of personal."

"What?" I asked.

"What happened with Cole, when he took you and you were so sick? And why did he come after you?"

I was taken aback by her question. Emily already knew so much about the whole messed up angel situation, it was strange she didn't know a lot about what happened with Cole, other than that he had been the leader of the condemned, black eyed angels. She had never asked what had happened and I wasn't exactly dying to tell my story of dying.

"You don't have to tell me if you don't want. I just want to understand what happened better. I should have been there for you more. I'm the only person that could understand even a little bit of what was going on, and I kind of shut you out. And honestly,

I'm morbidly curious," she said with a small smile.

I didn't answer right away, thinking about the answers to her questions. "I don't think he really knew why he came after me. He said he saw me at a trial and that he just had to have me. Maybe it was just the fact that I was alive, I don't know. It doesn't seem like a good enough reason to draw him out into the world of the living."

"That doesn't make any sense. He just had to have you? I bet Cole was lying to you about that. I bet there was a real reason."

I considered this for a moment. "That would make sense. He lied about a lot of things. Cole made me believe a lot of things that weren't true. He made me think Alex had found another woman, that Sal really did commit suicide. It was awful. He had me locked up in this room with no windows.

"And then he had the gall to ask me to be his queen of the condemned," I said disgustedly as I stared out at the grass in front of me.

"What?" she asked, confused.

My stomach knotted as I recalled the conversation with Cole. "Cole told me I was dying, which was actually the truth. He had me pretty much convinced I would be getting branded for myself. He said he could make the afterlife not as bad as it could be for me. He said he could even gain me a position on the council. All I had to do was agree to be his. He even had the nerve to tell me that 'hell's not that bad.'"

A shudder worked its way up my spine as I recalled how Cole had touched me after that horrific conversation, the way he made me want it in such a delusional and twisted way. It took me a moment to realize that Emily had not said anything in response to my revelations.

I glanced in her direction. She seemed to be in deep thought, as if heavily pondering over the things I had just told her.

"Cole is an awful man," I said, my voice coming out a little more harshly than I intended. "Well, not even a man." I immediately regretted saying this. Even though Alex was as unlike Cole as it was possible to be, they were still the same species, or whatever you classified an angel as.

"I know that," Emily said defensively. "He branded me too for eleven years, don't forget that."

Neither of us said anything for a moment after that. I didn't want to be having this conversation. I didn't want these wretched things to be in my past.

But they were; nothing was going to change that fact.

I glanced at my watch, surprised at how much time had passed already. "I'm sorry. Can we just pretend this conversation didn't happen?"

She was quiet for a moment then nodded her head. "Yeah. I'm sorry I brought it up."

"Why don't we just hang out today? We could go

back to my place and watch a movie and just be bums today."

"That sounds really good actually," she said with a smile. "It sounds like a nice normal day."

I drove Emily back to the athletic center where she picked up her car. We drove together back to the lake. I pushed the button to open the garage and pulled in next to the truck. Emily pulled in behind me.

We opened the front door, finding all of the lights turned off.

"Surprise!"

Alex and Sal popped up from behind the couch. Streamers were streaked through the rafters and balloons were tied everywhere, all in brilliant colors of lime green and hot pink – Emily's favorites.

"Thanks you guys!" Emily said in awe as she took in the decorated living room. I was surprised when her eyes turned red and a tear broke loose onto her cheek. Without saying anything, I wrapped my arms around her. When I stepped away, she wiped the tears and went to give Alex a hug. She knew better than to hug Sal who didn't like to be touched.

"Alex made a cake," Sal said, bouncing where she stood. I was still shocked to see her there. She had only recently started coming out of her house again.

"Well let's see it!" Emily said excitedly, causing Sal's excitement to build until she bounced on the balls of her feet.

We all rushed into the kitchen where, sitting in all its glory, was the cake Alex had made. It was three-tiered and looked like something right off the food channel.

"Wow!" Emily said with something close to a giggle. "You really are amazing when it comes to food, Alex."

"Glad you like it," Alex said with a smile, draping an arm across my shoulders.

It seemed a shame to cut into the beautiful cake, but everyone except Alex dug in after consuming more than our share of hamburgers, potato salad, and soda.

As we ate, my thoughts drifted to a few months previous, to my own birthday.

The weather had been amazing, considering it was still May. I had walked through the door after yoga and found a scene very similar to the one we had just created for Emily. Alex, Sal, and Emily had been there with one surprising addition.

"Dad!" I had exclaimed and bounded across the room, throwing my arms around his neck.

"Hey, Kid," he said as he patted my back, returning my embrace. "Happy birthday."

"I'm so glad to see you, Dad," I said into his neck, squeezing him tighter.

"Ouch," he grimaced, and I immediately released him and stepped back with a sheepish look on my face. "That's quite the grip you've got there."

"Sorry," I apologized as I beamed at everyone in the world that mattered to me.

We'd eaten dinner, cut the cake, and I'd opened all the presents. After Emily walked Sal home, my dad pulled me out onto the back deck.

We sat on the wooden swing Alex had installed only a few weeks before. It was almost completely dark by then, but the last of the evening light reflected on the water in the beautiful way of man and nature.

"I'm really glad you could come out for this, Dad," I said as I glanced over in his direction.

"Me too," he said with a grin and wrapped an arm around my shoulders.

We were both quiet for a while as the last of the daylight faded, the only light to see by coming from the windows. It took me a minute to realize there were a few tears streaming down my father's cheeks.

"Dad," I said in alarm. "What's the matter?"

"Oh, nothing," he said with a sigh and squeezed me a little tighter. "I just didn't think you were going to live to see your sixth birthday at one time. Now here you are, a twenty-one-year-old woman."

"It's thanks to you, Dad," I said quietly as I leaned against him and rested my head on his shoulder.

"I put you through hell for it though," he said, his voice rough sounding.

"It was worth it." I smiled as I sensed Alex

walking around in the house. Worth every second of it, no matter how terrifying it had all been.

He didn't say anything for a while as he composed himself. "I like Alex more than I imagined I would ever like a guy one of my girls would get involved with. But I can't say I'm thrilled at you guys living together like you do."

"It's not like that, Dad," I said, suddenly feeling very uncomfortable. "We haven't done… that."

I felt my dad relax a little bit at my uncomfortable response. "Well, why don't you two just get married? You practically are already."

It took a moment for me to respond to that. "It's complicated." My stomach knotted up.

Thankfully, my dad didn't press the subject any more.

"I told your mother where I was going, Jessica," he said quietly. I felt a rock form in my throat. I tried to swallow it but it didn't go down. "She asked if you were alright, how you were doing."

"And?" my voice came out shaky.

"She'd like to see you. She has a few things to say I think you should hear."

I sat up straight, feeling like all my insides had turned hard. I pressed my lips together tight and shook my head. "I can't talk to her. Not after everything that happened. She was going to have me committed, Dad."

"I know," he said, his voice sounding tight, as if he

was holding back tears again. "But she wants to see you. You're still her daughter."

"Am I?"

My dad didn't say anything for a minute, and I almost felt guilty for my harsh words. "You need to forgive her sometime."

"It's not going to be today," I said, my voice barely more than a whisper. Dad squeezed my shoulders and pressed a kiss to the top of my head.

"Well," he said as he stood up. "I'd better get going."

"Dad," I said as I rolled my eyes. "I don't know why you don't just stay here. The master bedroom is empty."

"I've got to leave really early in the morning," he said as we walked back in the house. "I've got to catch the red-eye flight, so I'm staying down by the airport."

I walked him to the front door. "Thanks again for coming, Dad," I said as I pulled him into a hug.

Just then Alex walked into the room. My father extended his hand and Alex shook it. "It was good to see you again, Alex."

"You too, Denis," Alex said with a smile.

We said goodbye and my father walked out to his rental car.

"Thanks again for all of this, you guys." I was pulled back into the present by Emily's voice. "I'll see you on Friday, right?" she asked me as she headed for the front door.

"Yep, I'll be in class," I answered as I followed her. We said our goodbyes and I closed the door. My eyes froze as I turned, caught by my own reflection in the mirror that hung next to the door. Swallowing hard, I tore my eyes away from myself and went to help Alex clean up.

CHAPTER TWO

JESSICA

The rain pounded the pavement, causing steam to rise from its black surface. It drove in a lot of people who normally might not have come into the bookstore. The flash storm had caught everyone by surprise; no one expected it, since the sky had been blue and sunny just a half hour before.

I watched people from the register, eyeing their movements, watching the way they interacted with things, other people. They seemed so different from myself now. They were so normal. They chatted and laughed with their friends. They picked up books, glanced over them, set them back down. They went about their everyday lives like there was nothing that existed outside of the norm. They knew nothing of angels, death, fear. I felt like a stranger in the human race, like I didn't belong here at all.

I envied them.

And yet, I could never regret the events that had happened in my life. They had brought more love and joy into my existence than I ever would have imagined possible.

"Will that be it for you?" I asked as I took the book from the young woman who came up to the counter.

"Yep," she said as she smiled kindly at me, her teeth perfectly straight from years of braces. It unnerved me that I could tell she had once had them. I shouldn't notice small details like that so easily.

"I've heard great things about this one," I tried to make conversation as I swiped her card. I wanted to feel normal. "The sequel is coming out around Christmas."

People bustled around the store. The crowd was making me uneasy. They were so *loud.* I heard every word they were saying, every intake of breath they took it seemed. Every time they swallowed or blinked it sounded like nails scraping against a chalkboard. I closed my eyes and took a deep breath, trying to block out the noise I didn't want to be hearing. The noise I *shouldn't* be hearing.

"Are you alright, dear?" Rita, my motherly boss asked.

"Yeah," I said a little too quickly, snapping back to the here and now. "I've just got a headache," I lied. I hadn't had a headache for four months, since I was nearly dead in Cole's basement.

"Why don't you go take a break for a little bit?" Rita said, her face kind and warm.

"Okay, thanks," I said as I stepped aside and let her take over the register.

People crowded the store, making me dodge them as I worked my way to the back. I nearly knocked a young woman over, her husband catching her before she fell. I smiled with an apology, swallowing the lump that instantly formed in my throat, and stepped out the back door. I sat on the steps and watched the rain pour onto the gravel just a few feet in front of me. My insides felt all twisted up.

A month or so after everything had happened, I had decided it was time for me to get a job. Alex was plenty willing to provide everything I could ever need, but I needed to feel some independence. I had taken care of myself since I was sixteen. Now that I was twenty-one I wasn't going to revert back. I could take care of myself.

I supposed pride played a large part in my decision to find a job as well.

I had also told Alex that I wouldn't take any money anymore for house sitting since he now lived there and so did I. It felt weird to be getting paid for it.

Downtown Books was located exactly where it said it was, in the heart of downtown Bellingham. I loved the smell of the place, the feel. I loved my boss and the owner, Rita Baker. She was a quiet, kind woman with wild red hair and vibrant green eyes. I had never heard her say a harsh word or treat someone unfairly. She was as much a mother to me as my own was now. Maybe more so.

I heard a car pull into the back parking lot and park next to my GTO. I gave a sigh as I realized who it was.

"Hey, Jessica!" Austin Andrews said with a wide grin as he ran up to the steps to escape the rain.

"Hey, Austin," I said, giving a halfhearted smile back.

"Rita said it's pretty crazy in there. She asked if I could come in and help for a bit."

"It's not really that bad. There's just a lot of people inside 'cause of the rain. Not too many people are actually buying anything," I said, half defending the reason I was sitting outside when Rita felt swamped.

"Yeah, she always panics when there are more than five people in there at a time," Austin joked as he walked up the steps. "You coming inside?"

"I'll be in in a minute," I said as I looked back out into the rain. The door slammed shut behind him.

Austin Andrews was Rita's nephew. He was a nice guy with brown hair and Rita's same green eyes. He wasn't very tall, but it was obvious he spent more than a few hours at the gym. He was easygoing and easy to get along with.

Unfortunately, Austin was a little too overly anxious to be friendly at times. It was plain to see he was interested. He smiled too much at me, always stood a little too close. I didn't think he even realized he was stepping over the boundary just a little too much. He knew about Alex and had met him several times. They seemed to get along well enough. Austin didn't act like he was trying to steal me away; he just wasn't keeping *himself* far enough away.

It was a little annoying, but he was still a friend. I could always use more of those.

The rain started to fade out and within a few minutes it stopped completely. As it did, I went back inside. It would be easier to deal with work without so many people around.

I got back to what I was supposed to be doing. Rita was best at working the cash register. She was friendly and really knew what she was talking about when it came to books. Me, I did a little better keeping the inventory organized and the shelves stocked.

I brought a box of books out from the storage room and started putting them on the shelves. I was putting a few books on the religion shelf when the title caught my eye. *Angels: Heaven's Messengers*. Glancing to make sure no one was watching me, I flipped through the pages.

Less than sixty seconds later, I snapped it shut. No one ever got it right. They all made them out to be wonderful beings with halos and harps that wanted nothing but good for people. No one knew what so many of them were really like.

I rubbed a hand on the back of my neck without thinking about it as I put the book on the shelf. The X on the back of my neck had long faded into a white scar, but it was never going to fade away. It was a permanent part of me, whether I liked it or not.

ALEX

The place needed a lot of work; there was no question about that. The ancient wallpaper was pealing and torn, the carpet was stained. There was a badly cracked window in one of the bedrooms. The entire place smelled just a little off.

"The seller is motivated," the realtor said as we walked back through the kitchen. The man wasn't what I had expected when I had talked to him on the phone. The guy was probably younger than I was. "It's a heck of a deal if you've got a little extra money to put into fixing up."

I nodded as my eyes traveled up, admiring the crown molding. "It's got potential," I said as we walked to the living room.

"So?" he asked, stuffing his hands into his pockets.

I nodded again, looking around one last time. "I'll take it."

A huge grin broke onto his face. "Excellent. I'll call the owner this afternoon and tell her the good news!"

"Thanks, Ryan," I said as I extended my hand and shook his. His palm was sweaty with nerves. I wondered how long he had had his real estate license. I heard his heart hammering with excitement. "I'll give you a call tomorrow so we can get all the legal stuff taken care of."

Ryan thanked me, gave instructions to lock up when I left, then let himself out the door. I stuffed my hands in my pockets and looked around the ancient house again.

My grandfather, Paul Wright, built his empire dealing in real estate. He'd made his first million before he turned thirty and that was even back in his day. The man knew how the market worked, what to invest in and when to get out. He'd had quite the reputation down in California. He'd left me a wide open legacy, passing everything down to me. It was time I started doing something with the knowledge he'd passed on. This house was the start of that. I'd fix it up and rent it out until the economy recovered enough to sell it.

The house just seemed to speak to me. It was nearly one hundred years old. It had so much history to it. I wondered about all the children who had been raised in it, how many couples had called this their home. How many lives had been built here.

My insides knotted up and a lump formed in

my throat.

Pushing those thoughts away, I took one last look around the house and let myself out, locking the door behind me.

My step faltered when I was halfway to my truck as a whispering piqued my ears. The sound was hurried, chaotic. It wasn't the sound of a far off conversation I was overhearing. It was coming from *within* me. The sounds of faraway chuckling caused the hair on the back of my neck to stand on end. The feeling of an ice cold shiver worked its way down my spine.

As I reached my truck, I braced my hands on the hood, my head hanging. The feeling of darkness started creeping from my chest out toward my limbs. The pull into nothingness was becoming a little stronger every day. My un-beating heart felt like it was sucking the life out of every part of my body. My hands started trembling. I'd be angry at myself later for making a dent in the hood.

And before I could even think to fight it, my wings burst out of my back, shredding my shirt.

I'd be grateful later for the fact that this house wasn't in a high density part of town.

I gasped for air, I didn't need it, but it was a natural instinct. My lungs felt squeezed, like they were caving in. My entire body felt like it was collapsing in on itself.

"No," I hissed. "You won't take me."

The sound of my phone ringing made me jump. My eyes grew wide in horror as I lost my concentration and my hands disappeared before my eyes. Shaking my head I dug into my pocket and pulled my phone out, hands again visible.

"Hello?" I said through clenched teeth, my eyes squeezed closed.

"Hey Alex, it's Ted," my lawyer's voice came through on the other end. "Can you meet later this afternoon?"

"Yeah," I said, my voice tight as I struggled to make it work. "I'll be there."

JESSICA

"Sorry," Emily said as she bustled about her small bathroom, prepping her face and hair. "I don't have too much time before I have to leave."

"Where are you going?" I asked as I sat on her bed, watching as she got ready.

"I have a date tonight," she said, staring at herself wide-eyed, applying a generous amount of mascara.

"With the guy you went out with the other night?"

"No, with some guy I met at the coffee shop today," she said as she started back in on her hair. "I may hate working there, but I do meet a lot of hot guys. Oh yeah, did I tell you I have an interview at the University?"

"No," I said as I shook my head.

"A position came open for a new instructor. I really hope I get it. The athletic center barely covers my rent, and I don't know how much longer I can handle my boss at the coffee shop. I would miss the guys though," she said with a little chuckle.

"What's with you and this dating spree?" I asked. Emily had been out with a different guy nearly every night for the last two weeks.

"What? Just because I've got a condemned brand on the back of my neck means I can't date? I'm just sick of hiding away all the time. Besides," she said as she applied some lipstick. "It's not like I can ever let it progress very far. How am I supposed to explain the wings and all? It's not like I can ever actually sleep with any of these guys."

I didn't say anything in response. I wasn't sure what to say to that.

"So," she said as she closed the door slightly. A second later, I started blushing when I realized she was going to the bathroom. "Have you thought any more about what I said? About Cole lying about why he came after you?"

"That's actually the reason I came over." I squirmed where I sat, not wanting to talk about this, but knowing it was going to drive me mad until I understood the situation fully. "I just can't make any sense out of it."

The toilet flushed and a second later I heard

the water as Emily washed her hands. "Well, there's the fact that you're human. There's a starter. Maybe he just wanted that long lost connection." She opened the door and stepped out of the bathroom, leaning against the doorframe. "But then there must be something about you specifically. I went through the trials too, and after discovering that you went through the same thing I did, there must be others out there like us. So it can't be that simple."

"That's really scary to think about," I said honestly, my eyes falling to the floor. "Why *me*?"

"If this was happening now, I'd say there was no question about it," she said. "You're the most unearthly looking human there is on the planet now. But that is only something that's changed recently. Not that you weren't beautiful before," Emily said with an apologetic smile.

"See, it doesn't make sense. What was so different about me, so compelling to him that it drew him out into the world of the living?" Goosebumps washed over my skin as I thought about the reasons, even though I had none.

"I think he was keeping something from you, Jessica. I'm guessing it's kind of a big deal for a dead angel to chase after you into the real world. There's got to be more to this."

My stomach rolled, and my body suddenly felt ice cold.

A honk from outside brought my head back into the real world.

"That must be my date," Emily said, a weird, almost forced smile coming to her lips as she grabbed her purse from off the nightstand. I followed her out to the front step. "Call me if you think of anything. I'm kind of morbidly curious about this now."

I gave a chuckle and Emily gave me a quick hug before she locked the door and bounded into a shiny red sports car.

Ten minutes later, I was back in my apartment, digging through my closet. My fingers closed around the manila folder, and I pulled it out with shaking hands. Enclosed were the drawings I had done when I was younger. I'd been pretty good, but when I realized how much they terrified my mother I'd quit. I hadn't drawn a thing since.

Taking a deep breath, I opened the folder and pulled the pages out.

My mother had been right though. The images of angels, wings, and brands were terrifying. In a beautiful and haunting way.

Even after everything that had happened, I still couldn't help but stop and stare at Cole's beautiful face. His features were stunning in every way. That kind of flawlessness shouldn't be allowed to exist. But perhaps the more evil or good you are, the more beautiful you are made.

Why me? I thought as I touched two fingers to the picture. In a way, I almost wished I could face Cole, just one more time, and ask him the question that was driving me insane.

As I heard the door open and close upstairs, I closed the folder and buried it again.

Alex came down the stairs and pressed a quick kiss to my lips.

"So how did it go today?" I asked, closing my closet door behind me.

"Good," he said, his signature smile beaming from his face. "I told him I'd take it."

"That's awesome!" I said enthusiastically. "I can't wait to see it."

"It needs a lot of work," he said with a chuckle. "I also spoke with my lawyer. How would you feel about taking a little trip?"

"A trip?" I asked, raising one eyebrow.

"Down to the house in southern California?" he said, his smile turning sly as he took my hands in his.

I couldn't help but return the smile. "I'll talk to Rita and see if I can get work off."

"Great!" he said as he pressed a kiss to my lips again then headed back upstairs. "I can't wait for you to see where I grew up."

CHAPTER THREE

JESSICA

It was strange to realize how tied down I was becoming to my life. It almost felt like a real life. Normal. I had a job I had to get time off of; I had someone who counted on me to help her out every day. I had responsibilities. I suddenly felt so old.

But Rita had been just fine giving me the three days off, saying it would give the new girl a chance to really get into the swing of things. Emily had easily agreed to help Sal out and Sal had even seemed alright with the arrangement. Maybe she didn't need me as much as I thought she did.

Alex had pulled out all the stops and wasn't holding anything back. He had arranged for a limo to pick us up from the airport.

"Okay," I said as I shook my head and slid in beside him. "I haven't wanted to ask before, but I have to ask now. Just how much money did your grandparents leave to you?"

Alex chuckled as he pressed the button that sent the privacy screen up between us and the driver. "Does it matter?"

"Of course not," I defended myself. "This is just so weird for me. I don't think of you as this super rich guy, but then I get these little glimpses and realize there is this whole entirely different part of your life I've never really seen."

"A lot has changed in the last year or so," Alex said as he took my hand in his. "It feels like a completely different life."

A strange pang formed in my stomach. I had really changed Alex's life. I'd completely turned it on its head and flipped it around until it didn't even look the same in any way, shape, or form.

"Hey," he said quietly as he placed his hand under my chin and turned my face towards his. "It's better now."

I could only manage a small smile and gave his hand a squeeze.

As we drove through the canyon, my heart started beating a little bit faster. I had been to Alex's home town of Laguna Beach twice before, when I had lived in central California myself. It was where Jason, my ex's, parents lived. I hadn't exactly been received in a warm manner. They had all thought I was a freak. As it turned out, so did their son.

The houses started getting bigger and nicer as we kept driving. Finally we turned into a driveway that was meticulously landscaped with palm trees, shrubs, and flowering bushes. My stomach did a strange quiver of anticipation.

The limo pulled into a circular driveway and stopped in front of the gigantic double wooden doors. I simply marveled at the house before us.

"Welcome to my childhood home," Alex said with a wide smile as he stepped out of the car and held a hand out for me.

It was all white with a clay-colored tiled roof. It was hard to tell how big it truly was, since it was well hidden behind the landscaping, but it looked as if it kept going and going. And to both sides of the house I could see the sandy beach.

"Wow," was all I could say as I followed Alex to the front door. He took out a set of keys and unlocked the door. The driver unloaded our bags, Alex tipped him, and then it was just the two of us.

"Come on," Alex said as he took my hand in his. "I'll show you around."

The entryway we entered into was dominated by a large abstract sculpture made of a mix of bronze and steel. "I always hated that thing. For some reason my grandpa loved it."

"It's...interesting," I said with a chuckle.

We entered into a living room, decorated lavishly, but comfortably. Pictures lined the walls, filled with Alex's face as he grew up. I paused at one, seeing familiar features in the man that looked to be in his thirties.

"That's my dad, Keith," Alex said as he came

to my side.

"I wish I could have met him," I said quietly as I looked into his father's brilliant blue eyes. Another pang struck me in the chest. I missed Alex's blue eyes more than I would ever admit aloud.

"Me too," he said. He gave me a sad little smile and grabbed my hand. He pulled me in a different direction. "Here's the kitchen."

"No wonder you like to cook so much," I chuckled. Any world-class chef would trade his soul for the granite countertops, the huge stainless steel fridge, the stove that had six, seven, eight burners. It made even me drool over it, and I didn't even like to cook.

"Yeah, I spent a lot of time in here," Alex said as he ran a hand over the smooth surface of the refrigerator. "Maybe I'll have to do some remodeling to the kitchen at home. Come on," he said as he took my hand again and pulled me out of the kitchen. "I've got to show you the best part."

As I had been looking at the pictures on the wall in the living room, I hadn't even noticed all the French doors that lined the other wall. They opened up onto a huge balcony.

"Oh my," I breathed as we stepped outside.

A light, warm breeze tussled my hair, the scent of the ocean water filling my nose. The balcony stretched about fifteen feet away from the house, a huge swimming pool beyond that, and past that, a perfectly sandy beach and wide open ocean.

"Why are you living at the house in Washington?" the words slipped out before I even really realized I was saying them.

Alex chuckled and pulled me into his arms. "Because you're not here."

"I think maybe I could consider relocating," I said lightly, unable to take my eyes from the ocean view before me.

"You hate California," he laughed in my ear. "And besides, your life is there. *Our* life is there."

"I don't hate California. But you're right, I would never want to live here again." I gave a content sigh and closed my eyes, leaning into Alex's chest. "It is nice to have a vacation together though. It almost feels like we're a normal couple."

Alex gave me a squeeze, pressing his lips to my forehead. "It's really nice to have you here, Jessica. But I don't think I could live down here again. The lake is home. It's where I met you."

"What made you leave here and go back to the lake house?" I suddenly asked. Knowing what was here, it seemed strange he had left it to go to the dated and much smaller house in Washington.

"It was hard being here, knowing my grandparents were gone. I didn't like being in the house alone. It felt so big and empty. And I don't know, I just always loved the lake house. I needed some peace."

"That's how I ended up there. I just needed an escape," I said as I burrowed my face further into his chest.

"See, that's home," he said as he pressed another kiss to my forehead.

We settled into Alex's old bedroom. I had a good laugh at all the old posters of basketball stars that still lined the walls. Alex reminded me that he hadn't been back in this house for more than a week or so since high school.

The next morning, Alex headed out to take care of business. All of the houses and apartments his grandfather had owned were managed by one rental agency that had recently gone out of business. It had caused quite a lot of havoc and rather than pay the several thousands of dollars to have his lawyer come down and take care of it all, Alex opted to come and take care of it himself. It was a little weird seeing the business side of him come out.

With little else to do, I hopped in his grandmother's small convertible and headed for all the shops along the ocean.

I squinted in the sun as I walked along the sidewalk. Everything was so bright here. I felt so exposed with the lack of towering evergreens around me. And there were so many people.

"Where do you want to go for lunch?"

"Did you hear about Alexis?"

"I think we should go to that party tonight. We can always sneak out."

I was hearing everything. Every conversation that was going on within a fifteen foot radius of me, not a word escaped my ears. I heard every intake of breath, every scratch as fingernails scraped over dried out skin.

Not even realizing where I was going, I bumped into a young couple. I squeezed my eyes and looked away as I got out of their way, noticing how the young woman was admiring the sparkling rock that was recently placed on her finger. My breathing came in sharp gasps as I pressed my hands to my temples.

Desperate for some quiet, I ducked into a café that looked to be fairly empty. I ordered a sandwich and a drink and went to sit out on the back deck that over looked the water.

I took a ragged, deep breath in, trying to calm myself down. The looks from the two guys working inside made my stomach squirm. The way my skin glowed in the pounding sun made me all the more uneasy. Maybe coming to California with Alex was a mistake.

I looked down at the sandwich on my plate and pushed it away. It was a waste of money to get it. I was never hungry anymore. I probably wouldn't eat more than a few times a week if Alex didn't make me. Just one more thing that was wrong with me.

At first I hadn't noticed the one other person who had been sitting out on the deck. But as I heard his voice coming from behind me, I froze. My palms started sweating and a huge lump formed in my throat. I would recognize that voice anywhere.

"Yeah, I'll talk to you later," he said and I heard a cell phone being hung up.

I made sure my hair covered my face, was extra self-conscious that the brand wouldn't be showing. My heart sank into my stomach as I heard him shift, heard the way his breath caught in his throat, heard him stand and take a step towards me.

"Jessica?"

I squeezed my eyes closed, swallowing hard.

"Jessica? Oh my…" he gave a small chuckle. "Is that you?"

And then he stepped in front of me. Jason Walker, the one who had driven me out of California and into Washington.

"It is you," he said with a little chuckle, his dark brown eyes narrowing, the dimple in his right cheek showing. "Hi."

"Hi, Jason," I managed to squeak out.

"What are you doing here?" he asked, his voice coming out more demanding than I hope he had meant it to.

"Um, on vacation?" I didn't mean for it to come out like a question.

"By yourself?" he asked as he sank into the chair across from me. It was amazing how little he had changed in the two or so years since I had seen him last. He still had the same clean-cut brown hair, his dark eyes just as penetrating, his mannerisms exactly the same.

I shook my head. "No, I'm with someone. You visiting your parents?"

"Yeah," he said as he nodded. His expression was almost puzzled as he looked at me. I saw that same expression cross my face sometimes when I looked at myself in the mirror. "Yeah, I have two weeks off in between semesters, so I came down to see them for a bit."

I nodded, unsure of what to say. If my nerves were on edge before, they were about to crack now.

Jason continued to stare at me for several long moments, that same puzzled expression on his face. "You're different," he said. His eyes never left my face.

I didn't say anything in response.

"In a good way, I think," he added.

I just chuckled and shook my head, my eyes glued to the table between us. I then noticed there was a gold band wrapped around one of his fingers.

"You're married?" I asked before I thought about what I was going to say. Guess I could have used a little more tact.

He glanced down at his hand. "For just over a

year now. We met at Stanford."

"That was quick," I said, a bit more sharply than I should have.

Jason's eyes narrowed, his expression hardening. "And what about you? How many guys have you scared away since me?"

My eyes fell to my hands in my lap. I felt like he had punched me in the stomach. "Do you really want to go there, Jason?"

"Sure, why not? Have you screwed with any other guys' lives with your nightmares? Your delusions?"

"I don't have them anymore," I murmured into my lap.

Jason just chuckled as he looked around us. "Of course. Why am I not surprised?"

I ground my teeth together, my fists forming into hard balls. I felt the hairs around my brand stand on end. From somewhere inside the café I thought I heard someone say "*Are you going to let him treat you like this?*". But then, why would someone say something in that context, right at that moment? I must have been imagining it.

"There is someone, you know," I said as I finally looked up to meet him in the eye. His smug look fell just slightly. "And he's far better to me than you ever could have hoped to be."

"Oh yeah?" he said as he leaned in toward me, his arms folding on the table. "And does this guy know about the angels?"

"He does," I said, never letting my stare back into his face waver. I wasn't going to let Jason hurt me again. I'd gotten over him long ago.

"And just how serious is this relationship?"

"It doesn't get much more serious."

"Then why don't you have a ring on *your* finger, Jessica? What's holding him back?"

I felt like my insides had finally cracked, and I became hollow inside. My eyes fell to the table once again, unable to take the cruel look that was building in his eyes.

"You see, Jessica. No one is ever going to be able to handle you. Your family couldn't. I couldn't. This guy eventually won't be able to. As long as there are 'angels' in your life, you're going to be alone."

My breathing sped up and black spots formed on my peripheral vision. And suddenly a familiar tingling started on the back of my neck. *"Why are you taking this from him?"* the words resonated from a place inside of me.

My fists clenched all the harder and my blood boiled. "You're wrong," I finally said. "I don't have to explain anything to you, about who he is, what he's done for me, what I've been through since you hurt me so badly I had to nearly flee the country. But you're wrong."

"Am I?" he asked with a cold smile.

I sat back in my seat, staring him in the eye. As I did, a strange expression came over his face. The calculating smile was replaced by a look of confusion, almost fear. But my blood was still boiling. "How did I ever waste any of my time on you?" I said coldly, shaking my head slowly.

Jason's eyes whipped around, looking for something I didn't see. When his eyes fell back on me, they were wide with unease.

"I have to go," he said, his eyes twitching from side to side again.

"Please do," I said, watching as he rushed out the doors. As he fled, I felt my brand prickle just slightly once more before a warm breeze washed it away.

It took several long minutes for me to collect myself enough to get up. As I headed towards the doors Jason had run through, I caught a glimpse of a set of dark eyes watching me before they disappeared. An all too familiar chill worked its way up my spine.

I spent the rest of the day trying to pretend the conversation with Jason had never happened, trying to pretend I hadn't felt my brand act up. It hadn't acted up since I had nearly died. I wasn't going to acknowledge that it was telling me something. So I pushed it all away and blew way too much money on things I didn't need.

Alex walked back through the doors of the

house looking worn down, but satisfied. "Crisis taken care of," he said as he wrapped his arms around me as we stood on the balcony.

"I'm glad," I said, feeling distracted as I looked out over the water, my cheek pressed into Alex's chest.

"Is something wrong?" he asked, his lips brushing the top of my head as he spoke into my hair.

I shook my head and pressed my lips tight together. "I just missed you."

"Come on," he said as he pulled me back inside. "Get changed. You've got to come try out the water!"

"You mean swimming in the ocean?" I asked, fear peaking my voice.

"Of course," he said as we stepped into his room. "You can't come to Laguna Beach and not go in the ocean."

"You know I can't wear a swimming suit," I said as I froze in the doorway.

Alex had just pulled off his shirt but froze and turned around to face me. The evidence of why I couldn't wear some skimpy bikini was evident on his own back. I saw emotions clashing in his eyes as he was brought back to our reality. Again I felt a pang of guilt for ruining his life.

"Never mind," I quickly recovered. "I'll just wear my tank top over it." That brought his smile back.

We didn't actually swim much. After a few minutes in the water we ended up on the beach as the light was fading in the sky, turning it a brilliant pink. I lay on my back in the sand, Alex propped up on one elbow looking down at me. The back of his hand traced down my jawline, creating tingling sensations. He dipped his head down and pressed his lips softly to mine. He shifted his weight, pulling his body on top of mine. One hand circled around my waist, pulling me as close to him as possible.

My head spun as Alex's lips trailed to my throat, his hand sliding over my stomach. Before I knew what was happening next, I was scooped into his arms and we were tumbling through the door and into the massive shower in the master bathroom.

I screamed and giggled as the icy water pounded my skin. My back met the tiled shower wall as the water slowly turned warm, Alex pressing tighter against me.

His hands came to my stomach again, sliding under the tank top I wore. As our lips moved together, he slid it slowly up until it came over my head and fell to the floor with a slop.

My hands wrapped around Alex's shoulders, sliding over his ridged muscles, trailing down his back. My fingers brushed over the heavy scars there, my insides doing strange quivers.

In one fluid movement Alex hoisted me up and my legs wrapped around his waist. His fingers were just drifting to the clasp of my top when he froze, his entire frame coming to a standstill.

"What am I doing?" he said with a ragged breath, placing a hand on the shower wall, his forehead resting against mine.

"Not as much as I want you to be doing," I moaned, at the same time disentangling myself from Alex. He chuckled, bringing his hands up to either side of my face, and biting his lower lip.

"I'd better be careful or I'll be earning my own brand in a second," he said. I tried to give a return chuckle, even though I didn't find any part of that statement funny. He pressed a quick kiss to my lips and took a step away. "Um, did you bring any concealer with you?" he said sheepishly, his finger touching the side of my neck.

"What were you trying to do?" I teased as I brought a hand to my neck to cover the mark that was apparently already blooming.

He merely gave a shrug with a wry smile and stepped out of the shower. He grabbed both of us a towel and we went back to his room.

After grabbing my clothes, I took an actual shower, a really cold one, and grabbed a drink while Alex showered after me. I lay on his bed, picking a piece of paper I saw sticking out of the end of Alex's bag. It was actually a picture.

It was taken the night on the yacht, down in Seattle. The night Cole had kidnapped me. It had been snapped just fifteen minutes or so before Cole had let me know he was there, even though he was invisible.

A reflection of the light brought my eye to my left wrist, the one that was encircled by the bracelet Alex had given me at Valentine's. The one I never took off, except to shower. My gaze drifted up to my fingers. There should have been another piece of jewelry there from Alex. The one I had waited every day to receive for the last four months.

Alex walked back into the room, only a towel wrapped around his waist.

"Hey now. I thought we had established that we were being good," he said slyly as he walked to his bag and pulled out some clothes.

"Oh, I'm not trying to temp you into bed with me. Yet," I added as I gave him a half smile.

"Close your eyes for a second," he said as he unfolded a pair of pants. I did as he said and less than two seconds later he told me to open them. He stood there in just a pair of jeans, his beautiful and perfect chest still exposed.

"Come here," I said with a smile and ushered him toward me with a finger.

A sly look crossed his face as he walked slowly across the room to the bed. He lay next to me and briefly pressed a kiss to my lips. He then took the picture from me and studied it.

"You looked so amazing that night," he reminisced as he stared at it. "It's too bad Cole had to come and ruin it," he joked.

"Yeah, too bad," I only half joked back. I studied Alex's face as he continued to look at the picture. "Cole told me you were going to ask me a question that night," I suddenly blurted. As I did, I felt Alex instantly stiffen. "Was he telling the truth?" I knew Alex knew exactly what I was talking about.

Again Alex was quiet for a long moment. I felt him relax a bit and he wrapped his arms around me, giving me a light squeeze. "Yes, he was telling the truth."

The tension I was feeling inside threatened to cause me to spontaneously combust as Alex didn't say anything more after that. "And now…?" I barely managed to whisper.

"Now…" his voice was very quiet but he kept his embrace tight and secure around me. "Everything has changed now."

I felt my heart sink as I heard his words, and I suddenly felt like I might vomit. I think I might have even felt worse in that moment than I had when I had been sick and dying just a few months before. "Oh," was all I managed to get out in a hoarse whisper.

"Oh, no, Jessica," Alex's voice sounded

panicked as he pulled me tighter into his chest. My emotions whiplashed as I realized with relief that I had misunderstood him. "That will never change. My feelings for you will *never* change. They seem to grow more intense by the day. There are days I worry they just might overcome me. I promise you that I will love you for forever and even longer than that. Don't ever, ever question that."

"But..." I said, feeling slightly comforted, but not understanding what the problem was.

"But, as I said, everything has changed. I'm dead, Jessica. I know you don't like it when I say that, but it's true. I'm not even human anymore. It's painfully obvious in pretty much every aspect of my life. I have no idea what is going to happen in my future."

"But the council, they said you could stay with me," I said, suddenly feeling panicky and oddly uncertain. I had never questioned the council of angel's graciousness to let Alex return to me, but my head was suddenly filled with doubt. It had been a *very* gracious move. I knew what most angels were like. They weren't the kind and giving beings most people believed them to be.

"I can't be certain about anything anymore," Alex said in a whisper as he released me and lay back on his back, staring blankly up at the ceiling.

I didn't like the fear, no, the terror, that was suddenly ripping through my body. My hands started shaking and my stomach was in knots. I propped myself up on an elbow and took Alex's jaw in my other hand, forcing him to look at me.

"You're not going anywhere," I said in a low but firm and steady voice. "I won't let them take you from me. If you have to go back, I'm going with you."

Alex's eyes hardened just slightly at this as he looked back into my eyes. "Don't say that. You're going to be walking this Earth for a long time. I made sure of that."

"This Earth isn't worth walking if you're not on it anymore," I said, feeling a loose tear fall from my lashes onto my cheek.

Alex pulled me into his chest again, pressing his lips into my temple.

"Please," I cried softly. "I've thought about this every day since Cole told me. It tortures me, feeling the anticipation and the anxiety that you never will actually ask it. I don't care about everything else, all the other complications. You're exactly what I want, exactly as you are."

He absentmindedly ran a hand down my hair, pausing briefly on the back of my neck where he knew the branded X was. "I can't make any promises or guarantees right now, Jessica, other than that I love you more than I can possibly tell you."

Despite his words, my insides finally crumbled and I hollowed out.

CHAPTER FOUR

ALEX

I coughed as a cloud of years and years' worth of dust billowed around me. I was thankful this was the last of the carpet as I carried it out and threw it onto the flatbed trailer I had rented. It was a good thing I didn't need to breathe or I would probably be getting very sick. If I could still get sick that was. Who knew what kind of stuff was living or had lived in the thirty-year-old carpet.

The blank walls stared back at me as I walked inside, and I felt an odd sense of excitement. I was enjoying myself a lot more than I ever would have expected. I'd patched all the walls since Jessica and I had gotten home. Now with the old carpet removed, I was ready to move onto the next phase of the remodel.

My mind wandered as I applied gallon after gallon of paint to the walls. It had been a mistake to go down to California. It had changed everything.

I felt completely torn, now knowing that Jessica knew I had planned on proposing. I was relieved that she knew. She should never doubt how much I loved her. And yet it made me sick that she did know. She would always think about what was supposed to happen, but now never could.

Jessica would hardly talk anymore. She moved about her daily activities. She still went to work, still attended Emily's yoga class, still checked in on Sal. But she wasn't there. She'd checked out, and I didn't know where she had gone to. But I knew I was the one who had sent her there.

I thought back, to where this had really all began. It was amazing how astronomically your life could change in just one day. It had come crashing down the day I had gotten the phone call while I was in Africa. The two most important people in the world to me were dead, their lives gone out in just a blink of an eye.

There had been hundreds of faces at the funeral. Endless faces came up to me and gave their condolences. Some I knew, and yet I couldn't specify a single person who had been there. They had all been a blur. And all I could think about was how I was finally alone. A true orphan. My mother had abandoned me as an infant, my father long dead, and now my grandparents were gone too.

I couldn't stay in that house. I saw them all everywhere. My grandfather sitting at his desk, my grandmother in the laundry room. My dad laughing from his bed. The lake had called to me.

And then I met this crazy girl on the stairs. I'd

actually been a little worried she really was going to hit me with the baseball bat.

There was something about Jessica, even from that very first moment. She was so different from anyone I had ever met. I wanted to be with her constantly, but didn't want to come off as a creep. And then I heard her scream that night.

She told me about the nightmares, about angels.

I had been filled with such conflicting thoughts after I left the next day to go back to California. I couldn't really believe the things she had said. What she had told me was impossible, or so I thought. It sounded crazy. Angels and nightmares, and about them being more than that. I hated to admit it, but I had thought she really might have been crazy. Those kinds of things didn't exist; angels weren't real, despite how convinced she seemed otherwise.

But I also knew I was starting to develop these intense feelings for her. I wanted her company again. I needed to see her, to make sure she was okay. I wanted to protect her. From what, I wasn't really sure.

After I had come home and found out what had happened to Sal, the scale had been tipped. I couldn't help it, seeing her so broken and open. I still wasn't sure what to think about the whole angel/nightmare situation but I knew my life would never be the same again without Jessica. When she showed me her scars I knew I would never love another person as much as I loved her. I knew the amount of trust and faith it had taken for Jessica to tell me the things she had, and even more so to show me the things she did. I was forever hers from that moment.

I also knew then that everything she had told me wasn't crazy. It was all real.

I loved her more than I could imagine it was possible for someone to love another. And now I was hurting her. It was killing me.

I had just hammered the lid back on a can of paint when my cell phone rang. I wiped the drips of paint off my hands onto my work pants and pulled it out of my pocket.

"Hey, Beautiful," I said.

"Hey," she said. The voice of a dead person. "I was going to stop at the store after work and grab a few things, but my wallet isn't in my purse. Would you check and see if it fell out in the truck?"

"Yeah, hang on a second," I said as I stepped outside. "It's here. Do you want me to bring it over? Maybe I could take you to an early dinner when you get off?"

"Uh, I'm not really hungry right now."

"Maybe some ice cream?" I hated how desperate I felt.

"Sure," she answered with a hint of a sigh.

"Okay, I'll be there in twenty minutes."

Exactly twenty minutes later I pulled the truck into the bookstore and walked inside. I looked around for her but only saw Austin working.

"Is Jessica still here?" I asked.

"She's in with Rita. They're talking about trying to get some author to do a signing," Austin said as he walked around the counter and leaned against it, his arms folded across his chest. He looked at me with a faintly arrogant look, though his eyes were hard and cold.

"Oh, okay. I'll just wait for her," I said as I leaned against a table and mirrored his stance. He just stood there and stared back at me.

I couldn't take the way-beyond-awkward silence for long. "So you and Jessica work together a lot now?" I blurted out. I had a bad habit of babbling when I felt uncomfortable.

"Most days," he said as he chewed on the inside of his cheek.

The uncomfortable silence stretched on again for a few minutes.

"Jessica's been different lately," he said as his eyes hardened even further.

"Oh yeah?" I said, my eyes finally dropping away from his. Austin – 1, Alex – 0. "How so?" I didn't see how letting on that I knew things were off would help.

"She's been kind of depressed."

I just gave a little nod as I kept my eyes glued to the floor just to the right of his feet. I wished Jessica would hurry out here so we could go.

"Maybe she should be with someone who would make her a little happier. Someone who would do anything for her."

I finally snapped. All the tension that had been threatening to burn me up since Jessica had brought up the fact that she knew I was supposed to propose came flooding to the surface. In a movement that was too fast, I had closed the small gap between us and had bunched up his shirt in my left hand. My nose only an inch away from his, I hissed, "You have no idea what we've been through together. What I *have* done for her."

Austin's eyes grew wide, and I saw fear consuming him from the inside out. He didn't seem to be able to say or do anything. I knew how I must look when I was angry. It would probably be the most terrifying thing a human would see in their life.

I counted to five and let out a slow breath as I released the boy that was trying to be so tough and heroic for a woman who wasn't his.

"I'm sorry," I muttered faintly as I stepped away, resuming my stance against the table. "But you really shouldn't say things like that to me. Or to Jessica. It might be bad for your health. You shouldn't put your nose where it doesn't belong."

Eyes still wide, he just nodded his head and

walked toward the back of the bookstore and tried to look busy. Less than thirty seconds later, Jessica came walking out of the office with Rita.

"You ready?" she said with a smile that was half forced.

"Yeah, let's go," I said as she grabbed my hand. I glanced back at Austin who quickly looked away. I was starting to get a little tired of all the guys who looked at Jessica like she was a piece of meat.

X

The next day, Jessica was pulled into work when another girl had called in ill. She hadn't even said goodbye when she left. I felt sick. Our ice cream trip had ended up in a huge fight. She had actually slammed her bedroom door in my face. She tried telling me she didn't care what happened, that she just wanted to be with me, and I tried to tell her that we couldn't have that anymore.

But in that moment I hated myself, everything I had become. I hated the angels who had tried to take her, I hated Cole for what he had done, I hated the entire afterlife. I wanted to fix this. But how could I do something so selfish?

The gravel crunched as I parked the truck in the tiny lot. I wasn't sure why I was here or what I expected to get out of this. I wanted some answers, for someone to tell me what was right and what was wrong. It seemed a church should be the place to find someone who could answer that for me.

The chapel was empty when I entered, as I should have assumed it would be on a Friday afternoon. I looked around, making sure no one would be watching from the shadows but my senses told me there was no one around.

I worried I might burst into flames as I knelt at the altar. I wasn't supposed to be here. Angels weren't supposed to walk the land of the living. I wasn't alive. But here I was, searching for answers as any mortal man might in the house of the Lord.

"If you're out there," I said quietly with my eyes squeezed shut. "Help me know what the right thing to do is."

I sat and waited. What was I supposed to be doing? Listening for words to be spoken to me? A feeling from within? I wasn't sure.

Nothing came for a good three minutes.

The sensation started in my fingertips and crawled up my arms to my chest. The air that flowed through the building suddenly sounded hollow and far away. My vision faded in and out, and I struggled to make my eyes focus on the marble floor at my knees.

A chorus of low chuckles resonated from the darkness. I heard them whispering my name, calling me to join them, to go back to where I now belonged.

I gasped for air.

"Are you alright, sir?"

The call of the dead dropped away instantly as a voice from behind me rocked me back to my senses. I realized then that I had dropped to all fours and was shaking violently. An itching like I couldn't describe ran under the skin of my back as I struggled to fight back what I was.

The priest who stood in the aisle behind me looked concerned and took a hesitant step toward me.

"I'm fine," I said as I shook my head and climbed to my feet. It took every ounce of concentration I had to keep my wings from erupting. That would make for a difficult conversation. Actually, it might kind of make this priest's life, seeing a real angel. It would also probably greatly increase the size of his congregation. "Sorry, I just got kind of dizzy."

"Why don't you have a seat?" the middle-aged man said as he indicated the front row pew.

I wanted to slip out and avoid this entire situation I had stupidly put myself into, but couldn't do it without offending the man who was trying to be nice. "Thanks," I said uneasily and sat beside him.

Neither of us said anything as we sat side-by-side and looked at the stained glass window featuring a baby Jesus.

"Do you believe in redemption, Father?" I blurted out before I could stop myself. *Ah crap.* I really didn't need to get into a discussion with a man of God in my current…condition, about redemption.

"Of course," he said with a slight smile as he looked at me. He had the same expression as most did when they looked at me up close. The look that something was wrong with me, but they couldn't figure out what. "Our Lord and Savior died so that we might be redeemed."

"Even if someone does something so selfish it could destroy someone else for the rest of their life? Even if someone does something to make themselves happier than they could imagine? Even if it's only for possibly a few days?"

"We all make poor decisions. Hopefully we think long and hard about them before we do something we will regret."

I nodded as I stared at the ground at my feet. My hand slipped into my pocket and found the small box there. My fingers rubbed it as they did a dozen times a day.

"But there is always forgiveness when we fall," the priest said in a steady voice.

I wished he hadn't said that last part. I still didn't have the answers I was seeking. *Try to make the right choice, but there is always forgiveness.* I wanted someone to tell me exactly *what* the right choice was here. I doubted you were still entitled to forgiveness after you died. "Thank you, Father," I said as I stood and walked out the door.

The water lapped at the rocks below us, the slight breeze bringing the salty scent up to where we sat on the rocky ledge. I picked a rock up and threw it out into the water.

Jessica sat next to me, reclined, propping herself up on her elbows. She stared out over the water, but I could tell she wasn't really seeing anything. She'd said less than ten words since we'd left the house and walked over the hill to the ocean.

"Are we ever going to be able to move past this?" I said as I my eyes fixed on the bracelet I had given her at Valentine's. The tiny white gold leaves reflected the bright sun.

Her eyes dropped to the ground too but she didn't respond for a while. "I hope so," she said softly.

"I don't want things to be this way," I whispered. She still didn't say anything.

"I don't know how to fix this, Jessica," I said. I could feel the desperation inside me start to boil up. "Things are so spun out of control I don't know what to do. I hardly know what is right and what is wrong anymore here. I never had a hard time seeing the line before in my life, but now I'm not sure where it begins and ends." I took a deep breath and glanced up into her face for a moment before my eyes fell back to the ground.

"I wish things could be different. I wish there was a different way we could have fixed this whole thing. But this is the way things worked out. It's not perfect, but it's what we have. As long as you're involved that's perfect enough for me."

Jessica took several shallow breaths, her eyes finally drifting from the ocean to my face. "I just don't understand why we can't just move on with our lives together," she finally spoke. "So what if things are a little screwed up. Believe me, I can deal with a screwed up life. I've done it my whole life."

"You don't understand," I said in despair as I pressed my hands into my face and dragged them down over my eyes.

"What don't I understand, Alex?" she said, her voice cracking. "What is it that I'm missing here? I love you, I'm pretty sure you still love me. I don't want to spend my life with anyone else. What more do we need?"

"Of course I love you, Jessica! But I can't control what is going to happen to me!" I shouted louder than I had meant to. I'd been telling her the same thing over and over.

"I don't care!" she shouted back as she got to her knees and came closer to me. She took my hand in hers and looked at me with pleading eyes. I could only keep my eyes fixed on the water below me.

"Marry me, Alex. Marry me."

I knew I couldn't look her in the eye or my already wavering willpower would crumble. I wanted to cry, to fall apart, anything. I felt like every crucial piece of me was shattering inside. I thought it was going to kill me when I shook my head. "I can't."

Tears started sliding down Jessica's face as she closed her eyes for a moment. She dropped my hand and in a movement that was too fast, was gone into the woods behind me.

CHAPTER FIVE

JESSICA

I was hollow after we left California. I moved around in a numb state, my actions automatic and mindless. My emotions were numb after Alex said the things he did, after he killed my hopes of someday calling him my fiancé. People don't come back from the dead, he would be staying an angel. While Alex was still an angel, he would never completely be mine.

I tried to find hope in this situation, to see a way around this, but you can't overcome death.

I felt myself pulling away from everyone, not that there were too many people to distance myself from. Emily got sick of my non-responsiveness fairly quick. She'd tried to get into an argument with me several times, tried to talk some life back into me, but there was little point when I didn't even respond. Rita was worried about me, but as long as I performed my duties at work there was little she could do. Austin backed off, for that I guess I could be grateful. Sal thankfully remained clueless. She didn't need anything else upsetting her life, she'd dealt with enough already.

Alex knew exactly what was wrong with me. He knew why I was so sullen and where my mind had gone to. He could change it all with four little words, but he was never going to.

I felt crushed. After dealing with the insanity that had been my life for so long, I had resigned myself to an existence of unhappiness and solitude. I was never going to have those things in life that other girls had. And then things changed. Alex had been able to accept the things that were happening. More than that, he had saved me from it.

Here was my once chance at a normal life. As normal as it could be, being in a relationship with someone who was dead. And now it was being cut off. Never allowed to continue to grow.

This would be my only chance at this. No one else would ever understand me the way Alex did. No one would ever accept me as I was and with all the impossible things my life involved.

And most importantly, I would never love another man like I did Alex. A love like that didn't come around more than once a lifetime.

But we were never going to move beyond this point. We were as far as we were going to go.

In a way, Jason had been right. As long as angels were a part of my life, I was going to be alone.

X

"Come on, *that* has got to make you feel a little better," Emily said as she smiled and waved at the guys across the club. They waved and smiled back. Even though I was trying not to look at them in return, I could tell it was me their all too probing eyes were turned upon. I didn't understand why, not with Emily standing beside me looking like a Greek goddess.

"*How* is this supposed to make me feel better?" I said as I pulled her toward a more secluded part of the club. "I just feel like a piece of meat."

"Well if you don't want it, I wish I was getting a little more of that attention," she said as she tried not to let her drink spill. Despite Emily's claim to be a terrible drunk, she had downed a few drinks already. Apparently I was going to be driving her home. "I don't think they can help it though, just look at you. I don't have that angelic advantage."

I shushed her and looked around to make sure no one had heard her. It was unneeded though; the music was pounding so loudly you couldn't hear anything unless you were right next to the person. The noise was hurting my head. I was a little worried my eardrums might burst.

Emily was right though. With the strobe lights flashing, there was something a little, well… weird with the way it danced on my skin. It seemed just a little too luminescent. It creeped me out a little.

I had come home from work earlier that day to find Emily waiting for me.

"I can't take this mopey, empty thing you've become anymore," she said as she hauled me into my bathroom. "We're going out. One way or another, you'll be coming back a little less miserable."

Just under an hour later she had me buffed, shined, and make-upped to perfection and here we were.

We found an empty table, and I tried my best not to touch its sticky surface as we sat down.

"So what's the deal with you lately?" Emily said bluntly as she turned her eyes on me. "Why have you been so…gone?"

"I haven't been gone," I said defensively, noticing another guy leering at me. *Why* did Emily think this would cheer me up?

"Ugh, don't even try to pull that crap on me," she said as she rolled her eyes. "I can hardly even stand to be around you recently. You can barely even look at Alex. And seriously, *it's Ale*x! What's up?"

I kept Emily's stare for a long minute, debating with myself on whether to finally tell someone what was devouring me from the inside out. It would probably feel good to just get it out. "On the night that Cole took me, he told me Alex was going to ask me certain *question* that night."

Emily seemed confused for a minute. I had little doubt her slow wit was connected to the drink in her hand.

"Alex was going to ask me to marry him that night," I spelled it out for her.

"Oh my gosh! Are you serious?" Emily gaped.

"Yeah," I said with a nod. "And then Cole came and screwed everything up."

"Well, why hasn't he proposed then? I mean, you guys are practically married already!"

I gave a sigh, not really wanting to think about it now. I should have just left things alone. "I don't really know. He just says that he's too unsure of everything now that he's changed."

"That's lame," she said as she took another swig and wiped a stray drip from her chin.

"That's basically what I said."

Emily downed the rest of her drink in one swallow. "Well, I don't see what it really matters. Like I said, you guys are basically married already. What difference is it going to make?"

I didn't answer Emily. I didn't want to tell her how to me it would make all the difference. I didn't tell her how badly I wanted to be Jessica Wright, how badly I wanted to call Alex my husband, or even just fiancé. I didn't tell her how badly I wanted to be with Alex, all of Alex. And I couldn't do any of those things until Alex asked me that life-changing question. What I had with Alex was more than I could ever have hoped for in a million lifetimes, but now that I knew what else was supposed to happen, it didn't seem enough. We just didn't seem…finished.

"I think you should get over this. You've already got the most amazing guy that has ever existed. What more could you want? Just enjoy what you've got." Her voice dropped just slightly as she added "At least you have someone."

Her last sentence caught me off guard. Guilt suddenly washed over me. "I'm sorry, Emily. This must sound really immature and selfish."

She just brushed it off, rolling her eyes at me. "Whatever. I can understand, I guess. Every girl dreams of their fantasy guy and their dream wedding dress and whatnot."

I gave her a half smile. Emily really was a good friend. Even though it wasn't really working, I appreciated her trying to cheer me up.

"Moping time is over," she said as she sprang to her feet and pulled me up with her. "Let's dance!"

I tried to relax and just enjoy myself. I didn't dance often; actually, I couldn't remember the last time I had danced. Several guys came and went, mostly dancing with Emily because she didn't clam up and shy away. Even if Emily thought it was just dancing, it didn't feel right to be doing it with another guy.

A pair of black eyes watching me from across the club caught my attention and my head whipped around to get a better look. The man turned and started walking away, his dark hair covering his face. I whipped around again as Emily danced around me.

"Are you okay?" she shouted at me.

I took two steps toward the guy when he suddenly turned toward me. Relief and embarrassment washed over me. I was getting paranoid. Of course it wasn't Cole.

"Do you want to go home?" Emily asked as I turned back to her, her face showing concern.

I gave a little half smile. "Only if you don't mind."

"Come on," she said as she looped her arm through mine. She dug into her handbag and handed me the keys to her car. "You're going to have to drive though."

X

"I have to go to work now," I said, frustration obvious in my voice. Not looking at Alex, I grabbed my purse off the table and walked out without looking back or saying goodbye.

I slammed the door to my car as I got in and hurled my purse in the passenger seat. Throwing the car into reverse, I backed out of the driveway too quickly, nearly hitting another car in the process. I got a nasty scowl from the man, but I didn't care enough to feel bad for nearly hitting him.

Two cars honked at me as I drove to the bookstore, evidence that I probably should not have been driving. One minute I was driving way too slow, the next I was speeding and swerving in and out of lanes.

I finally broke down as I pulled into the parking lot of the bookstore. My breathing came in sharp gasps. I could feel panic boiling up in my system, threatening to take me over. Tears sprang to my eyes and came down my face in angry torrents.

Alex and I had had another fight, yet the same one we had been having over and over again. I wanted to be his wife, to have all of him. And he wouldn't do it.

I hated that we were fighting, I wanted it to end. But I wasn't going to give up on this. On him. I would deny that he might not be with me someday until the day he wasn't.

I squeezed my eyes closed and leaned my forehead against the steering wheel. It felt good to let it all out. I couldn't let Alex or anyone else see this. But it felt good to release everything.

And yet it shredded me to pieces at the same time.

Taking a deep breath and wiping the tears off

my cheeks, I realized I was now almost ten minutes late. I pulled the sun visor down, checking my reflection in the mirror. My heart leapt into my throat as I caught the reflection of something moving behind my car, just a quick white blur. I whipped around in my seat, my eyes searching frantically for whatever it had been. I found the parking lot devoid of any movement.

The feeling that a pair of eyes were watching me made my skin crawl. Even though I couldn't see who the eyes belonged to, the gaze was intense. It took every ounce of courage I had to jump out of my car and run into the bookstore.

I clocked in and set to stocking a few shelves. My hands were shaking violently and my stomach felt queasy. This wasn't the first time in the last week or so that I'd felt invisible eyes watching me.

"Are you okay, Jessica?" Rita asked as she walked up to me, her expression concerned.

"Yeah," I sniffed and tried not to look at her. I realized then that signs of my breakdown must have still been evident on my face. Crying did horrible things to my skin. "I'm fine."

"Oh, Sweetie," she said as she placed a hand lightly on my shoulder. "You don't look like you feel fine. And you're pale as a ghost. Do you want to talk about it?"

I could only give Rita a half smile, touched by this woman who cared so much. I missed having a motherly figure in my life, one that cared about me and asked if I "wanted to talk about it." "No, it's fine. Thanks though."

"If you're sure," she said as she gave me a sad smile. "You're welcome to use my office if you need some time to yourself today."

"Thanks," I said again, fighting back the tears that wanted to spill now at her compassion. I tried to ignore the fact that Austin was watching a little too closely.

I pulled a few more books out of the box at my feet and set them on the shelf. My hands still shook violently.

My nerves were even more on edge the last week than normal. I couldn't shake the feeling that someone was watching me, even following me. That there was someone lurking in the shadows that I couldn't see.

And then there was the increase in fights between Alex and I. It had gotten so bad one night, I had nearly called Emily to ask if I could come stay with her for the night. I knew he wanted me to just let this go. How did he even think that was possible for me?

Not all of us are so noble.

My body froze as the words prickled somewhere in the recesses of my mind. It wasn't like I had even heard the words. It was more an impression of the idea.

...always waiting for you.

Black spots formed in the edges of my vision, and my knees started shaking.

This isn't real, this isn't real. He's gone. I repeated that over and over in my mind, trying to convince myself that it was true.

My eyes flashed back open as a pair of hands suddenly wrapped around my arms. I flung my hands at them, a scream escaping from my chest. That was when I realized it was Austin who had grabbed me, and I was half on the floor.

"Whoa, Jess," he said as he backed his face away from my hands. "You looked like you were going to pass out there. Calm down. Are you okay?"

He lowered me onto the ground, his eyes searching my face. I squeezed my eyes closed and shook my head. I hid my shaking hands in my lap.

"What happened?" he asked, looking around for what I assumed was Rita.

"I..." I stuttered, struggling to come up with an answer. "I just got lightheaded, that's all."

"Here," he said as he gave me a hand and pulled me to my feet. "Maybe it will help if you eat something. Have you eaten anything today?"

"No," I answered him. In fact, I probably hadn't eaten anything in three or four days. Alex and I had been fighting so much, he hadn't thought to force any food into my system.

Maybe that's all it was. My body needed food, and in response to its starvation, I'd had a delusion.

But I knew I was lying to myself.

That night, I lay alone, staring up at the ceiling. I glanced over at the clock on my nightstand. 1:37. I'd been lying awake in bed for the last two and a half hours, staring into the dark, telling myself that the impressions I'd felt earlier weren't real.

He's gone, I thought to myself again. *It wasn't real.*

I jumped violently as the phone rang. I reached over and picked it up after only one ring. Who was calling at this time of night?

"Hello?"

"Jessica," I immediately recognized Emily's voice. "I'm in trouble," she sounded like she was crying. "Can you come get me?"

"Of course," I said as I sat up and turned on the lamp. "Where are you?"

She gave me an address with a quick request that I hurry before we hung up.

I flung some pants and a jacket on before I grabbed my purse and headed upstairs. Alex was sitting at the kitchen table, working on something at his laptop.

"I've got to go pick up Emily," I said, not even looking at him.

"Do you need me to come?" he asked, worry in

his voice.

"No," I said shortly. I walked out the door and closed it behind me before he could say anything else.

As I drove to the address Emily had given me, I felt a bad vibe creep over me. This was a sketchy part of town in the middle of the day, it was downright terrifying looking in the middle of the night.

I found Emily sitting on the curb under a streetlamp, clutching a jacket around her shoulders. I pulled up and pushed the passenger door open for her. She climbed in and pulled the door closed.

I glanced at her as I pulled away. Her face was streaked with dried tears and running make-up. Her hair was tousled looking, her clothes looking disheveled.

"What happened?" I asked, feeling a large lump in my throat. I wasn't sure I really wanted to know.

She squeezed her eyes closed and shook her head. I glanced away from the road and saw the tears break free from her eyelashes, sending black trails down her face again.

"What am I doing?" she half whispered. "I'm going to get myself killed."

My heart hammered chilled blood as I considered what she said. "Are you okay? Did someone do something to you?"

She opened her eyes again, pursed her lips tight and looked out the window. "I went out with this guy. We went for drinks. He must have slipped something into mine. Most everything is a blur, but I remember fighting him off me and not knowing what to do. I found a payphone and called you. I didn't think to grab my purse. The creep will probably steal everything inside."

I didn't say anything for a long while. I didn't know what to say.

"Hey," she said as her awareness perked up a bit. "You just missed the turn off to my place."

I shook my head. "You're staying at my house tonight. There's no way I'm letting you stay by yourself the rest of the night."

Emily was quiet for a second. She reached over and gave my hand a quick squeeze. "Thank you, Jessica."

CHAPTER SIX

JESSICA

The night was cooler than it had been for a few weeks. I breathed it in and out, wishing it could clear out all the bad feelings I had coiling up inside of me. I took a seat on the front step and soaked the cool air up. It felt a little weird, sitting in the front when the back view was so much nicer. The back deck was just kind of *our* spot, and I needed to escape the turmoil that was surrounding Alex and I right now.

Alex had taken off to the new house, saying he needed to get a few more things prepped before they came to install the carpet the next day. The time apart came as a relief to the both of us. We both needed some air, some space to breathe. We'd still been arguing a lot lately, or at least I was doing a lot of arguing.

I'd only been outside for about three minutes when I heard a car pull into the driveway and looked up. I felt my stomach knot when I recognized the car and the man that got out of it.

"What are you doing here?" I asked as Austin

walked over, his hands in his pockets.

"I'm not really sure," he said, his face reflecting what he said. "I thought maybe you could use someone to talk to. You seemed a little down at work today."

"More than just a little," I sighed as I slid over on the step to make room as Austin joined me.

"Okay, more than just a little," he chuckled. When I didn't say anything for a moment he took lead. "So… what's up? Why all gloomy?"

"I don't know if I want to talk about it," I said as I stared across the small patch of front lawn.

"My mom and sisters say I'm an excellent listener."

I didn't say anything for a while, not really wanting to talk to the guy who was a little too interested in me about the guy that was the cause of my turmoil.

"Is there a little trouble in paradise?" Austin asked teasingly. "Something wrong between you and pretty boy?"

"Don't call him pretty boy!" I snapped, glaring at Austin.

"Whoa, sorry," he apologized, holding his hands up defensively. "Just trying to lighten up the mood a bit."

"I'm sorry," I said as I rubbed my eyes. "I'm just…dealing with a lot right now."

"You sure you don't want to talk about it?"

I finally looked over at Austin, met his chocolate brown eyes. They were soft and curious, yet they sincerely told me he wanted to help.

"Alex and I have been fighting," I finally blurted out, looking back out over the lawn. "I want him to do something, but he won't do it. He has his reasons but I… He's looking at this in totally the wrong way. We're supposed to be together, no matter what's changed in the last few months.

"And then, well, yeah, there's some other stuff I can't talk about," I caught myself before I started babbling about how I couldn't figure out why a sadistic angel had come out of the land of the dead after me. Or about how I was afraid he wasn't actually ready to leave me alone. "Everything's just so messed up right now. I feel like everything's spinning out of control. It's killing me."

"There," Austin said with a hint of a smile on his face. "You feel better?"

"Eh, not really," I automatically responded. "Well, maybe just a little."

He just smiled and we both sat in the quiet for a little while. He picked a long piece of grass from the edge of the steps and twirled it in between his fingers. "I know a lot about fighting," he finally said, his voice a little quieter. "My parents used to fight every night. I'd cry myself to sleep a lot as a kid. No kid should ever have to hear the things they screamed at each other. They finally got divorced my sophomore year of high school.

"You're fighting now. Things only get harder as life goes along."

"It's not like that," I said, feeling a lump form in my throat. My eyes stung as tears sprang into them. "No one could really understand what we're going through right now. Things will work out though. They have to."

Austin just looked at me for a long while. I could feel the mood turn all the more somber.

"I hope they do," he finally said and patted me on the back. "You deserve to be happy. Just remember, he's not the only option there is out there."

Before I could say anything else, Austin stood and walked back to his car. Before he got in, he looked back and waved. He then backed out and drove away.

It wasn't the same as talking to Emily, but it was nice to talk to someone who didn't know all the gory details.

I wasn't sure I felt any better after talking to Austin though. Two tears spilled down my cheek as the clouds rolled in and the sun set behind the mountains. A few minutes later, the rain started to softly fall.

I still hadn't moved when Alex pulled in the driveway and parked. He walked up the sidewalk and stood in front of me, his shirt slowly getting soaked as he stood in the rain.

We didn't say anything for a few moments, just stared at each other. Emotions pushed and pulled between us in unspoken hurt and grief. We didn't have to say anything. Everything that needed to be said had already been said.

"Can we just be us tonight?" he finally said. I hated myself when I saw the pain in his eyes, the worry and uncertainty that was there. "No worries about what's going to happen in the future? No fighting. Just me and you?"

I stood up and joined him in the light rain. I wrapped my arms behind his neck and looked up into his changed eyes. "I'd like that a lot actually," I said as another tear rolled down my cheek, camouflaged graciously by the drops that fell from the sky.

"Come on," he said as he took my hand and led me down the hill in the nearly diminished light.

The lake was perfectly quiet as the rain created endless patterns on the water. We were the only ones around.

Alex led me out onto the dock and just held me for several long minutes. It felt nice, to just be together like this, not worrying about things that felt out of our control. It reminded me of everything that was really important, why I loved him so much. This was home; this was where I belonged, forever.

He looked down at me and his lips found mine.

They worked together in practiced unison, never tiring of what they discovered together.

To my surprise, Alex's hands tugged at the hem of my shirt, lifting it up over my head.

"What…?" I started to question.

"Let's go for a swim," he said as our lips continued to move together.

"In the rain?" I asked against his lips. At the same time, I lifted his shirt off, my hands tracing the perfect panes of his chest and stomach.

"Why not?" he asked as that smile tugged at his lips.

I couldn't help but return the smile and just gave a shrug.

I pulled my pants off, only feeling a little self-conscious that Alex was seeing me in only my bra and underwear. My stomach did a little quiver as Alex stripped down to his boxers.

With a squeal, I jumped into the water with Alex's hand in mine.

It felt good, to just let things go and just be us. I needed some fun, to get back to the here and now. We chased each other in the water, creating a game of underwater tag. Alex of course won, cheating with his lack of needing to breathe.

It was totally black for nearly an hour before Alex gathered me back up in his arms.

He touched his forehead to mine, looking at me intently, though it was hard to make anything out with only the lights in the windows to see by. "You know I love you, right?" he said seriously.

"Of course," I answered.

"Okay, just never forget that. That's all that matters."

I pressed my lips to his, gently at first but ending with more force.

"I love you Alex," I breathed. "Don't *you* ever forget that."

It didn't change what I wanted from Alex, but after our night in the water I wasn't quite so depressed. I made an extra effort to not make Alex miserable anyway. And to make myself not so miserable to be around.

My recent paranoia of thinking Cole was stalking me brought that subject back front and center in my mind. The thought that Cole had been lying to me before about why he had come after me had never even crossed my mind before Emily had brought it up. I had also tried very hard to block the whole terrifying incident out of my head. But why would Cole lie about that? Had there been something more sinister and complicated behind it all the entire time? I felt like I was going in circles, always asking the same question and coming up with no reasonable, or even unreasonable, answers.

The more I thought about this, the more it drove me crazy. Of course the one person who knew me better than anyone would notice.

"Is something wrong, Jessica?" he asked me one sunny afternoon on the deck. "You seem really distracted lately."

"I don't know, I just…" I shook my head as I stared out over the water, watching but not really seeing the group of teenagers swimming. "Emily just said something a while back that I can't seem to get out of my head." I would leave out the part about Cole stalking me at all costs.

"What?" Alex questioned, his brow becoming furrowed. I lost my train of thought for a few seconds as I let my eyes wander over the perfection of his face.

"Uh…" I stuttered for a moment. "Well, Emily asked me about what happened with Cole when he took me, and I told her. She said something though about what he said as to why he took me. She thought he was lying, that there must have been some real reason why he came after me."

"You're worried there might have been more behind it?" Alex probed.

"Yeah," I said as I nodded my head. "Why me? Was it just because I'm human? Did he just want the long lost connection? He had to have known there was something different about Emily, that she wasn't the person on trial either. Why not her? And after finding out about Emily, there has to be other people out there who have gone through this too. Why not any of them?"

Alex's hands suddenly but very softly, lay on either side of my face and his steel gray eyes burned into mine. I felt myself suddenly relax and then realized just how worked up I had been getting over all of this.

"It doesn't matter," he said softly but firmly. "No matter the reason he came after you, he can't touch you now. Not ever. I made absolutely certain of that. You saw it yourself. You don't have to be afraid of him anymore, wherever he is."

My insides that had felt so twisted up for so long now suddenly relaxed. In truth, I had been terrified constantly for the last few weeks. Even if Cole really was following me around, he couldn't touch me. Alex was right. He'd given everything to protect me. And even if Cole could get me, Alex was more than capable of protecting me.

I felt myself relax, and Alex wrapped his arms around my shoulders and cradled me into his chest. Maybe I didn't have to be afraid of Cole anymore, but I still couldn't get the question of *why* out of my head.

Alex's phone started ringing. As he pulled it out and checked the caller ID, a smile crossed his face. "Hey, it's Rod!"

I smiled at Alex as he answered the phone with an excited "What's up!" and went back inside to give him some privacy.

Rod was Alex's best friend and could have been his twin if not for the extreme difference in their skin color. I had met Rod once, but had not exactly gotten to know him well since I had been having massive swings between normality and being within moments of death.

I went to the fridge and pulled out a bottle of water. I downed the entire thing in one breath, the same way I used to down caffeinated beverages when I went without sleep for days on end. It was the first thing I had drunk since Austin had poured a massive amount of hot chocolate down my throat the day I nearly passed out.

"Hey."

I spun around as I heard the door open and Emily walked in. She dropped her purse on the floor and flopped down on the couch.

"Hey," I said as I put the cap back on the bottle and threw it into the recycle bin. I then noticed the look of unrest on Emily's face and could almost cut through the unhappiness that was rolling off of her. "Is something wrong?"

Emily's eyes dropped and she started picking at a hangnail. "I heard back from the University today. I didn't get the teaching job. They said they found someone 'better qualified' for the job." She made quotation marks in the air with her fingers.

"Oh, Emily, I'm so sorry," I said as I crossed to the living room.

Just then Alex came back inside, a wide grin plastered on his face. "That was Rod. He said he's moving up here for the rest of the summer. He's found an apartment and needs some help moving in. I'm going to help him unload the truck. Sounds like it's in the same area as your place, Emily."

"Who's Rod?" Emily asked, irritation in her voice.

Alex gave Emily a slightly surprised look when he heard her tone. It lasted only a moment though before that brilliant smile was back. "My best friend from California. I'll invite him over for dinner tonight."

"You sure you want to do that?" I asked him. "Are you going to be able to fake eating an entire meal?"

Alex shrugged his shoulders slightly, his smile and mood undeterred. "I'll figure it out. I want you to meet him, Emily. And I want you to get to know him a little better, Jessica. As long as you don't mind him coming over, that is."

I gave a little chuckle at this. "It's your house. And of course I don't mind."

If it was possible, Alex's smile widened as he closed the gap between us and laid his hands on either side of my waist. "It's as much your house as much as it is mine," he said quietly. His eyes burned with such intensity, I couldn't form any coherent thoughts. He gently pressed a kiss to my lips, leaving my own burning and tingling in an intoxicating way. My head was spinning when he took half a step away, still keeping his hands on my waist.

"I'll be back tonight. You're invited too, Emily. I'm not sure exactly how long this will take, but I'll plan on being back by at least seven so I can get dinner made. I love you," he said as he pressed a quick peck to my forehead and headed out the door.

"I love you, too," I breathed. It was ridiculous how my entire body ached when he let go of me and walked out the door. Things may have been tense between us but I still knew the way I could light up whenever we were together.

I instantly regretted the smile that was plastered on my face when I looked back at Emily. The glare that was on her face literally made me jump.

"Emily…" I stuttered. "What…what's the matter?"

It took a moment for Emily to speak and I saw the blood build up under her skin as her face turned a bright color of red and purple.

"It's not fair!" she finally exploded. I took a step back. "It's not fair!" she screamed again.

"What?" I said as I took another step back. "Emily, what's going on?"

"It's not fair that you get to be so happy and

have mister perfection fawning all over you! It's not fair that you get the two most flawless looking men in all the history of the world chasing after you with their tongues hanging out of their mouths.

"Why can't I find someone who is so ridiculously in love with me that he would give his life for me? You guys might be fighting lately, but you're still gushing with so much love it almost makes me sick."

"Emily, I…" I tried to stop what I knew was only the tip of whatever iceberg had been turning Emily cold the past two months or so.

"He's so perfect, Jessica," Emily interrupted me, and I saw her eyes turn red and moisture pooled in them. "Alex is not at all my type but with a face like that how can you not drool over him? You have to see the way other women look at him when you go out. And he's with you. He's yours. There's no question about that, about how much he loves you. Even if you didn't know what he did for you. All you have to do is see the way he looks at you! It's enough to drive any woman insane! You have a literal *angel* who loves you I think more than any of us can comprehend!"

She paused for a moment and took a few sobbing breaths even though the tears had not broken from her eyes yet. I was in too much of a stunned shock to say anything.

"And I'm all alone. All these guys I've gone

out with lately, they're nothing. I'm just a body to them. I don't even have someone who has a schoolboy crush on me. I don't have some way beyond 'trophy' boyfriend to tote around and drive other women crazy. I don't have anyone to kiss me like Alex just did you, to tell me that he loves me. I'm all by myself."

When Emily fell silent I could only stand there in stunned silence. I hadn't had anyone blow up at me like that since Jason.

It took me a moment before I could make my brain work somewhat and move to the couch. I sat a foot away from Emily, debating whether to hit her or hug her. I still wasn't sure how to take everything she had said.

"I'm not going to step away from Alex," I said in a low voice, keeping my eyes on Emily's face as she stared straight ahead. "I plan on staying with him for as long as he will allow, perhaps even longer than that if I have to."

To my shock, Emily gave a barking laugh, wiping tears from her eyes. "Oh my heck, Jessica," she said with a half-smile, finally looking me in the eye. She suddenly looked very tired. "Believe me; I'm not looking to steal Alex from you. Like I said, he is *not* my type. I'm just…"

"What?" I encouraged, suddenly relieved Emily wasn't looking to steal the love of my life away. I didn't think I could compete with her;

Emily was one of the prettiest and most congenial women I knew.

"I'm jealous! And I know it's shallow and for mostly superficial reasons, but that's the way it is. I want my own mister perfection that makes every woman around jealous of me because of the fact that he chose to be with me and not any of them! I know that sounds terrible but," she paused for a moment here and I could tell she was choking back those tears. "I'm so tired of being alone."

She was quiet after that, and I could tell the worst of it was over. I cautiously wrapped an arm around her and when she didn't jerk away, I wrapped the other around her and pulled her into a firm embrace.

"There's someone out there for you too, Emily," I said softly. "Any man would be lucky to have you. You're one of the most amazing people I know."

"But how can I do that to anyone?" she whispered. "What I've done…how can I do that to a good man? By being with him? I'm already damned."

I felt my body freeze as she said these last words. I suddenly understood what the real problem was and what had been leading up to her explosion only moments before. In order to stop her own nightmares, Emily had made sure what her own judgment would be. She had murdered her sexually abusive step-father and the nightmares had stopped. She ensured she would be granted black eyes come her own judgment day and receive her own branding.

Emily was my best friend and I felt sick to my stomach that I didn't know what to say to her. What kind of friend was I?

Emily saved me from wallowing however when she took a sniff and sat up slightly, wiping the tears away. "Did you think any more about what I said? About Cole lying?"

I was taken aback by her sudden change in conversation but grateful for it at the same time. "Uh…yeah. I've been thinking a lot about it but haven't really come up with a reasonable explanation. I just keep asking myself *why*, over and over."

Emily considered this for a moment before she spoke again. "Where is Cole? Did he go back?"

"I don't know," I said, feeling like I was only telling a half truth. I had my suspicions. "I somehow doubt he went back to where he belongs though. Cole doesn't seem to like to do what he's supposed to. He's the leader of the condemned for a reason."

"Huh," Emily said and was quiet for several long moments that stretched into nearly a full minute. Finally she sat up straight, fixed her hair and face, and stood, clutching her purse. "I'm sorry

I snapped at you, Jessica. I guess I just needed to vent. You really are a good friend."

"Any time," I said with a slight smile as I looked up at her.

"I think I'm gonna go now," she said. I could see different emotions and thoughts mixing on her face, but she kept them under control. "I'll talk to you later."

"See ya," I said as she walked to the door.

X

"Are you going to eat that, Jessica?" Rod said as he eyed the last half of my steak.

I chuckled as I shook my head. "Go for it," I said, silently grateful someone wanted it. It seemed horrible to waste such perfectly cooked food. There were times when I wished I did eat more.

"Sweet!" he said as he stabbed his fork into the juicy meat and set it on his own plate. He cut a large portion off and shoved it into his mouth. "So do you have any other beautiful women in this town, Alex?" Turning to me he said, "You wouldn't happen to have an equally beautiful female friend for me, would you, Jessica?"

Again I laughed, as I had been doing all night. Watching Alex and Rod together was like watching a comedy routine. "Like I said, I wish I could get a hold of Emily. I don't know where the heck she is.

But she does live really close to your new place."

"I'll have to go and introduce myself to my new neighbor," Rod said with a wide, blinding smile. The contrast between the color of his skin and his smile was almost startling.

"You should," I said, internally really, *really* hoping that Emily might get along with Rod. She needed someone apparently. I didn't have high hopes though, Rod could have been Alex's brother, and Emily had said twice that Alex wasn't her type.

Alex had been quite sneaky in pretending to eat the food that had covered his plate. I just really hoped the small pile of food off the side of the deck where we ate wouldn't draw out the animals. At least Rod didn't have a clue. Apparently he wasn't totally oblivious to the fact that something about Alex wasn't right.

"So what did you do, Alex? Go and get plastic surgery? I was going to ask you all day, just couldn't make myself say it," he said as his brow furrowed and he looked intently in Alex's face.

Alex burst into laughter, but I wondered if Rod noticed the slight signs of anxiety on his face like I did.

"Come on, man," he chuckled as he stole a slight glance in my direction. "Why would I go and do a thing like that?"

"I have no idea, but I just wondered why you're all pretty boy now? And how many times a day are you working out now? Cause I know that you know how bad those 'roids are for you." Rod's face had suddenly become more serious than I'd ever seen it before.

Alex's face fell for just the slightest of moments, as if he didn't know how to explain away how he had suddenly gotten the face and body of an angel. It was quickly recovered though before I figured Rod even noticed it. "It's called aging gracefully. If you're lucky, when you get to be my age, you'll look as good."

Rod's face was serious for a second after Alex's necessary lie before he burst into laughter.

Alex didn't age at all anymore.

"Whatever man! But you do look good! Not too sure about the weird gray contacts, but you do look good."

I realized I had been holding my breath and let it out in one big whoosh as I joined in the laughter. I was glad Rod had assumed wrong about Alex's eyes, I was getting tired of lying all the time.

The night passed by in an all too quick state of perfect happiness. This was the way life was supposed to be. Spending time with the man I loved most, seeing him with his best friend, and laughing as if nothing in the world was wrong. As if that man I loved wasn't dead, wasn't constantly holding back a massive, beautiful pair of wings, as if I didn't have my own pair of wings raised directly in my skin and an X branded into the back of my neck.

CHAPTER SEVEN

JESSICA

I woke with a jump, the way one wakes when you hear a noise that doesn't belong. Or maybe it was the absence of it; the house was perfectly silent as I strained my ears, searching for the cause of my sharp awakening.

I was alone in the bed, but when I placed a hand on the sheets I found them still with traces of warmth, Alex had been in the bed within the last ten minutes or so.

"Alex?" I called, again straining my ears for any signs of life. Only silence met my ears. I swung my legs off the bed and walked out into the tiny living room.

"Alex?" I called out, only to be met with silence again.

The living room and kitchen were empty, as was the family room in the basement. I knocked on the closed door to Alex's room, and when I got no answer, I poked my head inside.

The room was devoid of Alex's presence. I noted however that Alex's red T-shirt was lying on the floor, a drawer of his dresser pulled open. This seemed a little strange, Alex kept his room obsessively clean, however little time he spent in it. It was unlike him to leave clothes on the floor.

I checked his bathroom next, only to find it empty. The walls of the shower were still wet though, evidence that he had been in there recently.

I returned to his bedroom and noticed Alex's phone, wallet, and leather wristband were sitting on top of his dresser. He never left home without those things.

A quick search of the house revealed he was nowhere inside. I checked the garage and found the truck, my GTO, and the motorcycle all still parked inside. After checking in the back, I found both the canoe and kayak in their places.

My mind reeled as I pulled on a pair of denim shorts and a tank top. It was unlike Alex to leave without telling me where he was going and he never went on walks without me as far as I knew. There was only one other place he could be.

I let myself into Sal's house after knocking once, as usual. Sal was sitting on one of her couches, the book I had brought home for her a few days ago clutched in her hands.

"Is Alex here?" I asked as I looked around.

"No, I haven't seen him," Sal said without looking up from her book for even a moment.

I checked around the house just in case. It

wouldn't surprise me if Alex had come to help Sal with something and Sal forgot he was here. But after only a few minutes, I ruled that Alex wasn't anywhere at Sal's.

"Do you need anything Sal?" I asked, feeling distracted and only asking out of habit.

Sal didn't say anything, or if she did I didn't hear or notice. I let myself out the door and walked back home. I had just gotten back into my apartment and grabbed the phone to call Rod when I heard the doorbell ring.

I dashed up the stairs to answer it, expecting anyone else in the world to be there than the person who was.

"Amber?" I said in disbelief as I took her in, standing so unpredictably there in my doorway.

I nearly didn't recognize my now eighteen-year-old sister. Not only had she been thirteen the last time I had seen her, but her face was slightly distorted looking, with a massive black eye, a split lip, and another dark shadow on one of her cheeks.

"Hi, Jess," she said with a sad half smile. The action caused her lip to split again, a thin line of blood forming on it.

"Oh my gosh!" I gasped. "Are you okay? Come in here!"

I grabbed her arm and pulled her inside, closing the door behind us.

"Amber, what happened?" I asked as I looked

closer at her, my brow furrowed.

She wouldn't look at me for a moment. She simply stared at where the stone fireplace rose up into the rafted ceiling. When she finally did look at me, there were tears swimming in her eyes.

"I couldn't go home. I couldn't let them see this, and I couldn't cover it up this time," she said, the last few words coming out as a sob. She unexpectedly threw her arms around me, nearly knocking me over. I realized then she was a good two inches taller than me now.

"Hey, it's okay," I said softly as I patted her hair, horrified to see the bruised imprint of fingers on her arm, just below her shoulder. "Who did this to you?"

"Todd," she said with disgust as she stepped away and wiped tears from her cheeks. I led her to the couch and we both sat on the aging leather. "I feel so stupid. He promised he wouldn't do it again. He said he was sorry and that he loved me. He knocked me out last night, Jessica, he hit me that hard."

"Amber, I'm so sorry," I breathed as I wrapped my arms briefly around her shoulders again. The anger and hatred that was stirring under my skin surprised me. I had never had violent feelings toward anyone other than Cole, but the emotions and the actions I wanted to take toward this guy Todd would surely earn me my own brand one day.

"I couldn't go home last night after I woke up. Mom and Dad tried to warn me. They told me constantly that Todd was no good for me, that he scared them," she took another sniffling sob. "They had no idea how right they were. But I…I was so sure Todd loved me, and I loved him. I didn't want to believe he meant what he was doing to me. And I couldn't tell Mom and Dad, I couldn't let them be right after all the fights we had."

Amber's sobs were coming closer together by this point. I took hold of her trembling hand and rubbed circles into it, trying to calm and comfort her, sensing there was still more to come and that it wasn't going to get any better.

"When I woke up, Todd was gone, and I just knew that I had to get out of there. I'm not sure I'd survive the next time he comes after me," she said, taking deep breaths.

Chills ran down my back as I listened to my sister. My thoughts drifted to Sal, who was the way she was because of an abusive husband. He had nearly killed her one night and she'd been lucky to have survived. She wasn't whole afterward, but at least she was alive.

"I couldn't stay in Ucon; Todd would always be able to find me. And I couldn't go home only to be told 'I told you so.' I didn't know where else to go, so I came here. I'm sorry to barge in on you like this, but I didn't know where else to go," she said with another sob as she collapsed into my arms, burying her face in my chest.

"Hey," I said firmly. "You're not barging in at all. Of course you're welcome, you're my sister."

She was quiet for a minute as her shaking and sobbing calmed. "Good thing I went digging through Dad's desk that day. If I hadn't found your address written on that paper, I don't know where else I would have gone."

I chuckled slightly. "I was wondering how you found out where I was. I worked pretty hard to make sure they couldn't find me. Dad managed to get to me though."

Amber was quiet for a while longer, her body becoming relaxed and limp against mine. "I've missed you, Jessica," she said quietly and sat up to look at me.

I noticed the bags under her eyes now, the way they were bloodshot. I then realized that to have gotten here at the time she did, considering she was in Ucon last night, she'd have had to drive through the night.

I gave her a small smile. "Why don't you go lay down?" I said quietly. "You look like you could use some sleep."

She gave a little chuckle. "I probably look how you always used to look."

I gave an uncomfortable laugh at this, unsure how to react to what she said. I would have rather pretended like my horrible past involving the nightmares and my family's reactions didn't exist.

Amber stood and followed me to the master bedroom on the main floor that was never used. She was asleep just moments after her head hit the pillow.

I closed the door to the bedroom and leaned against it. It was only after a few moments that I realized my hands were shaking violently. I came up with two reasons why. One, I was unbelievably furious with the man who thought it was okay to use my little sister as a punching bag, and two, I hadn't been prepared to see a member of my family today, the ones I had run away from. Especially the one who looked like a cloned, younger version of my mom.

I needed someone to talk to and with this desperate thought I remembered how Alex was unexplainably missing.

A call to Rod's cell phone yielded no answer as did Emily's. Just two cheerful sounding recordings of each of them, instructing me to leave a message.

A part of me was saying that I was over-reacting and being a clingy, possessive, and needy girlfriend, but another part of me knew something was off. This wasn't normal behavior for Alex. When you lived nearly every waking moment with someone, you learn their behaviors pretty well.

I couldn't go out and look for him. I couldn't leave Amber here by herself, and besides, I had no idea where to start, considering every means of transportation Alex owned were all still here.

I didn't know what else to do and trying to convince myself that I was just overreacting and that Alex was just fine, I set about doing laundry. Laundry had a way of clearing my head when I was upset or stressed. I needed something to take my mind off the worry that was eating away at me and laundry did the job of numbing it. Or at least I pretended it did.

The hours ticked away, every passing one driving me nearly crazy. There was no sign of Alex, still no answer from either Rod's or Emily's cell phones. I checked on Amber nearly once an hour just to make sure she was still breathing. I debated if I needed to take her to the hospital, but decided she probably needed her rest as much as anything else.

I was making a sandwich when some form of relief came. The door to the master bedroom opened and a groggy, yet slightly more refreshed looking Amber came stumbling out.

"Would you make me one of those?" she said, her eyes brightening slightly.

"Sure, you can have this one," I said as I handed her the grilled cheese sandwich I had just pulled off the pan. "I'll make another."

Amber took the sandwich with a pained looking smile and sat at the bar.

"How are you feeling?" I asked as I sliced some more cheese.

She swallowed her bite before she spoke. "My head hurts worse, but it feels a little clearer. You know I don't do well without enough sleep."

I chucked at this. It was strange remembering all these little details from when I had still lived at home. It felt like another lifetime ago. Things had changed so much since then, for the better.

"So what do you do to be able to afford such a nice house?" she asked, wiping crumbs from her hands onto the plate.

"Oh, um…" I stuttered as I flipped the sandwich over. "It's actually not mine. It's Alex's."

"Who's Alex?"

My brow furrowed as I looked over my shoulder at her. "Did Dad never tell you about Alex?"

"Dad didn't say anything about anyone, including you. I'm just now realizing he must have gone to see you those times when he suddenly ran off. He said there was some kind of emergency, but wouldn't say a word. He must have eventually told Mom though cause your name started popping up again in hushed conversations."

It suddenly felt as if there was a rock in the pit

of my stomach. My dad had told me my mother wanted to talk to me on my birthday. What had they been saying about me? Was he going to tell her how to find me?

"Alex is…uh, my boyfriend," I said, pushing that thought out of my mind. The word boyfriend didn't seem adequate enough to describe what Alex was. When someone gives their life for you, boyfriend just doesn't quite cut it.

"I never would have pegged you as the girl to live with your boyfriend," she said with a slight smirk.

"It's kind of complicated," I said with a smile, remembering the first night Alex and I had met. I had nearly attacked him with a baseball bat in the stairwell.

"Spill it, sister," Amber said with a smile creeping into the corner of her lips.

I couldn't help but smile as well as I launched into the story of how I care took the house, how Alex's grandparents had died, leaving everything to Alex. It was slightly more difficult telling how Alex and I had come to be in a more intimate relationship without saying anything about Cole and the entire nightmare situation.

"So where is he then?" Amber asked, her face alight with excitement. "When can I meet him?"

"Um…" I hesitated, feeling a hard, cold knot forming in my stomach. "I'm not sure where he is right now, actually. It's kind of weird, we're kind of inseparable pretty much twenty-four-seven."

Amber was about to say something when there was two knocks on the door. Before I could even take a step towards it to answer, it swung open.

"Alex, you'd better have a good reason..." Rod stopped short in the doorway as he closed it behind him. "Oh, hey, Jessica. Sorry, but I don't appreciate you holding my man hostage, causing him to leave me waiting at the court by myself for over an hour."

"Hi, Rod," I said with a smile. I might not have caught the teasing in Rod's voice if his personality wasn't so similar to Alex's. "Actually I've been hoping Alex was with you. I tried calling your cell a couple of times. I don't know where he is."

Rod got a puzzled expression on his face before reaching into his basketball shorts and pulling his cell phone out. "Stupid piece of junk," he said as he shoved it back in his pocket. "Sorry, it keeps shutting off randomly."

Rod then seemed to realize that there was another person in the house. "I'm sorry, I didn't see you there at first. Who's this, Jessica?"

"This is my younger sister, Amber," I said as I smiled at her. "Amber, this is Alex's best friend, Rod Gepper."

Rod crossed the room and reached out to shake

Amber's hand. I noticed Amber kept her gaze downward, as if trying to hide the violent marks on her face. I was surprised when after only a moment Rod laid two fingers very softly on the side of her face, just over the bruise on her cheek.

"Did someone do this to you?" he asked very quietly.

Amber didn't say anything, just kept her eyes on the floor.

"Tell me where to find him, and I'll make sure he can never do that to anyone again," I was shocked at the venom that filled Rod's voice, it was frightening in the way he sounded perfectly calm at the same time. When I looked over at him, I saw the intensity his eyes were suddenly burning with.

Amber finally looked up at him, with shock in her eyes. For a moment she almost looked fearful but after a second it melted away into a smile. "Thanks, but I really doubt he will find me here. He's about 900 miles away right now."

"Well, if he shows up and bothers you again, you call me, and I will take care of him for you," he said, his tone serious but a smile starting to spread on his face. I couldn't help but smile too. So did Amber.

"Did you say you don't know where Alex is?" he said as he broke his stare at my baby sister and looked over at me.

"No," I said, that knot forming in my stomach

again. "The truck is here, the motorcycle is here. His cell and wallet are still in his bedroom. I don't know where he would have gone. It's like he just vanished."

As the last few words came out of my mouth I felt my body go numb. Vanished. As if he suddenly wasn't in this world any more. As if he had suddenly been pulled back into the world he was supposed to be a part of now.

"Well, he was supposed to meet me at the basketball court over an hour ago, and he never showed. He didn't answer his phone either, so I decided to come looking for him."

I barely heard the words Rod said. I was suddenly trying very hard to keep from throwing up. "Are you okay, Jess?" I heard Amber say. "You're white as a ghost all the sudden."

"Yeah, I'm fine," I lied as I folded my arms across my midsection to try and hide the trembling in my hands. "Just wondering where Alex could be."

"I wouldn't worry too much," Rod said. "Alex likes to wander, but he always comes home eventually."

I nodded, barely hearing what he said. I wished I could take that as the answer to Alex's disappearance, but I had a feeling there was something much more terrifying and sinister to this.

The knot in my stomach never left the rest of

the night. Rod left after exchanging numbers with my sister. Amber went to bed early, again sleeping in the master bedroom. I sat on the leather couch the rest of the night, waiting for Alex to walk back through the front doors yet dreading that he wouldn't. I fell asleep there on the couch and had nightmares the entire night.

X

I felt numb the next morning when I confirmed that Alex was still not home. I called Rod who said he still hadn't heard from Alex. I only got Emily's voicemail again.

The temptation to call in sick to work was strong. I really did feel sick, but it was only from worry and the terrifying familiar sensation of dread that filled me. I sincerely hoped that work would distract me from my obsession. Amber seemed grateful for the time by herself in the quiet when I told her I had to go into work. Mondays were always slow in the bookstore. I worked the morning shift and Austin came in at eleven to help with the afternoon rush to the espresso and then take over in the afternoon. Today was no different; there wasn't a soul in the building besides me.

I ducked under the counter, grabbing for my purse that was stashed underneath. I set it on the wooden surface, digging through its contents for the book I had been reading. Pulling it out, I noticed there were two envelopes tucked inside. My brow furrowed, I pulled them out and set the book back down.

The envelopes were yellowed and aged looking. I noticed that one of them was sealed with wax, some sort of family crest pressed and then hardened into it. The writing on it was elegant and perfectly printed in a way you just didn't see any more. Upon a closer look, my blood ran cold as I distinctly recognized the handwriting.

Cole.

My head spun and little black dots started forming on the outskirts of my vision. I then realized that I wasn't breathing. My heart pounded and the sound of its thundering raged in my ears. My hands started shaking, making me nearly drop the envelopes.

I was terrified, horrified, but surprisingly, I was raging angry. Everything Cole had done to me, done to Sal, done to Alex, came rushing back at me and hit me like a punch in the face.

Before I even realized what I was doing, I had counted to eighty-one under my breath.

So I hadn't just been paranoid. Cole was still around. He had been watching me, closer than I could have ever realized. Sometime he had been in the house or had slipped into the bookstore and put the envelopes into my purse.

He could still be here right now.

"Cole?" I said aloud with a quivering voice. My system felt suddenly saturated with panic.

But I didn't feel any eyes on me like I had the past few weeks.

I could only pray I really was alone.

I opened the letter with the wax seal. I checked to make sure no one had entered the bookstore and that no one was around the front of the building. I leaned against the counter and pulled a yellowed piece of paper out. My eyes quickly glanced over it but froze at the date written in the corner.

1 June, 1759

I supposed the date should not have struck me as strongly as it did. I remembered Cole saying something about how he had not walked this Earth in a few hundred years. The reality that Cole had lived hundreds of years ago had not really occurred to me.

My Dearest,

Let me begin by first apologizing again for the things that happened with your father yesterday. I promise that I did not mean to anger him. Sometimes my temper seems to get the best of me. Please tell him again that I am sorry and that I take back what I said. I don't think that he fully believed me when I said so myself.

I did not get a moment of sleep all last night. As I stared up at the ceiling, all I saw was that horrific scene of me making a fool of myself, but more front and center was the horrified look that crossed your face. It was well deserved and warranted. I regret every breath I took that was used to produce the words that came out of my mouth.

Please, my dearest, I beg of you another chance to make it up to you. Your father never need know of me again, nor James. Even through all the times I have begged you to end it with him, through all the times you have told me that you simply can't, I will gladly desist if you will simply give me another chance.

I need you, my darling. I cannot live without you. Please.

Yours, always and forever,
Cole

I could only stare at the page for a long moment after I finished reading. The laughter that suddenly burst from my chest startled me, it was so bizarre. It was amazing, that even though Cole had lived over 250 years ago, he was still exactly the same. Dr. Jekyll and Mr. Hyde. Charming, yet hiding a monster inside. Always wanting what wasn't his and willing to do anything to get it.

It was out of pure and simple morbid curiosity

that I pulled out the other letter. This one was obviously a woman's handwriting.

8 June, 1759

I cannot even begin to describe the horror that filled me as I watched you and my father argue over what was best for my future. Father would not speak to me for two full days afterward. He would barely even look me in the eye and when he did it was with the utmost disappointment. He told James of it, I don't know why I should have expected anything else, father tells James everything. I don't think James took it as seriously as it actually was. He brushed it off without a second thought, for which I am grateful. The engagement is still on.

I find that I cannot stop thinking of you, though. The way you whispered those words in my ear that night haunts my every thought. The way you touched me in the moonlight in the barn sends my heart racing.

Cole, I have to see you again, please come as soon as you can.

All my love.

I felt sick to my stomach, the nerves setting it on edge. At the same time, my pulse raced. This only made me feel all the more sick. Whoever this woman was, I unfortunately knew what she was talking about. I remembered the crazed longing I felt to have Cole touch me again. Cole's words were compelling and had been for me mind boggling. Apparently Cole hadn't just gained this skill when he was granted a pair of wings and black irises. It was a well-practiced ability.

I was so absorbed in my own thoughts that I did not even notice how Austin had come in and was looking over my shoulder.

"Whoa, Cole huh? What about Alex?"

I jumped about two feet in the air when I heard Austin speak.

"Geeze, Austin!" I screamed at him as I put a hand over my heart, feeling it racing. "What are you doing?"

"Sorry," he chuckled and he bent down to pick a box up. "I thought it might be that order Rita was talking to me about last night. So who's Cole?"

"None of your business, that's who," I snapped at him.

"Man, Jess, calm down," he said, his expression a little offended. "I was just teasing you. I know that's not your handwriting."

I looked back down at the letter. It was folded in half so Austin had only seen the last half of it. He wouldn't have seen the part about this woman's father, James, the engagement, or the very old date.

"Sorry, for flipping out on you," I said as I put the letter back in the envelope and stashing both of them back in my purse and then under the counter. "Cole is, um…an old acquaintance." There, that was at least some of the truth. Cole was old, though acquaintance wasn't the right word for Cole. I wasn't sure what to refer to him as. My stalker?

"Is everything okay?" he asked as he started putting some books on a shelf. "You seem a little freaked out."

"There's kind of a lot going on right now," I said, not sure why I was talking to Austin. "I'm kind of not sure how to deal with it all."

"Are you and Alex still fighting?"

His question jarred me a little. I had almost forgotten the night he had come to the house and I had spilled my guts to him. I mostly remembered the other part of the night, the part where Alex and I had gotten nearly naked and went swimming.

"Oh, uh, not as bad. I just…I haven't been able to find him since yesterday. That's kind of weird for Alex."

"Why is that so weird?" he asked, his expression almost mocking as he continued to stock a shelf.

"Are you forgetting that we live together?" I asked as I raised an eyebrow at him. That reminder ought to put a damper on his ego. I felt a little bad, but he just didn't get it.

"Right," he said quietly and wouldn't look at me for a few moments.

I turned my attention to the inventory book and

started checking some things, trying to look busy. "Then my sister showed up yesterday morning too."

"I didn't realize you had a sister," he said, his attitude suddenly perking up. I could only roll my eyes at him. "Actually, I don't think I've ever heard you talk about your family."

"Exactly," I said as my eyes fixed on a blank spot on the paper before me, not really seeing anything. "I haven't seen her in about five years."

"Well why not?"

"I kind of left home when I was sixteen." Why was I telling him this?

"I bet it was good to see her though," he said. I was glad he didn't press on the last statement I had made.

"She ran away from home. Her boyfriend beat her unconscious. She came to me to hide."

"Dang," he said as he paused and looked at me. "Is she okay?"

"She's bruised, but I think she'll be alright."

"No wonder you're all worked up," he said as he broke down the now empty box.

"I just wish that was all I was dealing with," I said under my breath, thinking about the letters Cole had left for me and what they meant. Again, Emily's saying that Cole had lied brought up the question, *why me*?

And now I *knew* he was still around.

"I haven't seen Emily in a few days," I said, not

realizing I was saying it out loud. "She hasn't returned any of my phone calls either. And her class has been canceled."

"Your hot blonde friend?" Austin said. I didn't catch the joking tone in his voice, nor did I really even hear what he had said.

"Yeah," I replied automatically.

Great, just one more thing to deal with. Not only was Alex missing, Emily was too.

X

As soon as I got home, I made calls to all of Alex's other houses, the one in southern California, a condo in Hawaii, and a small apartment in New York City. There was no answer at any of them, just the sound of his deceased grandmother telling me to leave a message.

Luckily I didn't have to worry about keeping Amber company for too long. As soon as Rod was done with his shift at some part-time construction job, he came over. Apparently Amber wasn't going to have any problem moving on from Todd and apparently Rod wasn't going to miss having Alex gone too much.

As soon as they were gone, I headed down to the apartment to take a very hot shower. I fought back panic as I went into my bedroom and found four more letters sitting on my pillow. Cole had been inside my house. Was he still there now?

My stomach rolled as I sat on my bed and clutched the envelopes in my hand. I hated Cole more than I thought it was possible for me to hate someone, but I couldn't help but be curious to learn how he had come to be the way he was. How did one come to be the leader of the condemned?

The letters that followed the ones I had read earlier that day were rather embarrassing to read. They depicted two days in which Cole hid out in this woman's barn and her many long visits to such barn. The woman's recollection of the events was rather descriptive.

But the difference between the letter on June 14, 1779 to the letter on July 2nd was night and day. The former being full of desire, longing, and begging for another day, the latter was short and cold.

I fear father has begun to suspect you again. I cannot risk what my family has worked so hard to establish. This is the end, Cole. Goodbye.

I didn't get it. Why was Cole leaving these letters for me? Letters from and to another woman? It made no sense and if I was honest with myself, I wasn't sure if I really wanted to know the reason why. It was looking like there was more involved with Cole's obsession with me than I had first realized. That thought scared the crap out of me. As if the whole messed up situation with Cole hadn't been bad enough, now it seemed there was more to it than met the eye.

There was still no sign of Alex the next day. And he was still missing the day after that. I was a mess, a wreck. I knew I wasn't giving a good impression to Amber after having not seen me for years and years. I didn't care though. She could think I was crazy. I *was* going crazy.

In an effort to distract myself from the constant urge to throw up and break into tears, I pulled out Cole's letters again. I had found another dozen in my car the day after I had found the four in my bedroom.

Just as I was about to open a letter, my ears piqued at a sound and horrifyingly, the brand on the back of my neck prickled. I wasn't even sure what the sound was, almost like a choked off cry or a scream. I strained my ears to pick up on the sound again, rubbing a hand on the back of my neck.

I was all too familiar with that sensation.

"Amber?" I called, severely hoping for an answer from her. I heard only silence.

A familiar feeling of fear settled itself into the pit of my stomach as I climbed off my bed and walked into the living room. The apartment appeared to be empty, as I found the rest of the basement to be. An inspection of the upstairs revealed it too was empty, Rod's car gone and with it I had assumed Amber.

I didn't even register as I walked back down the stairs that I had already counted to ninety-seven.

Even though I had been denying and fighting it, I knew what the prickling on the back of my neck meant. Those feelings didn't come from this world and I had heard voices from the other side before. It was my body's response to the call from the dead.

Jessica.

I whipped around as I stood in the basement family room, searching for whoever had whispered my name.

The house was still empty though.

I fought panic as I quickly walked back into my bedroom and closed the door and the drapes. My breathing picked up and my hands started trembling. My brand prickled again.

Jessica.

The voice was a little louder now, sounding panicked and distressed.

"No," I whispered as a tear rolled down my cheek. I shook my head as I leaned against the wall and slid to the floor. "No."

Jessica!

And I knew why I was suddenly consumed by a fully-fledged panic attack. I knew the voice I was hearing. It was Alex.

Jessica! the voice screamed, this time full of pain and agony.

I suddenly knew exactly where Alex was.

CHAPTER EIGHT

ALEX

My fingers lightly trailed across her cheek, ever amazed at how perfectly smooth it was. Her nose twitched as I did, but she still didn't wake up.

The sun started creeping up in the sky, casting a golden glow through the window. The metallic glint reflected off of Jessica's shoulder, the wings exposed under the small straps of her tank top. They were the most terrifying and beautiful things I had ever seen, all at the same time. I recalled how my stomach had quivered the first time I had seen them. A sure and unarguable confirmation that everything she had told me was true.

A small smile crossed my lips as I briefly pressed them to her forehead and climbed out of her bed. My silent feet led me out of the apartment and into the shower.

As the scalding water poured over me I felt happy, content. I hadn't had that feeling the last few weeks. I hoped that maybe things were finally settling down, like we could move past this unsolvable problem and just be us again.

When I had gotten the call while I was in Kenya, I never would have guessed how my life was going to change. While I had lost the only two family members I had left, for I now really *felt* like an orphan, my world was finally going to be made complete. I'd found everything ever worth living for. And dying for.

I shut off the water, toweled off, and walked into my room. I opened a drawer and scrounged around for a shirt. Not really thinking about it, I grabbed a red one. It was Jessica's favorite color on me.

Before I even started putting it on, a sickening feeling sprouted in the pit of my stomach. The feeling as if a hole was forming in it and the rest of me was going to fall in. The pull of the darkness had never been so strong. A feeling of dread punched me in the chest followed by the sensation that all my insides were being sucked into nothingness. Like I was collapsing in on myself.

"No," I gasped.

The next second, I burst onto a narrow path of stone and into the world of the dead.

There I was again, standing before the ten dead beautiful creatures that would send millions to hell or paradise.

My wings ripped out of my skin as I caught my balance, my eyes growing wide as I stared down into the depths of the cylinder as I nearly fell. I looked up and my emotions crashed. My entire body shook with fear, terrified to be standing in this horrifying place again. At the same time, I was livid. Apparently they had decided my time on Earth was up and were going to finish up my trial.

"Alex Wright," the glorious man with blue eyes spoke. "We have called you back to ask you some questions about our brother who has escaped and failed to return."

"You mean Cole?" I asked. It felt like I had a huge rock in my throat as I tried to swallow. At the same time, I felt a little hope. Maybe they weren't going to keep me here forever.

"Yes," the man said, sitting still as stone, his eyes boring into me. "Unlike you, he has no reason to be in the world of the living. He needs to return and hasn't."

Maybe this wasn't about me. But I sensed where this was going and had my heart still been beating in my chest, my blood might have run cold. I didn't have any answers for them, and I sensed they weren't going to like that.

"Do you know where he is?" the glorious man asked, confirming my fears.

I shook my head and tried again to swallow. "No, I haven't seen him since he broke my neck and killed me."

"He lies," one of the beings with eyes black as the night sky interjected. "This man is with the object of the escaped one's obsession. He *must* know where he is."

"I don't," I insisted, panic forming in my system. I was very aware of the fact that there were ten of them and only one of me. And for every one of them, there were thousands more of them on their side.

"You have no idea where he has gone?" a woman with brilliant blue eyes asked.

"No," I said, my voice sounded hoarse. My mouth felt very dry suddenly.

"He is not to be believed," a condemned angel hissed at me.

"I swear!" I shouted.

"Liar!" two of them hissed.

Before I could do anything, four angels had ascended to the catwalk and each took hold of my wrists and ankles. A moment later, I was being dragged down into the fiery depths of the cylinder. Horrified, I looked pleadingly into the blue eyes of the ones above us. They only watched over the edges of their seats.

The heat engulfed us and threatened to choke me. Hands reached out from everywhere as we descended. I felt my feathers being pulled out, yanking my body in different directions as we fell. To my terror, I saw the five condemned council members following us as we plunged into sheer hell.

I was roughly shoved onto a landing that

sprouted off the wall of the cylinder. I tumbled to the ground, fighting to regain my footing. Before I could even stand, I was shoved back down by another angel.

"I've told you the truth!" I yelled as I backed up against the wall. "I don't know where he is!"

"That may be so," a man said as he took a step closer to me. "But it couldn't hurt to make extra sure you aren't holding anything back." My eyes widened as he drew a coiled whip. Two other angels grabbed me roughly and strapped coarse metal bands around my wrists before attaching the chain welded to them to the floor. I wasn't going to be going anywhere.

"Please, no!" I started to beg, pinned on my hands and knees to the floor. Just as the words escaped my mouth, the whip came down on my exposed flesh.

The beatings were unlike anything I could describe. I was whipped mercilessly for hours on end. But just as bad as the beatings themselves, were all the angels that watched and simply laughed and smirked. I was in more pain than I could even comprehend, and they were enjoying every second of it.

"Just tell us where he is and you will be released," a black-eyed being bellowed as he brought the whip down on my back again.

"I don't know!" I screamed for the thousandth time. "I don't know!"

"Liar!" the man screamed as he coiled his hand back to strike me again.

They came and went. After a few hours of my stifled screams, they would tire of the game and leave for a while. I waited, broken and defeated on the narrow ledge only to have them come back. They would ask the same question every time before the whipping started again. "Where is he?" My reply was always the same and always the truth. And they didn't care.

I waited alone on the ledge, my wrists still chained to the ground. I knelt on the stones below me, my forehead resting on its cool surface. No matter how I tried to block it out, I heard every word that was spoken above me.

"Down," a glorious female voice said.

"Down," another male sentenced.

All ten of them sentenced Nathanial Groves to a branding.

I heard it as his flesh seared and singed under the metal rod. I felt sick, thinking of Jessica having to endure this, over and over again. No wonder she went days on end without sleeping.

"Nathanial Groves, judgment has been placed."

I heard his screams. When the heckling and demented laughter started, I couldn't help but look up. As I did, I saw a mass of condemned angels grabbing their new brother and watched as they fell past the landing and into the darkness of the cylinder.

Countless hours later, I was released from my bonds and dragged back before the council.

"Are you sure you do not know where our brother is?" the leader of the blue-eyed ones asked me.

"No," I said as I shook my head, barely able to hold it up. "Please…" I tried to beg them.

"He needs to return," the man spoke again. "He has a duty here to perform."

"I think he is lying," a woman with black eyes said, her voice a hiss. It was disturbing that it was still beautiful. "He is hiding him."

"I'm not," I said breathlessly. I just wanted to collapse, to crawl into a hole and be left alone. "Please, let me go back."

The man who had taken so much pleasure in whipping me suddenly joined me on the catwalk, standing too close to me for comfort.

"The woman you came to us for. She is the object of our brother's obsession. She may know where he is. Perhaps we shall bring her here and question her."

"No," I said, panic burning in my system instantly. "No, she doesn't know where he is either.

You know he can't touch her, you promised!"

The man standing next to me gave a sick little smile, enjoying the new and much worse torment he was putting me through.

The blue-eyed council members just shook their heads. How could they do this to me? They knew this was unjust, that they were just wasting their time. They knew everything that was happening up there.

Not caring about anything I had said, two more of them grabbed me and knocked me off the ledge. Just before I fell, I thought I saw a familiar face watching from the staircase that wound up and down the cylinder, far above the council. The face looked much like I recalled my father's to be.

The crack of the whip seared my skin, and I could feel yet another welt blossom instantly. I was beyond tears of pain, had I actually been able to cry that is. With every connection of the whip to my skin I wished I could die, but then again I was already dead. I wished to simply never exist.

But that wasn't true. I had a reason for existing. A reason that I had to get back into the real world.

"Jessica!" her name ripped from my chest as the crack sounded. The pain was suddenly just slightly more bearable. Just slightly. If I focused on what made enduring this worth it, I would make it through somehow. "Jessica!"

CHAPTER NINE

JESSICA

The wind tore through the trees, making them creak and moan in a frightening argument of nature. The surf hit the rocks just feet below my shoes with pounding force, sending ocean spray into my face. I hadn't expected the storm today, but I was grateful for it. It meant there would be no hikers wandering by.

I closed my eyes, unsure of what exactly I needed to do to get their attention. "Please," I said, barely above a whisper. "Please give him back to me."

It seemed crazy, it seemed irrational, but I knew that they should be able to hear me. My father had made a plea for me before, Alex had made a plea that they had heard. Now it was my turn to make a plea.

"I want him back," I said, my voice slightly louder. I really didn't expect anything, but I opened my eyes, searching for any signs of my other half. Nothing had changed. It was still just the ocean, the rocks beneath my feet, and the towering trees at my back.

As I had sat in my room last night, feeling completely helpless, I couldn't deny anymore that there was really only one place Alex could be. I knew the terror that could come from that place. I also knew that once you went to that place, you weren't supposed to come back.

"Please," I said more softly, a single tear rolling down my cheek. "Please, give him back. I need him."

The wind picked up in intensity, whipping my hair all around my face. It pulled the tear from my face and carried it down into the salty water before me. Perhaps it was the increase in the elemental disturbance, or perhaps it was just the feelings of panic, uncertainty, and anger building up within me, but I was surprised as the words burst from my lungs.

"Give him back!" I screamed towards the heavens. "Give him back now! Or you will regret every second of his trial!" My voice dropped away after my last statement. What could I possibly threaten them with? How could I possibly tell them what to do? They had proved they had every bit of control over me for sixteen years.

The tears started streaking down my face as I sank to the ground. The sunset that colored the sky made me ache all the more. Alex had been gone for five days now. I felt as if all my insides had been ripped out of me. I knew there was a strong possibility I might never see Alex again, never feel his touch, never hear him laugh again. I had already lost Alex once, I had watched him die. I didn't think I could bear it again.

Knowing that even with my enhanced vision I

wouldn't be able to make my way back through the forest in the dark, I forced myself to get up and make my legs move. I felt drained and empty. I didn't see the ground moving beneath me as my feet carried me across the dirt, moss, and ferns. I couldn't feel any emotion other than a sense of loss, the sense of total emptiness. Somehow though, my feet knew the way back to the house on their own.

The moment I walked through the front door, I heard a clatter of sound, as if something heavy had been thrown against the wall in the basement. This was immediately followed by a high pitched scream.

"Amber!" I yelled as I sprinted for the stairs. My feet maybe touched two of them as I nearly fell down them.

I froze at the bottom of the stairs as I registered the scene before me. Amber was sitting on the couch, cowering, the TV turned on too loud. She was staring at a ball of perfectly white feathers that seemed to be pushing the shattered remnants of the bedroom door off of it.

"Alex!" I screamed as I shot across the room, clearing the remainder of the door off. It looked as if he had plowed right through it as he had suddenly burst back into the world of the living.

Alex gave a slight groan as he rolled onto his side, his eyes rolling around in their sockets. As my eyes adjusted to the dim light in the room, I was horrified to see the bruises and welts that covered his bare chest, arms, and face.

"Amber, turn on the light!" I shouted at her still shrieking and cowering form. I didn't see her move, but the light suddenly flashed on.

The bruises that covered Alex's body were deep purple and black. They spotted his skin, the largest one running from his shoulder, down his chest, and covering his ribs. Bands of red, raw skin ran around his wrists. Angry red welts also covered his back and some of them looked like they were trying to take on the coloring of the bruises. There was only one thing that could have made those marks. Alex had been whipped viciously.

"What is that?" Ambers shaking voice came from across the room.

My heart leaped into my throat as I registered what Amber was seeing. A winged, beaten man who had suddenly exploded into the room. "*That*," I said, my voice surprisingly calm, "is Alex."

"What?" I barely registered her gasp.

"Jessica," I heard Alex quietly gasp, his eyes still rolling around in his head. "Jess…"

"Alex!" I whispered as I scooped him into my arms and crushed him into my chest. He gave a gasp of pain, and I quickly released him. I didn't even notice the tears that were streaming down my face again. "You came back."

Amber's breathing was coming in shallow swallows, and as I looked over at her I saw she was swaying slightly, her knees trembling as they held her up.

"Go upstairs, Amber," I said firmly. "I'll come up in a while and we'll talk."

She didn't say anything, just stumbled toward the stairs and climbed noisily up.

"Help me up," Alex said, his voice shaky but getting steadier.

"Are you sure?" I asked, concern filling my face.

"Help me up," he repeated.

I pulled him to his feet, his face wincing with pain at every movement. He stumbled toward his bathroom, his arm wrapped around my shoulder to keep him steady. By the time I turned the light on, his wings were gone.

Alex staggered toward the shower, stepped over the tub wall, and turned the water on cold. With his jeans still on, he braced his hands on the wall and let the frigid water pour over his head. Wide-eyed, I watched as the bruises shrank, the welts smoothed out, and within a minute, all traces of whatever beating Alex had received were gone.

Seeing Alex standing there, trembling under the water, his eyes closed, finally broke me. Before I even realized what I was doing, I had climbed into the shower with him and buried my face into his chest. His arms wrapped around me and crushed me into his chest until it was difficult to breathe. Tears mingled with the flow of water and my sobs reverberated off the walls.

I wanted Alex to say something to comfort me. I wanted to say something to calm and sooth his trembling frame, but neither of us seemed able to say anything as the cold water cascaded around us.

I felt so relieved to have Alex back, safe and tangible in my arms. Yet at the same time, my nerves were so shot that I felt like throwing up.

We stood like that for a long time, both of us shivering and shaking. I finally found some bit of sense and turned the water off. I grabbed a towel off the rack and wrapped it around myself, then reached for another and when Alex held his hand out for it, gave it to him.

"I'm going to go put something dry on," I said, once I had stopped dripping everywhere.

Alex didn't say anything, just nodded his head and followed me out of the bathroom. He went into his bedroom and as I went into mine I still felt sick. I *had* to know, but I didn't *want* to know how Alex had gotten covered in bruises.

I quickly changed into a tank top and some comfortable cotton shorts and found Alex sitting on my tiny couch, wearing only a pair of basketball shorts. He reached for my hand and we both walked out onto the deck and into the darkening but still warm night.

The wooden swing that hung down from the upper deck creaked and groaned as we settled ourselves into it. I leaned into Alex's chest and he wrapped his arms around my shoulders.

Not a minute after we had sat down, I noticed Alex was trembling again and soon sobs were escaping his chest.

"Alex," I said, feeling horrified that I didn't know what to say to comfort him. I laid a hand on his cheek and looked into his eyes, though his gaze stayed in his lap. "Alex, it's alright."

Even though the sobs kept erupting from his chest, no tears came. I had never seen anything more heart-wrenching than an angel who couldn't cry tears.

"Jessica," he finally choked out. "They…they," another sob erupted, cutting off whatever he was going to say.

"It's okay now," I whispered as I wrapped my arms around him and cradled his head into my chest. I instantly regretted saying what I did. How were things okay? How could I know that?

"They tortured me!" Alex suddenly burst. "They tortured me when I told them I didn't know where he was! How could they not believe me? They know everything we do! I told them I didn't know where he had gone, and they tortured me!"

Alex's sudden outburst startled me. "Who, where who'd gone?"

"Cole," Alex said through clenched teeth as he sat up. "They wanted to know where he was, and I told them I didn't know."

Alex's form was still trembling, but I sensed a change in his mood. I was aware of how his jaw was clenched, how his fists were balled up, the taut way his shoulders were set. Alex shrugged me off and got to his feet. He stalked to the railing, resting his hands against it, his head hanging low. I could feel the anger and hatred rolling off him as if it were a physical, tangible thing.

"I could kill him right now if he were here," he said, his voice low but clear.

"Alex," I gasped when I noticed the wood beneath his hands was splintering as his fingers dug into it. "Don't talk like that."

"I would, Jessica," Alex suddenly spat. His harsh tone stung, but considering what he had just been through, I tried not to be too harsh on him. "I could kill him for everything he's done to us."

"You can't kill a man who's already dead," I said softly, realizing that Alex probably needed a little time to himself. "I'm going to talk to Amber."

"What are you going to tell her?" Alex asked quietly as he looked out over the pitch-black lake.

"I'm not sure, but I don't think I can lie about what she saw," I said as I walked through the door and closed it behind me.

They had tortured Alex to find out where Cole was. Alex didn't know. But I did.

I wasn't sure if my nerves could handle talking to Amber, but I knew it had to be done. I was physically exhausted, partly because I hadn't eaten in almost two days and I hadn't slept the night before.

Amber was in what was now apparently her bedroom, sitting on the bed, her back propped against the headboard, a pillow clutched tightly in her arms. I closed the door behind me and leaned against it.

Neither of us said anything for several long moments.

"So do you want to explain to me what the crap just happened down there?" she finally said, a sharp, accusing edge to her voice.

"I don't know if I can," I said, my voice small and exhausted sounding. "Alex was missing, now he's back."

"That wasn't just some great costume, Jessica. I saw the wings, you couldn't fake that. And he just appeared out of nowhere. I was just watching a movie and all the sudden the door explodes as that…that…" she didn't seem to be able to find a word for what Alex was. "Came blasting through it."

I didn't say anything as we stared at each other for several long moments. "So what is he supposed to be Jessica? An angel?"

"Yes," I said simply, the answer catching in my throat.

Amber didn't seem to have a response to this. At first she seemed like she was going to laugh at my answer, but her face slowly grew serious, her mind seeming to be somewhere else.

"Angels," she said quietly, her eyes looking distant. "You… you used to always tell Mom and Dad about the angels. They… they hurt you. That's why you didn't sleep, you said."

I had often wondered how much of my twisted past Amber remembered or knew about. Apparently she knew enough.

"That was all real." she whispered. "Wasn't it?"

I could only nod.

"Mom always said you needed help, that you were having hallucinations or something. It was real though."

We were both quiet again for another moment before Amber rose from the bed and came over to me. Her eyes were hesitant as she approached me, and I was surprised to see the tears that welled in them. I was taken off guard as she suddenly wrapped her arms around me.

"I'm sorry," she said, her voice shaky with the tears that broke free.

"For what?" I whispered as I wrapped my arms around her.

"For everything. For Mom, for not believing you, for not being there for you."

"You were just a kid," I tried to comfort her. "You shouldn't have had to deal with any of this, no kid should."

"But you did," Amber said.

"It's over now," I whispered. "I don't have the nightmares anymore. Alex is the reason for that."

Amber looked down into my face, her eyes searching, but I felt that she didn't want to know any more than she did now. "Can I meet him?" she asked as she wiped her tears away. "For real? Seeing him explode into the house doesn't count."

I felt the smile creep onto my face. It felt good. It felt like it had been ages since I had really smiled. I nodded and knowing I didn't have to raise my voice any louder than if I were speaking to Amber and said "Alex."

Before the look of confusion could fully develop on Amber's face, a soft knock at the door surprised her. I opened it, my heart leaping in odd ways in my chest as I took in Alex's glorious, now more composed face. I took his hand as I pulled him through the door.

"Amber, this is Alex," I said, knowing the smile that covered my face probably looked ridiculous, but not caring. He was finally back. "Alex, this is my sister, Amber."

A smile crept to one side of Alex's face as he extended a hand to Amber, who took it with shaking hands. "It's nice to meet another member of Jessica's family."

Amber didn't say anything as she stared at Alex's face. Her eyes, the blackness now gone, her face totally healed, were slightly wider than normal, her jaw hanging slightly slack. I couldn't blame her for the way her eyes traced downward; it didn't mean that it didn't bother me just a little bit.

"Sorry," Alex said clumsily. "About earlier. I didn't mean to scare you. Kind of couldn't help it though."

A knock at the door made everyone but Alex jump, and Rod's voice was calling for Amber a second later.

"Amber's not going to say anything about what she saw or knows to anyone," I said, my voice low as I stared her in the face. "Right?"

Amber continued to stare at Alex for a moment longer before she seemed to register that I had asked her a question. "Right," she finally said. "Right. Besides, who would believe me anyway?"

"Amber?" Rod called again.

Amber stepped around Alex and walked out into the living room, Alex and I following her.

Rod seemed surprised to see Alex and stopped short. "Finally decided to return, huh?"

"You know me," Alex said, trying very hard to keep his voice light. "I just felt the itch to go out for a while."

"Well you could have told someone about that itch. I think Jessica was about to have a mental breakdown."

Alex managed a small smile, wrapped an arm around my shoulders, and gave a firm squeeze. "Sorry," he said. I wasn't sure who it was directed at but it didn't matter. "Is anyone hungry?"

"I'm starving actually," Rod said, a grin spreading on his face.

Glad for the distraction, Alex walked into the kitchen and opened the fridge.

"Whoa," Rod marveled as he looked after Alex. "Those are some nasty scars. What happened?"

"I got in a fight with a really nasty guy," Alex said, his head buried in the fridge. "Over a girl."

CHAPTER TEN

ALEX

"Thanks for meeting with me on such short notice," I said as I sat in the leather chair.

My lawyer, Ted Kennedy, sat at the large desk in front of me and unbuttoned his suit jacket. "Anything for Paul's grandson. What can I do for you today, Alex?"

My hands gripped the armrests, I had to be careful not to crush them. The sick feeling that had been in the pit of my stomach since I had exploded back into the world was still there. What had happened had shaken me far more than I ever wanted to admit. "I want to transfer all of my assets to someone. Everything."

"Okay," he said, drawing out the word, his eyebrows rising. Ted was well aware of just how much "everything" was. "To who?"

"Her name is Jessica Bailey," I answered, still unable to look up. I felt strangely hollow, like something hadn't come back with me into this world, had been left behind.

"And may I ask who Jessica Bailey is?"

I felt a little irritated at all of Ted's questions. What did it matter to him as long as I paid his bill? But I supposed I could understand why he was asking them. He was curious as to who I wanted to hand the Wright fortune to. "She's everything to me."

"But you two aren't married, right?" he asked, his voice unsure.

"No," I replied simply. "I don't want her to know I'm transferring everything to her though."

"Well, there's no way I can transfer everything into her name without a lot of signing of papers. There's no way she wouldn't know what was going on. I mean there would have to be title transfers, account papers. We can set up a trust fund if you want or we can write up a will."

"A will should do just fine," I said, feeling sick. I seriously wanted to throw up.

"Is something going on that I should know about, Alex?" Ted asked as he leaned forward, folding his arms on the desk. "You're scaring me a little, if I'm being honest."

"I'm just dealing with some stuff right now, and I want to make sure everything I have goes to the right place," I said as I finally looked up into Ted's face.

"Are you sick or something?" Ted asked, his face concerned.

"I guess you could say that."

Ted was quiet for a moment as he looked at me. After a moment though, he was back to business. This was the one instance when I was appreciative of Ted being such a businessman. He would act concerned over my "sickness," and maybe he was, but he was quick to move away from personal stuff and back to business. He would get every penny he could out of his clients. But it wasn't like he wasn't worth the bill. That was why I had chosen him. "Well, let's go over all of your assets and discuss what you want to go to Jessica."

"Everything's to go to Jessica," I said simply as I sat forward in my seat. "My houses, my accounts, the cars, everything."

"Are you sure, Alex?" he asked as he shifted uncomfortably in his stiff chair. "We're talking about a lot of money here. Your grandfather passed quite a lot of wealth down to you."

"Just do it," I said, again feeling irritated.

Ted looked at me with disbelieving eyes for a moment. "I'll pull your file," he said, his expression back to business.

It had taken a lot more clarifying than it should have, but I walked out of there five hours later with a will in hand. Apparently "everything" didn't seem clear enough to Ted. It felt weird working on a document that was applicable to my death, as I had already died. But we had worked it that even if I were to disappear, Jessica would get everything.

My phone vibrated in my pocket, pulling my mind out of the ominous future. I flipped it open. "Hey, Rod."

X

I could smell something burning slightly as I walked through the door. That smell always made me cringe just a little. I found Amber working at the stove. I tried not to let it bother me, having someone else in my kitchen.

"I made dinner for us," Amber said as she poured something in a bowl. "Jessica called and said she is going to be working late tonight."

"Oh, uh…" I struggled for words as I sat at the bar. "I don't…actually eat." It felt unnatural talking about the whole angel thing with anyone other than Jessica or Emily. It was a pretty big secret to be letting other people in on.

"What?" she said with a disbelieving expression, as if I was trying to make a joke. "Oh," she said after a second, her face turning serious. "Yeah, the whole wing thing, right?"

I chuckled. "Right."

"Wish I would have known that before I cooked up all this food. Rod is working tonight as well."

"Sorry," I apologized. "Believe me, if I could eat it, I would." Maybe. I didn't trust too many other people's cooking than my own.

"It's alright, I'll save some for Jessica." Amber dished up a heaping plate and sat next to me at the bar.

"So how are you liking Washington so far?" I asked in an attempt to make conversation. I hated the fact that I really didn't know more than one member of

Jessica's family.

"It's better than Idaho, that's for sure," she said with a chuckle, forking some salad into her mouth. "And it's really nice to see Jessica again. I missed her a lot."

"I bet."

"It really freaked me out when she left. We didn't know what happened to her. She could have been dead for all I knew. She just disappeared off the face of the planet."

I hadn't really considered this before, what it must have been like for the ones Jessica left behind. I had only felt sorry for Jessica. What must things have been like to just up and leave like that?

"I can't blame Jessica though. It was really bad. She didn't really have any friends. Everyone just thought she was a freak. There was a lot of fighting at our house."

"Were things really as bad between Jessica and your mom as she says?" I asked, my eyes glued to the tiled surface of the counter.

Amber swallowed her bite. "Probably worse than she says. Things were really bad toward the end. Did she tell you mom was going to have her committed?"

I nodded. That was the hardest part to believe, even though I knew she was telling the truth.

"That tells you how bad it was. Mom just couldn't handle it anymore. I think that's the biggest regret of her life though." She paused, staring down into her food. "Mom cried for days at a time, after the reality of why Jessica had left set in. She was still terrified of Jessica, but she knew it was her fault, Jessica running away."

She took a few more bites, mulling something over.

"She called yesterday, you know. Our mom."

"Really?" I said, surprise obvious in my voice. "What'd she say?"

"She didn't know it was me who answered. I'm not ready for her to know where I am. I just asked to take a message. She just said she wanted to talk to Jessica. She said she wanted to make things right."

"Have you told Jessica yet?" I asked, odd excitement building in my system at the possibility of finally getting to meet all of her family.

Amber shook her head. "I haven't decided if it's the right thing to do. My mom hurt Jessica really bad. I'm not sure if telling her is right."

"I think it's up to Jessica to decide if she wants to speak to your mother," I said as I looked into Amber's face. She looked back at me, her eyes studying me.

"You really love her, don't you?" she said quietly, her eyes not leaving mine.

"More than I can say," I half whispered.

She studied me silently for a few more moments before she spoke again. "Why does she look a little sad when she looks at you? I know she loves you and that you make her happier than I ever thought she could be. But why does she look like something hurts her every time she looks at you?"

My eyes finally dropped away. I cleared my throat uncomfortably. "I was going to ask your sister to marry me a few months ago. I even bought the ring. Things changed really fast though. I changed. Into what I am now. I know she doesn't fully understand it, but I can't ask her anymore."

Amber didn't respond for a long time, just forked a few bites into her mouth. "Things will work out somehow. They have to."

"I hope so," I said as I glanced over at her, a sad smile clinging to my face.

CHAPTER ELEVEN

JESSICA

I had never seen the bookshop so busy. Being the middle of summer and a beautifully clear day brought everyone out and into town. Rita had called all of the employees to help out and I had been wrangled into helping out at the espresso machine.

"That will be $7.34," I said to the balding man at the counter. He paid and the next customer stepped up to the counter.

The last week I felt like a machine working. My hands were doing what they were supposed to, but my mind was just not there.

I should have been happy after Alex came back. Things seemed to be going great. Sal was happy and healthy. Rod and Amber were getting along, perhaps a little too well. Alex was as loving and attentive as ever. Even the fact that I still hadn't been able to get a hold of Emily shouldn't have brought me down as much as I was.

Everyone seemed to sense something was wrong. Amber had asked if there was anything bothering me, apparently even Rod sensed something was up. Alex asked if something was wrong, though he was always very careful in how he asked. I think he knew what was in fact wrong, but he tried to dance around it. He didn't want me unhappy, but he wasn't willing to fix the actual problem.

And then there was the fact that I continued to find letters. I still occasionally felt eyes watching me, felt a presence from the shadows. It just made the situation between Alex and me all the worse. I knew it was shallow, but I didn't want Cole seeing that we were having problems. I could just imagine the smug smile he was wearing.

The high school-aged girl before me had to tell me twice what exactly it was she wanted. A few minutes later I found I had still gotten it wrong, and the girl decided cursing at me was going to help.

"Why don't we switch places for a little while?" Austin offered mercifully.

I gave a sheepish smile and gladly stepped aside. "Thanks," I said. "I've been feeling a bit off today."

He probably thought I wouldn't hear him, I *shouldn't* have heard him, as he muttered, "more than just today."

I held back the urge to turn around and bite his head off. I felt more than a little irritated as I set about to making the drink orders that kept piling up.

He didn't know me or anything that was going on in my life.

I searched around for a knife to open a new box of cups and distractedly set to hacking it open. Who did

Austin think he was? He had no idea what I was dealing with.

I should have been paying more attention to what I was doing. It took me a second to even realize that my hand had slipped. The blade was burrowed into the soft patch of skin between my thumb and index finger on my left hand.

The scream of pain that wanted to jump from my lips was barely contained as I stared horrified at the knife that was lodged into my hand. The sensations of pain dropped away however as I waited for the blood to start flowing. It didn't.

I couldn't make sense of what was happening. The knife had to be sticking at least a half-inch into my skin but it wasn't bleeding. It hurt like I couldn't believe but there was no blood.

"Jessica, did you get that…"

I yanked the knife out of my hand when I heard Austin's voice just behind me, biting back another scream. I spun around to see him looking wide-eyed at my injured but un-bleeding hand.

"Whoa," he said as he blinked hard. "That was weird. I swear I just saw that knife sticking out of your hand."

I chuckled uneasily. "Guess it's been a long day for you too," I snapped back.

I knew I'd been too harsh when he only gave me a forced half smile then turned back to the register.

My hand was shaking as I looked back down at it. The half inch gash in my hand closed up and healed before my eyes. There was nothing but a thin white scar seconds later.

X

Three weeks after Alex' return, I had to do something or I was going to explode.

I waited until Amber and Rod were gone and found Alex out in the garage, working on something that had been squealing for a week in my GTO.

"I can't take this anymore," I said as I closed the door behind me and sat on the top step.

Alex looked up at me from under the hood, wiped at something invisible on his forehead, only to leave a greasy, black smudge there. He looked into my face for a long moment before giving a barely audible sigh and setting a wrench down on my battery.

"Why are you doing this to me?" I demanded as I folded my arms across my knees. "You know what I want. You must have wanted it too at one point, you bought the ring."

"You know why not, Jessica," he said quietly as he walked around the car. He leaned against it and folded his arms across his chest.

"It's not a good enough excuse," I said as I held his eyes steadily. It wasn't an easy thing to do. Alex had the most piercing eyes I had ever seen, except for maybe Cole's. And the steel gray color was unnerving. "The council told you that you could come back, to be with me, did they not?"

"You know they did," he said, exasperated.

"Then what is the problem?" I nearly yelled.

"I told you before, I can't be sure about anything now, Jessica," Alex sighed. "I think what happened a few weeks ago is just further proof of that."

"Then why are you wasting time?!" I shrieked. "If what we have is limited, then why are we wasting it?"

"Because I won't leave you alone!" Alex suddenly burst. "Who knows if I will be able to stay around for much longer, and I won't leave you alone like that! What if we were to go ahead and get married and then the next day I get pulled back for good? It could happen at any time! They could take me whenever they want. I won't make you a twenty-one-year-old widow, Jessica!

"That doesn't even make sense! I'm already dead!"

Alex's sudden burst of furry frightened me, it was so unlike him. My eyes slipped from his gaze to the cement floor. "Don't say that," I whispered.

"It's true, Jessica! I know you don't like to admit it, but it's true! I feel like I'm already being selfish enough staying. I'm not supposed to still be here but here I am! I must be the most selfish man there is because there is no possible way I could *not* be with you."

I couldn't say anything after that. My insides quivered and my stomach felt sick. I clutched my arms around my waist and squeezed, trying hard to keep myself from falling apart.

"Don't you think I want to?" Alex said softly, his voice trembling. I heard him take a step closer. "Don't think that *I* don't think *every day* about how you were supposed to bear my last name now? How badly I want to call you Jessica Wright now?" He was standing right in front of me now, and even though I still couldn't look at his face, he pulled me to my feet and wrapped his arms around my waist. "I think every day of how you would have looked, dressed in white. About how the veil would have looked in your hair. How you would have been the blushing bride. About how our wedding night could have been. But how can I give you that anymore, only to have it all ripped away? My time here isn't even mine anymore. I have no control over anything."

Tears streaked down my face. "But I don't care about any of that. I'll deal with it when or if that time comes. I just want you."

"You already have me," Alex whispered into my ear, his lips brushing against my skin. "I am yours in the deepest sense of the word I can conceive."

I didn't say anything for a long while, just clung to Alex's strong frame, trembling even though the tears had stopped. "I love you, Alex," I said quietly, my face buried in his chest.

"I love you, Jessica," Alex whispered. "As much as I think it is possible for anyone to love someone else."

X

I hated it, but one person wanting something out of a relationship that another wouldn't give reminded me of the letters.

After Alex had left to go off and do something "adventurous" with Rod, I sat alone on my bed and pulled out one of the last letters. I hadn't received any more in over a week. The last one I had received was addressed to me personally. I had yet to find the courage to read it. And yet I had finally felt the eyes disappear. Something inside of me told me Cole was finally gone, and that he wouldn't be coming back.

12 December, 1762

My Dearest,

I am realizing now just how truly hopeless this relationship is. I understand now that any feelings you had for me at one time are gone, if there truly even were any feelings at all. The hole that has been ripped into my chest can never be repaired as I know any chance of us being together again is impossible. No other woman could ever replace you, though.

I will never understand how you could reject my affection, after the hundreds, perhaps thousands of times I confessed my eternal love for you. James never has and never will love you as I do. That love will not end when I leave this Earth.

Even if you must be rid of me forever, I beg of you,

let me see my son just once more. I cannot bear the thought that I will never see William again.

My chest feels hollow and empty, and with nothing more to say, I bid you goodbye.

Cole Emerson

Despite everything I knew of how things went between Cole and this woman, whose name I still had not learned, I too felt hollow and empty as I read his words.

Cole had been a bad man and his actions that led up to his branding and position were hinted upon in these letters, but one thing was certain, he loved this woman. He may have been obsessed, but I never doubted he loved her.

As far as I could tell, Cole had met this woman when he started to do business with her father. I wasn't sure what the business was, but it sounded like Cole had been over to their house when the woman arrived home from boarding school. She had just graduated and had immediately become engaged to this man, James. They had been friends for a long time but the woman had not appeared to have ever had any romantic feelings for poor James.

An affair quickly started between the woman and Cole, consisting of a lot of sneaking around and dodging her father and James. Cole continually begged her to break it off with James. He was more than wealthy enough to please her parents and take care of her, but for some reason it appeared the arrangement with James was more beneficial.

The relationship appeared to have constant ups and downs of this woman telling Cole it was over and then telling him that she could not live without him. She went ahead with her marriage to James, but the affair continued. A year and a half after the wedding, the woman became pregnant and when the baby arrived it couldn't be denied that the father was not James. Apparently James was oblivious to the fact that William looked nothing like him, though.

Despite Cole's willingness and desire to be a part of William's life, the woman pushed him further and further away. James caught Cole trying to sneak into their house one day and had him arrested. This had apparently been the end of the relationship for good. The last few letters had gotten no response from the woman.

I threw the letter aside, felling disgusted. I didn't want to feel sorry for Cole. The fact that I did made me feel sick. Cole had never changed. He had well known that Alex and I were together and still tried to pursue something. And this other woman was *married,* and he still had the gall to continue to pursue her.

But I still couldn't deny the fact that I knew how much he had loved her and still couldn't help but feel a little sympathy toward him. I knew what it was like to want something from someone and never get it.

My torment from a few weeks earlier returned as I

read this last letter. He had said he would never love another woman and that no one could ever replace her. So *why* had he come after me?

I shook my head, trying to clear it. Why did it matter why? Cole couldn't touch me, he couldn't hurt me. I needed a distraction.

The phone just rang and rang before Emily's chipper voice told me to leave a message. I had tried to dismiss my worrying thoughts of Emily, but it was going on four weeks now with no word from her. Her yoga class had been shut down and the owner of the building had told me he had not been able to get a hold of Emily for weeks either. It was time to figure out what was going on. I would have called the police weeks ago if it wasn't for the fact of Emily's very convictable past.

Whatever Alex had done to the GTO worked because it didn't squeal anymore as I made the drive to Emily's apartment. The sun shone bright and brilliant in the sky, but it didn't do much to lift my mood. I was tired of always feeling so down lately, but I didn't know how to dig myself out of this hole.

I knocked on Emily's door hard and waited for her to open it. I knocked again, listening for any sounds from inside. There were none. I tried the door and to my total surprise, it was unlocked.

Feeling like I was encroaching upon Emily's privacy, I let myself in. "Emily," I called as I walked from the living room to the kitchen. When I didn't see any signs of her, I moved onto her bedroom and stood in shock in the doorway.

Emily was normally a very tidy person but her room was a disaster. Clothes were strewn everywhere, a jewelry box over turned, its contents strewn across the top of the dresser. Shoes were spilling out of the closet. I found her bathroom in much the same state.

My first thought had been that someone had broken in, but I quickly dismissed this. If she had been robbed I was pretty sure her flat screen TV and other valuables would be gone. No, it looked as if Emily had done this herself. She had packed and left in a hurry.

I combed the apartment carefully, looking for any signs of where Emily may have run off to but found nothing. Had someone caught onto her and come to take her to prison? Maybe she'd gone on the run.

I had just closed the door behind me when a very overweight man came walking toward the door, a bright yellow sheet of paper in hand.

"Is Emily in there?" he demanded, his voice sounding irritated.

"No," I answered, shielding my eyes against the bright sun. "I haven't been able to get a hold of her in a while."

The man gave a grunt, reached around me and taped the paper to the door. It was an eviction notice.

"She's three weeks behind on her rent," he explained when he saw the surprised expression on my face. "If I don't get the money by the day after tomorrow I'm going to have no choice but to toss all her stuff in the dumpster."

"You haven't seen her around then?" I asked, dismay in my voice.

"Not in a few weeks. She always comes and pays the rent in person. She didn't show up this time though. No phone call, nothing."

"Does it matter who pays the rent?" I asked as I pulled my wallet out of my purse. "How much is it?"

The man's face lit up as he looked at my wallet. "Don't matter to me as long as I get some money. It's four hundred plus utilities. Those are billed directly to the tenant, though. You can usually get away with not paying those for at least a month or two before they shut them off."

I had a hundred and fifty in cash in my wallet and wrote a check out for the rest. "Will you give me a call if you see or hear from her?" I asked as I wrote my number on a piece of paper and handed it to him with the money.

"Sure, whatever," he said as he ripped the eviction notice off of the door, leaving the tape and a traces of the paper stuck to it. Without saying anything else he turned and waddled away.

Emily seriously owed me, wherever she was.

X

I stopped for gas on the way home, and by the time I arrived the sun was starting to set. Rod's car pulled away from the curb just as I pulled in. He gave a wave and a smile, but I was glad he didn't stop to chat. I wasn't in the best mood.

Amber wasn't home yet. She had gotten a job as a receptionist at a temp agency not long after she had arrived. Apparently she was planning on staying a while. I suspected Rod had a lot to do with that. When I had found out about the job, I called my dad to let him know where Amber was. He wasn't happy with her for not letting him know where she had run off to, but he had figured she had found me.

I found Alex pulling the bag out of the garbage can. He glanced up at me with a smile but I caught the hesitancy in it.

"Missed you," he said as he tied the drawstrings closed and leaned over it to press a kiss quickly to my lips.

"I missed you, too," I said genuinely but feeling my mood start to sour again. "So what'd you guys do today? What was your big adventure?"

I saw the slight way Alex stiffened, the way his jaw clenched. He suddenly seemed very uncomfortable. "I kind of don't want to tell you," he said honestly, sounding like a twelve-year-old boy about to get in trouble.

"Why not?" I asked, feeling hurt, offended, and defensive all at the same time.

Alex sighed slightly before he sat at the bar, ignoring the bag of garbage on the floor. "We went shopping. Didn't get anything yet, but we went shopping."

"Shopping?"

"Looking at rings," Alex said, his expression becoming more uncomfortable by the moment.

"Rings?"

"Engagement rings."

I was confused for a moment, hope rising for a brief moment before it was painfully crushed. Alex had already bought my engagement ring. Alex had gone with Rod.

"He's going to propose?!" I suddenly bellowed, connecting the dots.

"Yeah, he's planning on it," Alex said quietly.

"But it's only been…" I trailed off. I did the math in my head, counting how long Amber had been here. It had been just over a month now. I was about to protest and say they hadn't known each other long enough to be talking about getting married but I then remembered that Alex and I had only known each other for about a month and a half before he planned to ask me to marry him.

"Huh," I said quietly. It felt as if that rock had settled itself back into my stomach again. My limbs suddenly felt heavy and as if all the blood in them had been turned into ice. "Good for them."

Without waiting for a response from Alex, I walked toward the back door that led out to the upper back deck.

"I'm sorry, Jessica," Alex said quietly as I pulled the door open.

"Don't be," I whispered. "It's my fault things are

the way they are."

Before Alex could protest or try to reason uselessly like I knew he would, I closed the door behind me. I hoped he wouldn't follow me, and I was glad when I heard his footsteps walk across the floor to the garage, taking the trash out.

I sat on one of the lounge chairs and pulled my knees up to my chest and wrapped my arms around them. The sun started to set, dyeing the sky an angry blood red. It stretched from the hilltop behind me, over my head, before giving way to the darkening cloudy sky in the east.

I didn't realize there were tears pouring down my cheeks until the muffled sob that escaped my chest made me jump. All of my insides trembled and rattled. I felt weak and tired, yet my limbs held their form stiffly as I tried to hold myself together and prevent myself from shattering from the inside out like I felt I was about to.

The desire to scream at someone filled me. I wanted to scream at Alex. To tell him to just do it and stop giving me his excuses that made no sense. I wanted to scream at Cole, for telling me in the first place that Alex had planned on proposing. I wanted to scream at everyone in the afterlife, for trying to take me before it should have been my time to go in the first place. If they hadn't have tried to take me, Alex wouldn't have had to sacrifice his own life to save mine.

But what was the point? Screaming wasn't going

to change anything. The council had already been gracious enough to give me *any* time with Alex. I somehow knew that Cole was gone now, so screaming at him wasn't an option. And I knew, no matter how mad I was at Alex, I could never scream at him. I owed him so much. I wouldn't be here if it wasn't for him. And besides that, I loved Alex.

I still wanted to scream though. I was tired of always crying so maybe screaming would have been a nice change.

When I heard the door open, I didn't turn to look and see who it was. I was enough of a freak now to recognize the sound and way everyone walked. Amber was home.

"Are you and Alex fighting?" she said as she sat in the chair next to me.

"Kind of," I muttered against my knees and wiped a tear away. "How'd you guess?"

"He just seemed really depressed. Didn't even say anything. I could just feel it rolling off him," she said as she mirrored my stance. "Want to talk about it?"

"Not really," I sighed. "It's complicated."

"Does it have something to do with the feathers?" Amber asked quietly.

Amber couldn't seem to make herself refer to Alex as being angel, whenever something came up she just referred to "the feathers" or "the wings."

"Yeah," I whispered as I wiped at a tear that had escaped onto my cheek.

"Whatever it is, you two will work things out. You two are perfect for each other. I don't think I've seen two people more in love."

I gave my sister an appreciative smile. "Speaking of which," I said, trying to change the subject. "How are you and Rod doing?"

I didn't even have to look at Amber's face to see the way it lit up. "Amazing," she burst. "Jessica, I've never felt like this about anyone before. He's the most amazing man I've ever known. I'm so in over my head."

"I can tell," I said as I met her smiling face, trying to smile back.

"I think…" she said, her gaze dropping to her knees for a moment. "I feel so sappy for saying it but, I think he's the one!"

I just smiled at her for a minute, trying to keep it genuine. "I'm happy for you, Amber. You deserve someone perfect for you." And I meant it. It didn't mean I wasn't almost violently jealous that she was about to get what she wanted and it seemed I never was.

CHAPTER TWELVE

ALEX

I set the groceries on the counter and went to answer the phone as it started ringing. Jessica followed me in, carrying another brown paper bag.

"Hello," a female voice on the other end said. "Is Mrs. Wright there?"

"She passed away a few months ago," I answered as I watched Jessica start to put the food away. I couldn't help but smile as I watched her fluid movements. It was so weird to see her move that way, it still freaked me out just a little.

"I'm sorry to hear that sir. Mrs. Jessica Wright?"

Hearing Jessica's name paired with mine jerked me back into paying attention to what the woman on the line had to say. "Uh, there's no one here by that name," I said as I looked away, feeling guilty or something for some strange reason. It wasn't like Jessica could hear the woman. At least I didn't *think* she could.

"Well sir, perhaps you might be interested in our special offer today…" she started her pitch.

"Ah," I groaned, realizing this was a sales call.

"Not interested. Thank you!" I tried to say nicely as I hung up the phone.

"Who was that?" Jessica asked as she bent over and put something in a lower cupboard.

"Just a sales call," I said with a half grin on my face. I couldn't help but stare at Jessica. I tried to be the nice guy, but I was still a guy.

"What are you looking at?" she asked with a sly smile as she stood up and caught me staring.

I chuckled as I walked up to her and wrapped my arms around her tiny waist. "The most beautiful thing known to man," I teased as I bent my head and pressed my lips to hers. "And she's mine."

Jessica only smiled in return as she moved her lips with mine. Not thinking about what I was doing, I lifted her off the floor and her legs wrapped around my waist. Distracted, I made my way to the leather couch.

She had no idea, the amount of restraint it took to keep from hurting her when we were together like this. I had to watch every movement I made with my hands, check every embrace, just to make sure I didn't crush her. Had she been a normal person, she would have constantly been covered in bruises. Jessica was far from normal though.

"Alex," she moaned into my throat. "I really don't want to stop."

"Me either," I growled as I moved my lips against her neck. Before I even realized what was happening, Jessica had peeled my shirt off and unbuttoned my pants.

And then the door suddenly opened and in walked Amber.

"Whoa," she said as she diverted her eyes from us as we scrambled to get off each other. "Sorry to be interrupting something. You know you two *do* have rooms?"

"Shut up, Amber," Jessica chuckled as she tried to tame back her impossible hair. I loved it when it got crazy like that.

"Nice going though, Jess," she chuckled as she walked into her room. "They don't come better sculpted than that."

I could only smile uncomfortably as I tried to tug my shirt down over my head.

JESSICA

I stared back at my reflection in the perfectly calm ocean water, searching my face. There was something hidden inside of me that wasn't really a part of me. It was different than me. It felt like an enemy.

My mind replayed over all the things that were happening lately. What was it about me that drew Cole out? Why didn't I bleed the other day? Why was I so scared to look in the mirror these days?

What was wrong with me?

I splashed my hand through the water, sending endless ripples crashing across my reflection. My chest felt tight as I straightened and looked out over the water. The islands were perfectly visible today.

I turned and started running through the trees.

What is wrong with me? I repeated that question over and over in my mind. It rushed around me in a maddening circle, showing me no answers.

The ground became a green and brown blur beneath my feet, and I didn't even see my surroundings as they whipped by. I wanted to out run it all, to leave all the impossibilities and insanities behind. I'd had enough of it all.

The next second there was nothing but air beneath my feet.

The next the Earth came crashing against my body.

All the air was forced out of my lungs as I slammed to the rocky ground. I rolled onto my side, my eyes struggling to focus on anything. I was confused at first. There was a huge rock wall that rose up to the side of me. It took me a moment to realize that I had run right off the edge of the twenty-five or so foot cliff.

I pulled myself up, wincing as every part of my body screamed at me. I shook the debris out of my tangled hair. Looking back up to the top of the cliff, I swallowed hard. I should have easily broken both of my legs, at least one of my arms, and done plenty more damage.

As I did an assessment of how I felt, I realized I felt perfectly fine.

I climbed to my feet. The pain faded away, and I started walking again.

Perfectly fine. That was the wrong description. I

felt like I freak. I didn't feel human. There was something terribly, horribly wrong with me.

How long had I been like this and not noticed? I had known something was different since I had nearly died but had *this* been the "different?"

My head spun, and I suddenly wondered if I even could pass out. My feet stumbled, one in front of the other, back in the direction of the house. Before long I was running again. The trees fell away behind me in a green and brown blur. Literally. I felt like I was flying, except that my feet were still pounding the springy earth beneath me.

I came to the river that flowed out of the lake and crossed it in one bounding leap. My feet felt light, my entire frame moving with a grace that felt foreign to me. I didn't even realize I was close to home until I shot across the narrow road and crashed into something both soft and hard at the same time.

"What the…" the something shouted as we crashed onto the driveway. I then realized that the something was Alex.

Pain exploded from my forearm and as I looked down at it my stomach rolled when I saw that it looked like a cheese grater had been taken to my skin, little pieces of rock and dirt embedded into it. Despite everything that had happened in the last five minutes, I was still horrified when no blood surfaced. It closed up in just a few seconds, the gravel dropping to the ground.

I looked up into Alex's face, his eyes staring wide

at my arm. I looked away quickly, pushing myself up to my feet.

"You want to explain what just happened?" he said as he too stood up.

"What are you talking about?" I said lamely as I walked toward the front door.

"Excuse me?" he said as he followed. "Are you going to just pretend you weren't moving at the speed of a rocket and that you suddenly seem to have regenerative powers?"

My bottom lip started trembling as I opened the front door and stepped inside. Alex silently closed it behind me, his frame standing near enough I could feel his body warmth against my skin.

"Well?" he said, his tone softer now.

"Yeah," I said, my voice cracking as I did. "Yeah, I am going to pretend that it didn't happen."

"Hey," he said softly as he placed a hand on my shoulder and turned me around to face him. When he saw the tears that had finally broke from my eyes, he wrapped his arms around me. "What's going on?"

"I don't know, Alex," I said, my voice cracking again. At least I could still cry. "I don't really want to talk about it. Enough is already wrong right now."

"You sure?"

I just nodded my head, unable to say anything else.

ALEX

I felt a little irritated at all the people that were on

the road around the lake these days. There were so many of them as I drove to the freeway on my way to meet up with Rod. I enjoyed the quiet lifestyle I had become accustomed to, and they were infringing on my new world. It was strange that they all bothered me. I was from Southern California, where there were millions of people. I had always liked people. Now they just stared open mouthed and tried to reason why I looked the way I did.

I tried to reason what I had just seen. What Jessica had just done was impossible. She had been moving almost as fast as I did. She had crashed into me like a torpedo. I still wasn't even sure if her skin had healed like I thought it did, or if that was just something my imagination had made up. Maybe I had gotten a concussion when she knocked me down.

I knew I hadn't though. I couldn't get a concussion.

What Jessica had done scared me beyond belief. Something was wrong with her. And it wasn't just what I had seen her do today. She still didn't eat much, maybe a meal a day. If I forced her. I wondered if she even still needed to. And she still only slept every other night, at the most.

I knew my limits and what I was capable of, but I also knew *what* I was. I was dead, I was an angel.

I wasn't so sure what Jessica was.

How much of her was human and how much of her was dead and more like myself, I didn't want to know. The things she was capable of though proved she was probably more angel than human. I didn't think she even realized this herself. She had no idea how close she had come to death. How much had she transitioned before I stopped it?

An involuntary shudder rippled through me at this thought. I had been so close to losing her. When I had found the gun she had been about to use on herself, my world started crumbling apart. I probably would have used it on myself had Jessica taken herself out of this world.

Surprisingly, the decision I made to trade my life for hers was easy to make. I was going to lose her one way or another. She was going to die; there was no question about that. I had expected to have to move onto the afterlife when I made the trade, so either way I was going to lose her. I would forever be grateful for this extra time we had been granted.

Everything changed after that horrific day though. I knew the things Jessica was capable of before it all happened was impossible. Before I died, she still shouldn't have been able to survive on as little sleep as she did. She didn't used to eat often either. Everything had been so much more enhanced after though. While I had freed her of the nightmares, she was still far from normal. She might not have realized I noticed, but I knew she was stronger than any man I had ever met. And her senses were closer to mine than a human's.

There was something else that was off about Jessica since that day. I couldn't pinpoint it exactly.

When I looked at her there was something that was different about her than everyone else I knew. Not just all the things that I already knew were different. Something else about her had changed, but I wasn't sure what.

And that was the part that terrified me the most.

CHAPTER THIRTEEN

JESSICA

I hung the phone up and gave a frustrated sigh.

Where was she?

Panic was starting to eat me up. It had now been a full month since I had seen Emily. I still had no idea where she had gone to. I'd been calling her phone three times a day lately, never getting anything but her voicemail.

"Hey, Jessica?" Austin's voice came from behind me. I turned around, trying to get my face composed.

"Rita just asked if I'd take this order up to some old lady who lives up in Ferndale. She said you could go with me if you wanted."

"It is a little dead," I said as I looked around the bookshop. It was completely empty besides the three of us.

Austin chuckled. "You want to come?"

I hesitated for a moment, hoping he wouldn't read anything he shouldn't into this. "Sure."

We let Rita know we were leaving and headed out to the parking lot. We paused in a momentary awkward second, unsure of what car to take.

"We can take my car, but we will have to stop for gas on the way. I'm almost empty," I said as we stood there.

"Let's just take mine then. I've got a full tank."

I slid into the passenger seat, pushing aside the food wrappers that were scattered on the floor. It smelled just a little off inside. I tried not to wrinkle my nose.

"Sorry," Austin's face flooded with red. "I was going to clean it out yesterday. Guess I kinda forgot."

"Don't worry about it," I said, giving a half smile.

He put the key in the ignition and went to start the car. It gave a high pitched squeal but didn't turn over.

"Maybe we should just take the GTO," I said as I pointed in the direction of my car. "Yours isn't really seeming up to the job today."

"No, it's okay," he said. I heard the undertones of frustration and embarrassment. "Just give it a second."

He was right. The next try it jumped to life, though the high squeal didn't die away. We pulled out of the parking lot and headed toward the freeway.

"Thanks for coming with me," Austin said as he turned his blinker on and merged into the flow of the light traffic. "I've taken an order into this lady before for Rita. I was stuck there for nearly two hours while she ranted on and on about I'm not even sure what."

"So you tricked me?" I said in mock horror. "You're going to let her take me prisoner too?"

"Not going down by myself," he chuckled as he

glanced over at me. "Like they say, misery loves company."

I gave an awkward smile. I had always applied that expression to the condemned angels.

"So have you heard from your friend that's been missing?" Austin asked, his eyes focused on the road in front of him.

I shook my head. "I'm getting really worried about her. No one has heard from her for over a month now."

"Have you talked to her family yet?"

"Emily isn't close with them," I said awkwardly. That was the understatement of the decade. "They don't talk."

"Well, have you filed a missing person's report?"

I shook my head again. "She's got kind of a shady past. It would only get Emily in even more trouble to get the police involved."

"What, like, she's a fugitive?" Austin asked with a chuckle as he gave me a disbelieving glance.

"Sort of," I said as I looked out the window. Wow. I'd said way too much. How stupid was I?

"That's kind of hot," he said with a hint of amusement in his voice.

"Okay, change of subj…Austin watch out!" I screamed.

It all happened so fast, but I didn't miss a single detail. The semi-truck in front of us had suddenly slammed on its breaks, causing the trailer behind it to jackknife across both freeway lanes. Austin swerved to the right to avoid hitting it, but there was no prayer.

The front left side of Austin's car slammed into the trailer. The car was suddenly airborne and I saw alternating views of freeway and open fields of the countryside as we flipped.

One second I watched as Austin was catapulted out the driver's side window that had been rolled down.

The next second everything turned black and very quiet.

ALEX

I set the dusting rag down and went to grab my cell phone off the counter as it rang. I didn't recognize the number.

"Hello?"

"Is Alex Wright available?" a female voice said on the other end.

"This is him," I answered as I looked around the house. I was nearly done with all the remodeling.

"This is Sandra from St. Joseph's hospital in Bellingham. Do you know a Jessica Bailey?"

My stomach suddenly dropped out. I wanted to throw up. "Yes. She's my girlfriend."

"There's been an accident. She's in the emergency room right now. You should come down as soon as possible."

"I'm on my way right now," I said as I locked the front door behind me.

It was amazing I didn't get a speeding ticket as I

screeched down the streets. Horrible visions filled my head as I couldn't push the truck fast enough. Was she okay? How badly had she been injured? What had happened?

But what if she hadn't been hurt? I'd seen her heal before my own eyes. There hadn't even been any blood.

I parked across three spaces as I pulled into the parking lot of the hospital. Moving faster than I should have, I sprinted through the doors of the emergency room.

"I'm here to see Jessica Bailey," I said to the girl who sat at the reception counter.

"She's in room 124," she told me as she looked something up on the computer, after asking for my name. "Officer Barrington is here to talk to you."

I turned around and saw the police officer that had been standing in one corner of the waiting room. I shook his hand as he extended it to me.

"Is she okay?" I asked, my voice frantic as we walked down the hall.

"It was a really bad accident," he said, his face grim. "She and the other boy were just getting into Ferndale when it happened."

"Wait," I said as I paused in the hall. "Other boy?"

"Miss Bailey was in the car with a boy she works with. They were driving his car, running a delivery I believe."

"Austin?" I asked. Even as I did I glanced into the

room to my right and saw a nurse propping a pillow under the very guy's right arm. His eyes met mine, panic seeping into them.

"I'm so sorry, Alex," he said, anxiety about to overtake him. "It was an accident. I'm so sorry!"

My eyes grew wide and panic filled me. "Jessica!" I yelled as I turned and ran down the hall, my eyes searching franticly for room number 124. "Jessica!" I bellowed again as I half fell through the right door.

She was lying on the bed, her eyes closed, her hair fanned out around her face. Monitors beeped and there were tubes hooked up to her arms.

"Is she alright?" I half whispered as I stood five feet away from the bed. I couldn't seem to make myself move any closer.

"It's nothing short of a miracle she made it out of there. A witness says she saw the car fly about fifteen feet before it hit the ground. It rolled about five times before it landed on the roof. The boy was thrown from the car almost immediately. He has a broken arm, but is fine other than that.

"Jessica was trapped inside. She was knocked unconscious. We had to use the Jaws of Life to pry her out. The car basically balled around her. I honestly don't know how it didn't crush her to death."

I bit my lower lip, squeezing my eyes closed for a minute. Just then there was a knock at the door and a graying man in a white lab coat stepped in.

"I'm Dr. Russell," he said as he shook my hand.

"I've been assigned to Miss Bailey."

"Is she okay?" I asked, my insides quivering. I felt like I was going to shatter at any moment.

"Excuse me," the policeman said as he stepped toward the door. "I have to go talk to the boy again." He closed the door behind him.

"Is she okay?" I asked again.

It was a few seconds before Dr. Russell spoke. "This is nothing short of a miracle, Mr. Wright. The EMTs told us that Jessica was completely wrapped up on the remains of the car. She really shouldn't have survived."

"But she's okay?" I felt like screaming at the man. I just wanted to know if Jessica was alright and no one would answer me straight.

"Jessica doesn't have a scratch on her," the doctor whispered as he glanced at her still form. "Not a broken bone, not a cut or even a bruise."

I cursed under my breath as I looked back at Jessica.

"We've taken x-rays of most of Jessica's body. Forgive me for saying this, but this woman has the most perfect body I have ever seen. I don't see evidence of a single broken bone, ever. And her structural make up, well, bodies like this just don't exist. She's…well, perfect."

My vocal cords didn't seem to want to work as I just stared at her. I was terrified.

"She's just resting right now. She woke up for a few minutes earlier, but she was disoriented. I think her body's trying to recover right now, despite the lack of damage.

"We would like to keep Miss Bailey here overnight for observation. If everything goes well I see no reason why she couldn't go home in the morning."

I gave a nod to indicate that I had heard him.

"I'll give you some time alone with her. Things are going to be alright, Mr. Wright. She's perfectly fine." The doctor laid a hand on my shoulder, giving me one of those all too familiar searching stares. After a moment he let himself out.

Jessica may have been perfect, but that just proved she was not *fine*.

I finally moved to Jessica's side, pulling a chair up close to her bed. I took one of her small hands in mine and pressed my lips to her knuckles. It terrified me to see her like this, looking so helpless.

She belongs with us...

You must return...

We are waiting...

The whispers built up slowly, so quiet that I didn't even realize they were there at first. They grew in intensity. They became hurried, frantic. Excited. I closed my eyes, focusing everything I had into pushing them out.

My breath caught in my chest as my insides started to quake. Everything inside of me felt like it was shifting, disappearing and reforming again. My hands shook, and I had to let go of Jessica's hand to keep from crushing it.

I braced my hands on the edge of her bed, my head hanging between my arms. I gave a gasping breath, trying to force air in and out of my lungs that felt like they weren't there anymore.

"No," I said through clenched teeth. "No."

The whispering built in intensity, becoming chaotic. I couldn't even distinguish actual words. But I was getting their message loud and clear.

"Alex?"

Air flooded my lungs and my insides felt whole again as everything dropped away and my head jerked up. Jessica was looking at me with her wide hazel eyes.

"Jessica!" I cried in relief as I pulled her into my arms.

"Where am I?" she asked as she returned my embrace and looked around. "What happened?"

I sat back a bit, hovering at the edge of the bed. "There was an accident."

I saw the memories come back to Jessica before I even finished my sentence. "The semi. The car flipped. Austin flew out the window. Is he okay?" Her tone was suddenly panicked.

"He broke an arm, but other than that I think he's fine," I said as I brushed a stray hair behind her ear.

Jessica took in her surroundings again. "I'm in the hospital." It was a terrified statement. "I can't be here Alex. There's something wrong with me. They're going to find out."

I glanced at the closed door, my insides knotting up. She was right. I had to get her out of here. Now.

I jumped up from the bed, digging through every drawer and cupboard. "Here," I said as I found Jessica's clothes. "Put these on."

She didn't protest or even say anything. She just got out of the bed, keeping her backside covered as best she could with the hospital gown. I turned around as she pulled her clothes on.

"They're going to ask questions," she said. "What have they seen?"

I squeezed my eyes closed. "Enough." Too much.

I didn't realize she had finished getting dressed until she stepped around in front of me. Her face was tight with mixed emotions.

"They can't know whatever they might have seen," she said as she looked up into my eyes. I could see the conflict in her own. "You're going to have to fix this."

"What?" I asked, my brow furrowing.

"They can't remember I've been here. None of them." Jessica's face was stark white.

I swallowed hard as I stared back at her. "I'm not like him. I can't do that. It's wrong."

Jessica bit her lower lip, her eyes dropping away from my face for a moment. When she looked back up at me they were tight. "They can't know. There's something wrong with me Alex. They'll do whatever they have to in order to figure it out."

And I knew she was right. Dr. Russell would start to wonder what was going on with Jessica. He had seen proof on the x-ray that there was something off. She was too perfect.

"I don't want to do this," I said with a quivering voice.

"I know," she said, her voice husky sounding. We stared at each other for several loaded moments. "I'll wait in the truck."

I felt my insides harden as I watched her go out the door. It felt as if the afterlife had sunk their claws further into me. I was getting forced into being what I was.

My jaw was clenched as I walked out the door and into the hall, all traces of Jessica gone. I walked down the hall and stepped into the room I had seen Austin in.

"Alex, I'm so sorry," he started in again.

"For what?" I asked. I was focusing everything I had toward Austin. "You have nothing to apologize for. You were in an accident."

Austin's face was saturated with confusion as he looked back at me. "The car. Jessica almost came on the delivery with me. She would have been killed if she'd come!"

"Get better soon, Austin," I said as I started back toward the door. I paused with my hand on the doorknob and looked back at him. My insides felt sick.

"Thanks for coming to see me," Austin said with a

small smile. "You're a good guy, Alex."

I couldn't even return the smile as I gave a nod and stepped out.

I didn't feel like a good guy after altering Austin's memories. It was wrong to mess with people's heads.

CHAPTER FOURTEEN

JESSICA

He hovered above me, his eyes gleaming black, the excitement and anticipation blurring their focus. His hands stroked both my arms softly, sending shivers down my spine. As his lips brushed mine, my pulse raced and my own hands brushed his bare back, my fingers rising and falling over the coiled muscles. They froze as I felt the feathers.

My eyes, which had started closing in blissful anticipation, shot open, gaping wide at the ones that stared back at me. Black, not steely gray.

I wanted to scream as Cole's hands continued their exploration of my skin. And just when I thought I could bear it no longer without screaming, it wasn't me he was touching anymore. The woman I was watching him with seemed to be enjoying what was about to happen.

With morbid curiosity I watched as Cole reached for something, realizing it was a length of rope. The woman seemed blissfully unaware of whatever it was Cole intended to do with it or that he even had something in his hand. Before I even understood what was happening, Cole had the rope wrapped around her neck before she could even scream.

Sweat covered me as I woke up, panting, my insides squirming in disgust. I felt dizzy and the branded X on the back of my neck prickled slightly.

I was glad to see that Alex wasn't lying beside me. Alex didn't need to see me having nightmares. It just wasn't fair to him. When I looked at the clock and saw that it was already ten, I knew why he wasn't still there. It was Saturday and Rod liked to go play basketball on his day off. It probably wouldn't be too long before he would come home. Alex needed a distraction too. Ever since he had made everyone at the hospital forget I was even there, he'd been off. I didn't blame him. There was something wrong with messing with people's heads.

As if these new nightmares weren't disturbing enough, I had the sickening feeling that they weren't just nightmares. They felt so real and they were *so* vivid. Each one had been slightly different yet all too similar, all five of them. Every one started with Cole charming the woman in the dream, always starting out as me, followed by some romantic escapade that included having a portrait painted of myself. Just as it seemed I was unwittingly about to make love to Cole it thankfully wasn't me anymore and Cole choked the life out of the other woman. He murdered them.

The part that worried me, that made me think the nightmares might be real were the surroundings. I wasn't dreaming of any time period I had ever lived in, was never dressed in the current trends of today. Everything looked very mid-eighteenth century, exactly when Cole had been alive.

I had never known all the deeds Cole had committed that led to his branding, but I saw this could be a strong possibility. He had a reason to hate women.

I climbed into the shower, feeling desperate to get my skin clean, even though I knew Cole had not in fact touched me in any way. I still felt dirty and defiled.

The bathroom was filled with steam when I got out. Maybe I had tried too hard to scald off the feelings of filth that weren't real. I wrapped a thick white towel around myself and opened the door to my bedroom to get dressed. I was halfway to my closet when I heard him move and felt his arms wrap around my waist as he came out from his hiding place behind the door.

Alex's lips traced a path from my shoulder, up my neck, to my ear. He did that to get a rise out of me and it worked. He knew I didn't like him playing with my ears, I thought it was just weird, not sexy. I turned in his arms, a smile playing on my face, a blinding one plastered on his.

"Good morning, Sleeping Beauty," he said quietly as he pressed a soft kiss to my lips.

"Morning," I said as I touched my forehead to his, biting my lower lip as the smile spread on my face.

Alex's hands traced my skin upwards, leaving tingling trails, up to the raised wings that spanned my back. I saw the way his eyes danced as he looked into mine, making my blood surge and rise in my veins. I didn't know any other way to respond when Alex looked at me like that.

My hands fisted in his hair as our lips met again and Alex crushed me into his chest. I wondered about the restraint he must have had to use to not totally crush my every bone, but for some reason this excited me all the more. Even though the fact that Alex was an angel struck terror into my heart at times, at others it made me want him in a nearly painful way.

Things ended the way they always did for us, in the bed but with neither of us completely satisfied and both our consciences clean.

"One of these times…" Alex trailed off as he lay on his back, looking up at the ceiling.

I smiled slightly, but my mind was in other places by now. Back to a few months before, to a scene very much like this one. It had led to a trip to Seattle, a decision made by Alex, a ring bought somewhere in the middle, and ended with a kidnapping.

I couldn't seem to think of anything other than the fact that Alex was never going to ask me to marry him. It was going to consume me until it drove me totally insane.

"Let's go for a ride," I said as I stood up and made my way to the closet. "But I want to drive today."

"Okay," Alex said, a slightly surprised look

crossing his face. I never drove the motorcycle on our rides.

"Now get out for a minute so I can change," I said with a small smile when Alex just sat there and stared at me with an almost drugged looking smile on his face.

He just shook his head with that smile as he stood and left, closing the door behind him.

"I think maybe you should slow down!" I heard Alex yell from behind me. "You're going to get pulled over!"

I ignored Alex as I gunned the bike faster, the towering trees whipping past us. I wasn't too worried about any cops out here. I still had yet to see any signs of life on these rural roads.

I knew I was being stupid and reckless, but the speed seemed to have a way of releasing some of the pent up emotions that threatened to explode from me. Maybe it was the tight leather I wore, a gift I'd received from Alex a few months previous, maybe it was the way I knew I looked in it, maybe it was just the way something under my skin knew something was wrong. But I needed to get out and do something stupid.

"Jessica!" I heard him yell. "Seriously, slow down!"

I still ignored him and a small, satisfied smile spread on my lips when I saw that the speedometer indicated I was pushing ninety-five miles an hour.

And just like that, it felt like my stomach had leapt out of my throat as iron bands gripped my waist and the motorcycle threatened to buck out of my hands. We came to a screeching, smoking halt.

As I killed the gas, the wheels spinning and skidding against the road, I turned around to see that Alex had slipped off the back of the bike. His hands gripped my sides hard enough there should be bruises later, if I still bruised. A trail of chewed up pavement made paths to his feet that were buried into the ground. Alex had pulled us to a grinding, halting stop.

"What the crap are you trying to do?" he demanded as he let go and pulled his totally unnecessary helmet off. His eyes were wide, angry, and confused at the same time. "Are you trying to kill yourself?!"

I was still in shock over what Alex had done, and I didn't have anything to say in response. My body was confused. I wanted to be angry, but my brain seemed to still be waiting to catch up with me. I pulled my helmet off without even thinking about it.

"What's going on, Jessica?" he asked, his voice exasperated. "You're all over the place lately. You're normal one moment, then you're depressed or angry the next. And now you're acting like you think you're invincible. Is this about Rod proposing to Amber last night? About how I haven't?"

"Everything is about how you haven't!" I suddenly shouted. All the anger, frustration, and sadness finally seemed to have caught up with me.

"You know that! I can't get over it, Alex! I can't keep going about day-to-day life like you don't have a ring for me, like things can never be the way they're supposed to be. And the most frustrating thing is that I know that things will never change. It is just going to keep going on like this!"

Alex's face was stunned for a long moment. "What are you saying?" he said quietly. "Do you want me to leave? That you can't keep doing this? Us?"

It felt like Alex had slapped me across the face. I could only glare at him for a moment. "You're *insane* if you think I could ever live without you," I said, still feeling frustrated and angry but horrified that this was how Alex had taken what I had said. But thinking back on what I had said, how could he have taken it any other way? "Forget I said anything. Let's just go home."

"Jessica, I…" he trailed off. He let out a frustrated sigh. I knew how he felt. We just kept arguing in the same circle, without being able to find a solution. There wasn't anything to be said that hadn't already been said. But we both knew there was no way we could live without each other. The very thought was a nightmare too horrible for us to comprehend. "I'm driving. You're just going to get yourself killed."

I then remembered what Alex had said about thinking I was invincible. Maybe I was. After everything that had happened lately, it kind of looked that way.

I couldn't help but think as I climbed on the bike behind Alex that maybe that would solve our problems. We couldn't seem to find a way to be together as we should be as human and angel. Perhaps the only way to solve this was to fully become an angel myself.

Neither of us said anything as Alex drove us home at a legal speed. I felt ashamed for what I thought about becoming an angel. The fact that I had even had the thought scared me. I was ashamed for behaving so horribly the last few weeks. I didn't want to feel like this, and I hated that Alex and I were fighting.

I still didn't know how to get over this, though.

Alex eased the bike into the garage and shut the engine off. I slid off and pulled my helmet off. Alex swung his other leg over, but remained sitting on the bike as he took his helmet off as well and just stared at me. I had a hard time looking at him, with those piercing gray eyes that looked so sad, knowing I was the reason they looked that way.

"I'm sorry," I said quietly. "I just…I'm going to go check on Sal."

Alex didn't say anything, but I felt his eyes on my back as I walked out the garage and up to the road.

As soon as I knew he couldn't see me, I doubled over and threw up on the side of the road. I walked to Sal's front door with shaking legs.

I knocked on the door twice before letting myself in. I could tell from the mounting mess that filled her house that the house cleaner hadn't been by in a few days. They must have been coming by tonight or tomorrow.

"Sal?" I called as I closed the front door behind me.

"Down here!" I heard her call from the floor below.

I found Sal in her office, sitting at the huge desk, gluing something in a book. I realized it was a scrapbook, and she was adhering a picture of Alex and me into it. There were stacks of pictures Alex had taken and printed out for her spread out on the desk.

I didn't say anything as I sat down and watched Sal get the photo positioned just right. Sal seemed better lately, since Cole had left and she had been discharged from the institution. She had more lucid times and a lot of the time she seemed nearly normal. But when she had her bad moments, they were usually worse.

"What is wrong, Jessica?" I hadn't even realized Sal had finished and was looking into my face with a concerned expression.

I wanted to reassure her that nothing was wrong, but I couldn't. I didn't have the strength and I didn't have the willpower to try and deny the feelings that were raging and storming within me.

"I yelled at Alex," I said honestly.

"Alex is a nice man," Sal said, a slightly sharp tone to her voice. "You shouldn't yell at him."

"I know," I said softly, my voice sounding hoarse. "I didn't want to, and I'm sorry I did, but I was mad at him."

"Why?" she asked, absolute interest in her face.

"Because he won't do something I want him to," I answered. As I said the words I realized how childish and selfish I sounded and was being.

"There must be a reason," Sal said as she looked at the pile of pictures, picking one out. "Alex would do anything for you. He loves you. I wish Roger had loved me like Alex loves you."

The fact that Sal had said her ex-husband's name surprised me. I couldn't recall her ever saying it out loud before, other than when she screamed it out in her sleep.

"I know," I said with a sigh.

"Maybe he knows something you don't. Maybe that's part of the reason," she said as she cut off a portion of the picture and then glued it to a page. It was a picture of me and my father, from my birthday party.

I made an agreeing noise, not thinking too much about what she said. I could sense one of Sal's more out-of-it moments coming on. "Do you need anything?" I asked as I stood up.

"More glue," she said without looking up at me. "And four mangos. Oh, and a jar of peanut butter."

I chuckled internally at her request. Sal was severely allergic to peanuts. She had probably forgotten. I would keep the peanut butter off my shopping list. "All right, I'll get them next time I go to the store."

Sal reached into a drawer, drew out a wad of money and threw it in my direction. It was more than fifty dollars, but I knew better than to try and give some back to her. She would be offended and would likely scream at me.

"I will see you later," I called as I walked out the door and up the stairs.

I was feeling slightly better as I started the short walk back home, but as I thought back over Sal and my conversation, something she said struck me.

Maybe he knows something you don't. Maybe that's part of the reason.

Some horrible things started to click together in my head as I thought about Sal's words. Alex had repeatedly said that he didn't know what was going to happen to him anymore. That he didn't have any control over his time. I recalled the scene Alex showed me, of his own unfinished trial.

The council members had been telling him something as Alex closed the vision or whatever it was. What they had started to say seemed important, and it now felt very deliberate that Alex didn't let me hear the rest.

Even though I kept walking, I felt my body freeze up. What did Alex know that he wasn't telling me?

My every nerve seemed about to shatter as I got to the front door and opened it. This new thought terrified me and made me feel immature and stupid for behaving the way I had been lately. This was Alex. What Sal said about Alex doing anything for me was true. He'd already proven that. If he wouldn't marry me when I had told him I didn't care what happened afterward, he must have had a pretty powerful reason why.

ALEX

As soon as Jessica was out of sight, I lost it. It was stupid and pointless, but I plowed my fist into the wall. I barely even felt it as currents of electricity raced up my arm. Great, now I was going to have to fix the sheetrock *and* call an electrician.

I went inside and slammed the door closed behind me. I flipped the TV on in an effort to distract myself, but turned it off less than thirty seconds later. I nearly punched the screen out for no good reason.

I leaned against the wall, slid down and buried my face in my hands. What was I doing? I kept telling myself that I couldn't marry Jessica because I wouldn't do that only to possibly be taken away the next day. But why? Jessica had told me dozens of times that she didn't care, she'd take anything we could get. My holding back wasn't making her happy. It was making her totally miserable. It certainly wasn't making me happy.

So why was I holding back?

My shoulders suddenly felt lighter as my thoughts resolved. I was going to do it. Today. As soon as Jessica walked back through the door. I would drop down on one knee and I would ask Jessica to marry me.

I got to my feet, excitement coursing through my system. I felt relieved that we were finally going to move past all the depression and hurt. Damn the consequences. Damn whatever might happen tomorrow.

As I reached into my pocket for the box I had carried around for the last few months, I felt something else vibrate and pulled my cell phone out. The screen display said I had just received a new text message.

Yet again my stomach felt like it was hollowing out as I read it.

I couldn't ask Jessica to marry me. Not only because it could crush her, but because there were worse things that could happen to me than just being pulled back into the afterlife permanently. They could still do horrible things to Jessica once I was gone. They could torture her, just as they did me, for the location of a certain dark angel.

JESSICA

I wondered if this was what shock felt like. I couldn't remember actually walking into the house and closing the door behind me. I didn't even realize that Alex had walked into the room and had said something to me. "Jessica?" he said, a look of concern on his face. "Is something wrong?"

His voice sounded far away and muffled as I tried to clear the suddenly dead feeling from my head. "Yeah, no, I..." I said as I shook my head, closing my eyes deliberately before I opened them again. I then realized that Alex was extending his cell phone to me. He must have said something earlier about it that I hadn't heard. "Sorry, what did you say?"

Alex's face was a mess of emotions as he looked at me. "I just got this a few minutes ago. I think you should take a look at it."

I took the phone from him, wondering what he could be talking about. It appeared to be a text message, and I noted the name of the sender was Emily's.

Tell Jessica that I'm fine.
She can stop calling.
I found Cole.
I finally have what she does.

I blanched as I read Cole's name and my knees felt weak. The dreams I had been having of him lately flooded my memory.

Emily was *with* him.

Without realizing what I was doing, I pushed the call button and held the phone to my ear.

"I already tried," Alex said. "It just went straight to her voicemail."

He was right; that was all I got.

"Why?" I stammered. "I don't…Why would she go after Cole? She knows what he's capable of. He branded her too, hundreds of times. Why would she go to him?"

I looked up at Alex and was surprised to see that he looked…almost angry. His jaw was clenched tightly, and his fists were balled up. It took me a moment to understand his reaction. Alex had been pulled back into the afterlife and tortured for Cole's location. He hadn't known, but apparently Emily did or had found it out.

"How'd she find him?" I said softly. "Where is he?"

Alex didn't say anything, just shook his head, his lips pursed in a thin line.

Neither of us said much else the rest of the night. I could tell Alex was furious, and while I couldn't blame him for feeling angry in general, I didn't exactly think it should be directed at Emily. Maybe that was because I too had known where Cole was for a while.

My last conversation with Emily haunted me as I recalled it. Emily was jealous of what Alex and I had. She wanted someone to love her the way she thought only an angel could love someone. And so she had gone and found the only other angel she knew of.

I sent Alex out that night, claiming to want some ice cream. As soon as he was out of the house I went into my closet and unburied the last letter Cole had left for me.

I took a deep breath as I sat on my bed with it in my hands. How many days had it been that I'd been too afraid to open it?

My hands wanted to shake as I tore the envelope open and pulled the single sheet of paper out. It took every ounce of strength I had to unfold the page.

Goodbye, Jessica. Eventually we all have to face our demons. I've gone to face mine. Perhaps someday I can help you face yours.

X

I had never felt so emotionally exhausted as I climbed into bed that night. My emotions had been pulled in too many directions. First with being angry with Alex, being terrified of what Alex might not be telling me, and the revelation of Cole and Emily was just too much. And what was Cole's letter supposed to mean?

I should have known better than to think that sleep might bring some sort of relief for me.

I had another nightmare of Cole that night. This one however was distinctly different from the others. This time everything was modern, the clothing, the music that played in the background, the way people talked. The biggest, most horrifying difference however was that this time I knew the woman Cole strangled in the end. It was Emily.

CHAPTER FIFTEEN

JESSICA

Cole's house looked exactly the same as it did when I had been there last. The glass was still broken in the back door where Alex had punched it out in order to get in. There was evidence of water damage from the rain getting in, but other than that, the front area looked the same. I wondered if Cole had even come in when he had come back to stalk me.

There were no good memories attached to this house. I had been held a dying captive here for over a week. I had nearly killed myself within these walls, twice.

This house was about the last place on earth I wanted to go back to, but I had to do this. I knew I had to find Cole, *now*, and I didn't know where else to start looking for clues as to where he might have gone. Emily obviously wasn't going to answer her phone, unaware of what might possibly be looming in her future. I had to find something to point me in the right direction. I didn't know how much time I had, if any. If the nightmares I had been having were real, Emily could already be dead.

I wandered down the hall to my left. The first door I tried was a bathroom, completely empty of anything, no soap, shampoo, or even toilet paper. The second door revealed a bedroom, also empty of absolutely anything other than a double sized bed, made up with stark white sheets, pillowcases, and comforter. I knew what was going to be behind door number three before I even opened it. I had seen into it once before, all part of a terrifying chain of events.

I knew what was going to be in the room but I wasn't prepared for the state it was going to be in. Books had been pulled off their shelves, files emptied and dumped on the floor, CD cases lying open and cracked. The place had been ransacked. Someone else had been here before I had, and I knew it wasn't Cole who had done this.

It seemed that if there was going to be any clue as to where Cole might have ran to, it would be in this room. Apparently someone else had thought that as well. There was only one other person who would have tried to find Cole. Emily.

Not knowing exactly what I was looking for, I started sifting through the mess. I started by picking up the CD cases. I didn't see anything that might give me any clues. I didn't recognize any of the band names, I wasn't into screamer rock. I next started into the books, quickly flipping through them, looking for anything that might help me. Cole had quite a collection of classics, written from the time period he had lived in. He also possessed volumes of poetry from people I had never heard of. I wondered why he had bothered getting them. He had only been back in the world of the living for a few months.

I couldn't make any sense of most of the documents I sorted through. Some looked legal like they were possibly closing documents on this house, his shiny black sports car, a house full of furniture. Nothing looked helpful as I cleared page after page from the floor.

A small feeling of hope surged in my veins when I saw the ancient-looking leather bound book half buried on the desk. I had seen it before, just briefly. Cole had been pouring over it the day I had seen his brand and realized his true identity. My hands shook and my insides quivered as I ran my hand over its worn and cracked surface.

Some sort of crest had been tooled into its cover, and I could barely make out the word at the top. *Emerson.*

I opened the cover and began thumbing through its pages. It was an extensive family tree, filled with names, dates, and places. I finally found Cole's name, written below Marcus Emerson and Annabell Florence's. Cole had apparently been an only child. I felt mixed emotions that the line ended there, knowing that Cole's blood had in fact been carried on.

The following pages contained maps, drawings of property boundaries, leases of real estate, and a lot of other information I had to hope would lead me to where I was now sure Cole would be.

It seemed so clear and simple where Cole had gone. Home. He'd gone to face his demons.

I just couldn't understand where any of these places were supposed to be. The entire Emerson legacy was bound on paper before me, but I had no idea where any of it was.

I was about to close the book when I noticed that there was still more. In the final few pages there was yet another family tree, written in ink that looked much newer and fresher than the rest of it all. The name at the very beginning took me a moment to process and understand who it must have been.

William Anthony.

Cole's illegitimate son.

I still didn't know Cole's lover's first name, but I now knew her last.

There were no places written with these names, but dates spread down through seven generations. I didn't recognize any of the names but at the bottom, when the dates reached years the final people could have still been alive, Cole had penned in

No connection.

I didn't understand what it meant, but it didn't matter. I closed the book and put it under my arm. I would take it home and Alex would help me figure out where the Emerson estate was. He had traveled around the world; perhaps he would see something that would otherwise never mean anything to me.

I don't know why I did it. I had no reason to and I regretted it the second after my feet met flat ground.

I walked with shaking knees down the stairs, descending into the shadowy second floor. As I did, dark memories surfaced, feelings I didn't want to remember flooded my mind.

The bottom floor was smaller than the rest of the house. To my left at the bottom of the stairs was a small theater room, to my right was a bathroom. Straight in front of me was a windowless bedroom.

I flipped the light on in the bedroom and froze in the doorway.

It looked exactly the same as when I had run out of the room six or so months before. The sheetrock was buckled in all over the room. I winced as I recalled the way Cole had thrown Alex's body against the walls. The sound of all the breaks echoed in my brain. Spatters of blood stained the light-colored carpet everywhere. There was a pool of it where it had drained out of Alex's nose after he hadn't been able to move.

One break in the sheetrock held my eyes locked. It was the smallest one but the most significant. Alex told Cole that he had made a deal, his life for mine. As Cole realized he could never have me, he had slammed Alex's head against the wall.

I recalled seeing how Cole's knuckles turned white as he squeezed Alex's neck.

And then the snap as he broke Alex's neck. And killed him.

I squeezed my eyes closed, holding my hands over my stomach. Why had I come here?

When I opened my eyes again, something else caught my eye. Lying on the ground, among the splatters and smears of blood, was the gleaming gun I had tried to turn on myself.

That was all it took to send me running back up the steps.

I took a dozen gasping breaths as I stood back in the living room. My head wouldn't stop spinning for a few minutes.

It seemed unnecessary, but I decided to check the other rooms on the main floor. I tried to keep myself from throwing up as I walked down the other hall. The first door was just a storage closet containing only towels. The second door opened to what was supposed to be the master bedroom.

It shouldn't have creeped me out as much as it did, to be in Cole's bedroom. Angels don't sleep, so the fact that there was a perfectly made bed in the room should have looked like anything else in Cole's home. It was probably one of the most unused pieces of furniture in the house. It still sent a slight shiver down my back to look at it.

There wasn't much in the room. The bed, a dresser, most of the contents piled on the floor in front of it, a nightstand Emily seemed to have gone through as well. There was a large walk-in closet off the room, though it was mostly empty. The bathroom that was attached was mostly empty as well.

I was about to leave when a painting on the wall caught my eye. It was a simple seascape scene, but it seemed oddly out of place for the frame it was in. The painting seemed like a cheap, mass reproduction, something anyone could buy for twenty dollars or less. The frame it was in, however, looked ancient and carved in intricate detail. It was obvious it had been done by hand and there were no repeat patterns. Every surface of it was different on all sides, yet blending perfectly with itself. It looked expensive as well, a tarnished gold look. As I touched a tentative finger to it, I was pretty sure it was gold leafed.

My fingers accidently brushed the paper of the painting, surprisingly ruffling it. I then realized that the picture wasn't mounted to the frame right, it appeared to only be attached at the top.

With curiosity, I lifted the paper to see what was hidden underneath. Half a second later, I wished I hadn't.

My mind couldn't make sense of what I was seeing at first. I was sure I would find another painting behind the false one, but at first glance I thought it must have been a mirror. Except the elegant twist wasn't the way I had done my hair this morning, the intricate and detailed dress exposing my shoulders wasn't the gray T-shirt I had put on earlier.

The woman in the mirror could have been my sister, no, my twin, if not a painting of myself in different clothes and a fancy hairdo. My skin crawled and the scar on the back of my neck prickled.

I searched the woman's face and wasn't sure if I was relieved or not when I found the subtle differences. Her eyes were much more green than my hazel, her bottom lip fuller than my own, her nose slightly more narrow. The woman in the painting wasn't me, but like I said, she could have been my twin.

Only after the mix of horror and bewilderment started to ebb somewhat did I notice the words that had been painted in the corner.

My Dearest

It landed on me like a pile of bricks. This was the woman from the letters. The woman he had had an affair with, created a child with, and the woman he could never have.

And she looked almost exactly like me.

X

We were both getting frustrated in trying to figure out where Cole's hometown was supposed to be. The documents were difficult to decipher and we had nearly exhausted all our resources except for having to pay a professional to take a look at it. We weren't against that, we just didn't know where to start.

The names that were attached to land parcels weren't towns as far as we could tell. They were names of families who had owned them, or other names that had no meaning to us. And we couldn't decipher a location from the hand drawn maps.

I had stayed up all night with Alex, poring over the book. I felt mentally exhausted and I could tell it was getting to Alex that we hadn't figured it out yet. I understood his drive to solve the mystery. He had been tortured for Cole's location. In some way, I think we were both afraid he might get sucked back into the afterlife and be terrorized again.

I was almost glad when Amber hauled me into her bedroom to work on wedding plans. I needed a break.

"You know you have to call and tell Mom and Dad sometime," I said as I flipped through the third bridal magazine.

"Ugh," Amber groaned. "I know. I'll do it tomorrow."

"No you won't," I half teased, yet knowing it was true.

"You don't know that."

"Yes, I do."

We sat on Amber's bed, flipping through magazines that were scattered across it. I was being forced into the quest of finding the perfect wedding dress.

"Well you're going to have to call Dad if you expect him to pay for a wedding," I said as I tossed the magazine aside and rolled onto my stomach. I may have been giving Amber a hard time about this, but I understood why she hadn't called. I had run away from my parents myself.

Amber didn't say anything as she looked intently at something on the page.

"So have you picked a date yet?" I asked as I grabbed Amber's left hand, again inspecting the ring on her finger. Rod must have come from some money like Alex had; the ring was stunning with a wide band and probably a dozen diamonds on it. I wouldn't say it out loud but I was jealous, even if that jealousy wasn't driving me crazy anymore. Sal's reasoning had fixed that. Who would have guessed it would be Sal who would finally talk reason into me?

"November fifth," she said as she turned the page.

"Wow, that's kind of fast," I said in surprise. "Only two and a half months away."

"Neither of us sees any reason to wait," she said as she set it down and looked me in the eye as I released her hand. "Even November seems forever away," she said wistfully.

"Are you sure you're ready to be Mrs. Amber Gepper?" I asked in a teasing tone.

"Yes!" Amber practically squealed as she scrunched up her nose, a gigantic smile plastered across her face.

I could only smile in return.

Amber gave a sigh before checking her phone for the fifth time in the last five minutes, looking for a text from Rod who was supposed to be getting off any minute. "So what about you and Alex? You two already live together. And don't try and tell me that you don't sleep in the same bed, I know you do."

"Yes we do, but it's not like that," I sighed as I shifted my position on the bed. "And actually, Alex doesn't sleep. Things are…" I hesitated, not knowing how to answer. "Complicated I guess. You know what Alex is. We just don't know what is going to happen. I told him I don't care but he's not willing to risk that something might happen to him."

Amber didn't say anything for a minute as she just looked in my face and took my hand. For some reason, I suspected she had already known the answer to her question before she had even asked it. "Everything will work out. It has to. You and Alex are perfect for each other. I keep telling you that. And just look at what you two have been through together. You have to finish the fairytale."

I couldn't help but laugh at this, and Amber joined me. I didn't think that fairytale was the right term. It all seemed like a nightmare with a few blissful chapters inserted into it.

Even though I wanted to be helping Alex figure out where Cole had gone to, I knew I needed to spend some time with my sister. Getting married was a big deal. And the fact that Amber had asked me to be her maid of honor made it an even bigger one. We had a lot of lost years to make up for.

Within an hour or two of being hauled into her room, Amber and I had chosen her colors and had a pretty good idea of the type of venue she wanted to have the wedding and the reception at. She still didn't have any idea what kind of a dress she wanted though. Maybe the fact that Alex and I had no wedding in the foreseeable future wasn't such a bad thing. This was going to be a lot of work and even more money.

It was well past three before I got out of Amber's

room and back out to find Alex. He was seated at the dining table, his laptop set in front of him, and had just set down his credit card and clicked on something.

"Sorry," I said as I walked to his side, resting one hand on his shoulder. "Um…I, Amber," I stumbled through my words.

"No, its fine," he said as he placed a hand over mine, his eyes still on the screen as he continued working. "This is important. You should be helping her."

"Any more luck?" I asked as I looked at what he had on the screen. It looked like a confirmation page for airline tickets.

Alex clicked over to another page which brought up a map. "I think I finally figured it out. I did some more research online and I'm about ninety-five percent positive that I've found it. It used to be called by something else, but a lot can change over a few hundred years. This is it though," he said as he indicated the map.

I peered at the screen but it didn't mean anything to me. "You're sure?"

Alex nodded. "I just booked us flights for tomorrow morning," Alex said as he finally turned toward me. He placed a hand on either side of my waist and maneuvered me until I sat in his lap. "I thought we could head down to Seattle tonight, get a hotel so we don't have to leave so early in the morning?"

The smile that spread on my face couldn't be

helped. "That sounds great," I said as I pressed a kiss to his lips briefly.

"Good," he said as he tucked a lock of hair behind my ear. "I booked a suite. I think you're really going to like it."

"We could be staying in a cardboard box and I wouldn't care. Just so long as you're there." I would have felt embarrassed for sounding so cheesy if what I said wasn't so true.

"Why don't you go get packed and we'll head out?"

"'K," I said as I bit my lower lip to prevent my face from cracking from the smile that was spreading there.

CHAPTER SIXTEEN

JESSICA

It was hard to explain to Amber why I had to leave. I knew the whole angel thing was already confusing and frightening to her, so I didn't know how to explain the whole mess with Cole. In the end we just left it simple. I needed to go help my friend before something bad happened to her.

After a quick introduction, Amber met Sal and I carefully explained to her that Amber would be helping her while I had to be gone for a while. I really, really hoped Sal could get along with Amber. It made me sick; it felt a little like leaving my own child behind in someone else's care. I didn't have any other choice though.

I went into work to tell Rita that I was going to be gone myself. She was in a hurry to leave so I only had a few moments to tell her that I wouldn't be coming into work the next day and that I didn't know when exactly I would be back. If my boss had been anyone but Rita, I was sure I would have been fired right then and there. She only said for me to call her when I knew when I was going to be back. It was so easy to love a woman like her.

"Are you in trouble or something, Jessica?" Austin asked as I stepped out of Rita's office.

"Were you listening?" I asked, my voice harsh.

"Where are you going?" he ignored the accusing tone in my voice, putting it in his own.

"It's not really any of your business," I said as I started toward the front door. "But if you have to know, I found Emily."

"Is she alright?" he asked, following me.

"Not really. She's in a lot of trouble," I said with a sigh as I paused at the door, seeing Alex waiting out in the truck for me.

"Is there anything I can do to help?"

I just looked at him for a minute, suddenly feeling incredibly guilty for having to have Alex mess with his memory. My eyes dropped to the cast on his right arm for a moment. He scratched at a spot where his cast ended. "No, but thanks, Austin."

The drive both flew by and crawled at the same time. I felt a sinking sensation in the pit of my stomach at the thought of going to England to find Cole. The last time I had actually seen him was when he killed Alex. I wasn't sure how I was going to react to seeing him again but I was sure it wasn't going to be good. And the panic and urgency I felt to get Emily out of a situation she didn't fully understand was getting more frantic by the hour.

And yet at the same time, I felt a rising anticipation at the evening before us. The memory of a day so similar in the past haunted me. The day we spent in Seattle just bumming around and the night on the yacht when Alex was supposed to propose to me. I wasn't getting my hopes up that Alex might change his mind, but it still sent warm, tingly feelings throughout my body to think about it.

Alex had been right when he said I was going to like the suite. It was on the top floor of the hotel and had an immaculate view of the water. The whole suite was twice as big as my apartment. It looked like something right out of a travel magazine.

Once we got our bags into the room, I found myself out on the balcony, soaking up the summer sunshine. Alex came up behind me and wrapped his arms around my waist.

I closed my eyes and smiled in sheer bliss. Alex's familiar scent filled my senses and the warmth of his body radiated throughout my skin. It was amazing the emotions he invoked in me. I didn't have words for how much I loved him or for how happy I was.

Before I even realized what I was doing, I had turned around and pushed Alex back into the room with much more force that I should have been capable of. My lips greedily found his, and the two of us tumbled onto the plush carpet.

We might have gotten carried away if it hadn't have been for the sudden explosion of Alex's shirt and my scream. In Alex's loss of concentration he had lost control of his ever constant struggle to keep his wings contained and they had burst forth with blinding glory. My scream of surprise sent both of us into a fit of laughter immediately after.

The wings might have frightened me, but I

hesitantly reached a hand towards them as we lay on the floor, gently tracing my fingers along a few of the feathers. I had never felt anything so soft and perfect. Even though I didn't meet his eyes, Alex stared intently into mine. His body was still half on top of mine, propped up on his muscled arms, just staring at me as I stroked the feathers.

"Let's go do something fun tonight," Alex finally said. "When was the last time you went dancing?"

"Uh…never?" I said hesitantly. "Well, I guess that's what Emily tried to get me to do when she took me out that night. I don't think that really counts though." I shuddered at the memory.

"I'm going to take you dancing. I heard of this really cool club. I think we should go."

I bit my lower lip in uncertainty. My last experience at a club hadn't been great. But if Alex was involved, I was willing to do anything. And besides, this might be the last chance I had to do anything just for the heck of it in a long time. Terrible things were going to be occurring soon and were probably already happening. "Okay."

Alex gave me a quick grin, and the next second he was gone and I heard the shower turn on.

I simply smiled as I sat up and then blushed when I saw his clothes in a heap at the foot of the bed. As I heard the shower curtain being pulled open then closed, I noticed a few things had fallen out of the pocket of his jeans. I bent to pick them up, wanting to make sure he didn't lose them. My heart froze for a moment before breaking out into a throbbing race as I saw a small black box lying next to his keys.

The velvet on the box looked worn and had quite a bit of lint stuck to it, as if it had been in Alex's pocket for months. I knew what this type of box was for. There was only one thing Alex would have carried in his pocket for weeks and weeks like this.

I felt sick and excited at the same time as I held the box. I wanted to see the ring more than anything, yet at the same time I knew what it was going to do to me emotionally. It was going to crush me again. I didn't want to go back to feeling like that again, and I didn't want to make Alex have to deal with that either. We had bigger things going on right now.

My stomach sinking, I put the keys and the box back in Alex's pocket and arranged his pants so they wouldn't fall back out again.

I had just pulled some new clothes out of my suitcase when Alex walked out of the shower, water beaded in his sandy blond hair and streaking down the bare skin of his chest. I blushed when I noticed he was wearing only a towel.

A soft moan escaped my lips as I walked toward him. "Are you *trying* to torture me?" I teased as I pressed a brief kiss to his lips before locking myself in the bathroom so I wouldn't do anything irrational.

X

I might have felt embarrassed for the looks I was receiving from about half the guys at the club if it wasn't for the looks Alex was getting from *all* the women. I couldn't blame them for staring. Alex was unquestionably the most beautiful creature walking this planet, but the lights that flashed and pulsed around us only seemed to enhance the unearthly effect. And I had to stop and stare at myself when I caught a glimpse of me in a mirror. There was most definitely something wrong with me.

There was something intoxicating in the air that night. Maybe it was the pulsing music, the flashing of the lights. Maybe it was the way we all moved, surging and flowing in a throbbing mass of dance. Whatever it was, I liked it.

We stood in the middle of the dance floor, the crowd pushing in around us. I noticed her across the club, watching us as we moved. She had curves any porn star would have sold her soul for and blonde hair that looked like it had leapt straight out of a fashion magazine. After a moment, I realized it wasn't us she was watching. It was just Alex.

The edges of her lips curled up and she worked her way through the crowd. Her eyes never left Alex's face.

In that moment, I saw every girl who had called me a freak and made fun of me in high school. I would never be like them.

Much to my satisfaction, as soon as Alex noticed her, he pulled me all the closer as the song changed and the tempo picked up. As I caught the woman's eye she simply winked at me, a slight smile on her face, and walked the other way, her eyes scoping out her next victim.

I knew Emily had been right, I had seen the way

other women looked at Alex, but I had never seen the effect he had on women like she had said. I would bet any other woman here would do anything to have Alex dance with them like he was dancing with me. And he was mine.

I could only imagine what my parents would think if they saw the way everyone in the club was dancing, myself included. I had never moved this way before in my life. Something felt alive in me in a way I had never felt before. A hungry feeling for more. Maybe it was the time Alex and I had spent in the suite that had gotten me feeling this way. Maybe it was just Alex and the way he was touching me.

A strange excitement spread from my stomach out to my toes and fingers as our bodies melded into one. Alex's lips played at my neck, his breath causing goosebumps to rise on my flesh. Of one thing I was certain, I didn't want this night to end. I was seeing a slightly different side of Alex I had never seen before. It was one that didn't want to hold back. I liked it.

And yet the pounding music was also causing my head to throb. My eyes ached from it all. I smelled all the alcohol that was being passed around, smelled the smoke that held on to people's breath. It felt like the whole building was about to collapse in on me.

"I'll be right back," I yelled over the loud music. As soon as I did, I realized yelling wasn't necessary, Alex would have heard me even if I had whispered it.

As I walked toward the bathrooms, I hoped I wouldn't come back and have to battle a hoard of women off Alex. Considering all the hungry looks he was getting, it seemed likely.

The smell in the woman's bathroom was enough to make my stomach roll. Evidence of human waste was obvious, cigarette butts had been left in the sink, the garbage can was overflowing. There was another person in the stall next to me and after a minute I realized there were actually two, both wearing heals. I got in and out, trying to touch as little as possible. After I made my escape I stepped out the back door to try and get some fresh air, afraid my stomach wouldn't handle any more of the stench.

The night was still warm, but at least the air wasn't so muggy like it had been inside. The symphony of the city sounded around me as I stood in the heart of it.

I was about to go back inside when a noise from just a few yards away made me jump, the cacophony of garbage cans getting plowed into. It was followed by a yell and a curse.

The smart thing to do would have been to go back inside and not think twice about it, but my curiosity got the best of me. I stepped cautiously forward, my eyes adjusting to the dim light.

For a moment my blood ran cold and all sound dropped away. A flash of metallic light and feathers came into sight for the briefest moment. I might have wondered I had imagined it but the face that looked up at me from the ground told me I hadn't. It was also different from the one I expected.

"Adam?!" I shrieked as I backed away a few steps, my back pressed to the cold brick wall.

"What?" he gasped as he struggled to stand up. His

clothes were dirty and wrinkled and I was horrified to see a small hole in his shirt above his left breast, blood soaking it.

"What happened?" I said, my voice suddenly hoarse and quiet.

He looked down at his shirt and squeezed his eyes shut and shook his head. He placed his hands on either side of his head. "What year is et?" he said with a heavy Scottish accent that took me even more off guard than I already was.

"What did you say?" I whispered again. I was still so in shock to see him here in the real world, this man who had bound and transported me from a cell to the place of judgment thousands of times.

"What year is et?" he repeated as he looked me in the eye, the same steely gray as Alex's.

I told him, my voice quivering. My mind struggled to catch up to what was happening.

"Holy shize!" he cried. "Et's been eighteen years?"

"Eighteen years since what?" I asked, unsure if I wanted the answer.

"Since I wus shot!" he exclaimed as he stuck a finger in the hole in his shirt. "Since I wus left ta die, bleedin' in the streets!"

I didn't know what to say or how to react. How could this keep happening to me? I thought I had escaped the world of angels, save Alex, but here another one was, yet again. "Alex?" I called, my voice unsure and weak.

Not two seconds later, the back door burst open and Alex's perfect form was at my side.

Had I been normal, things would have happened too fast for me to see. Surprise and uncertainty spread on Alex's face as he took Adam in. The next moment Adam was in Alex's face, Alex's shirt bunched up in his hands. For a moment, terrifying malice filled Adam's face, quickly replaced by one filled with awe.

"You're the one they allowed ta return?" Adam's voice was filled with amazement. "You're not the escaped one."

"I most definitely am *not* Cole," Alex said, a hint of disgust in his voice.

"Do ya know where he es?" Adam asked as he released Alex.

"We're leaving tomorrow to find him," I said quietly as I stepped closer to Alex's side.

"Ya have ta let me come with ya," he said, his eyes pleading and fierce.

"We can handle it," Alex said as he grabbed my hand and started walking away. "Just go back. I'll make sure he finds his way back to you."

"Please, ya have ta let me come with ya," he pleaded again. "They won' let me move on 'til I make him come back."

I had wondered many times why Adam had had to wait to be judged. Whatever the reason, here was his chance to finally move on. It was unfair that he had to wait so long.

"Alex, let him come," I whispered, even though I knew Adam would be able to hear me.

"You know what he is, right?" Alex asked me, looking me in the eye.

I simply nodded.

Alex looked like he was debating with himself, but I somehow sensed it didn't matter what his answer would be. I was sure Adam would get to Cole one way or another. If there was any way to speed this up, I was willing to do it. I didn't see how it would hurt to have Adam come with us.

"We're flying out tomorrow, bright and early," Alex finally said

"I don' have any money," Adam said, his voice sounding slightly downfallen. "At least I don' think I still have a bank account since I've been dead for eighteen years. But I have ta go."

Alex sighed and shook his head. I couldn't blame him for feeling a bit annoyed. "Come on," Alex said as he continued down the alley.

"Thank you," he said as he followed us. "Ma name es Cormack by the way. Cormack MacKenzie."

Not Adam. Guess I should have figured that wasn't his real name.

CHAPTER SEVENTEEN

JESSICA

The international flight was nearly full. Cormack was lucky we were able to get another seat and located so close to ours. We had gotten two end seats and he got the one right across the aisle from us.

I still couldn't believe what was happening. Adam, or rather Cormack, the man from my dreams who never said a word as he transported me to hell, was sitting not three feet away from me. Now Alex wasn't the only one getting open-mouthed stares from everyone. Cormack too was beautiful and just slightly not right looking. He might have better passed for human last night with all the dirt and grime on his face from suddenly reappearing into the world into a garbage can, his hair wild and messy. But with his flawless skin now clean, his thick black hair now washed and combed, it seemed it should have been obvious what he was.

The three of us said little as the flight prepared to take off and the attendants bustled around. Once we were in the air and on our way I couldn't hold back the questions anymore.

"So why were you at the club last night?" I asked. Even though the noise in the airplane was loud I didn't speak any louder than I normally would have. I knew both Alex and Cormack would be able to hear me, just as I would be able to hear them.

"I came to America about nineteen years ago, unsure of what to do with ma life, just knowin' I wanted somethin' different," Cormack said as he leaned slightly toward me in his seat. "Seattle seemed like an interestin' place, so I settled. I'd been livin' there about a year when I went out for a little fun one night. Went into the same club you came out 'a and this fellow tries robbin' me. I wus a complete idiot and tried to put up a fight, and the man shot me. Right in the very place I exploded back into the world 'o the living."

It made sense. You came back wherever you were taken out of this world. Alex had been dead less than a full day but his body hadn't been moved. He had come back into the same room. The day he went missing, he had been getting dressed in his room. When he came back he exploded into his room and mangled his bedroom door. I wondered where Cole had died and then come back to.

"Now, let me ask you a question," he said, his eyes narrowing. "How did ya know what I was? How did ya seem to know exactly what was goin' on? How do ya know who *I* am?"

It hadn't occurred to me that while Cormack may have known what Alex was right away, and more specifically known *who* he was when he saw Alex's gray eyes, he would have had no idea that I knew exactly who *he* was and *what* he was. Looking around to make sure no one else was paying attention to us, I lifted my hair from my neck and showed him my brand.

"Holy…" Cormack breathed. "But you're not…ya can't be…I knew there was somethin' different about ya but…"

"She's not an angel," Alex interjected. "Not completely anyway."

Hearing Alex finally say it made a rock form in my stomach.

The confusion on Cormack's face was obvious. It was difficult to explain everything that I did know and did understand of their world. It wasn't something I liked talking about, and it wasn't pleasant to think about the events that led up to my partially transforming into one of them. But there was obviously no other way to answer his questions.

"I'm not the only one who's gone through this," I said as Cormack's face continued to be full of wonder. "I know someone else who went through trials too. She just had to do it for different reasons. That's the main reason we're going to find Cole. She's with him."

"Es she daft?" he gaped. "That man es the leader of the condemned for a reason. Does she know what he's done? To a dozen different women?"

My blood chilled at his words. "Do you?"

"I know every deed every angel in the afterlife has committed. The deeds of your life may only be read once, but no one ever forgets or lets ya forget what you've done. Cole's ended a lot 'o women's lives. Along with countless other wicked deeds."

"She doesn't understand what is really going on. She knows who he is, but she…" I faltered unsure of how to explain the situation. Before long I had divulged Emily's whole story, from why she went through the trials, how she stopped them, and how she had wanted what Alex and I had.

"How could she be so resigned?" Cormack mused. "She believes she's truly condemned herself enough that she's willing ta seek out the king of the damned and give herself ta him?" He paused for a moment. "There's always hope. You should never give up fighting. It's worth it to keep fighting."

With his words my heart swelled. If Cormack could wonder at the outcome of Emily's trial, then surely her fate was not as set in stone as she thought it was. "Thank you," I said quietly as I reached across the aisle and gave his hand a little squeeze.

The attendants came around, taking drink and food orders. I was grateful I didn't need to eat as often as most people did. I hadn't ever heard anything good about airplane food.

Using the break in conversation, I turned to Alex, needing to tell him part of this whole thing I hadn't had a chance to yet.

"I found something else when I went to Cole's house," I said quietly, even though I knew Cormack would be able to hear me. I grabbed my backpack from the floor and pulled out the rolled up canvas. After all the horrible things Cole did to me I shouldn't have felt guilty for cutting the painting out of the frame, but I did. This was the woman he'd loved and I'd defiled her portrait by hacking it out of its frame.

"Holy..." Alex didn't finish his sentence as I

unrolled it, revealing the woman who could have been me. "What…? I…"

"She was his lover," I said as I looked her face over, so similar to my own. "They had a son together, but she was married to another man. She wouldn't give him a chance."

"I guess now we know why he came after you," Alex said as he took the painting from my hands to look at it closer. "She could be your twin. Or at least your great-great-great something grandmother."

At Alex's words, something in my mind sparked. "Give me the book," I said, excitement in my voice.

Alex dug Cole's family history book out of his carry-on bag and handed it to me. I flipped toward the back, to the page that started with William Anthony's name. My eyes again read down the line to the last words.

No Connection

The words that I had overlooked before suddenly made perfect sense. The whole screwed up situation just became all the more messed up.

"Cole was checking to see if we were family," I whispered. I pointed to William's name. "This was Cole's illegitimate son he had with that woman," I said as I pointed to the painting. "He was checking to see if we were related."

"Oh, that's jus sick," Cormack said. Apparently he had been listening in. Of course he had been.

"Tell me about it," I said, feeling a little queasy.

ALEX

"Just look at him, what I wouldn't give for a night with that," someone four rows back whispered.

"What is it about them?" someone else said in a low voice. *"There's something just...different."*

"I'm going to try and talk to her when we land. Maybe I can get her to the bar for drinks later."

"She looks just..."

The whispers were flying around the plane. Even though they probably thought no one would be able to hear them over the airplane noise, I heard every word, and I suspected Jessica heard most of it too.

They were right. There was something different about Jessica. Her skin was so flawless, it was all I could do at times not to reach out and touch it. Her eye color was just a little too vivid. The way she moved was mesmerizing. I could only stop and stare at times.

I grabbed Jessica's hand and tried to rub reassuring circles into it as I heard someone whisper something about how Jessica wasn't good looking enough to be with someone who looked like me. The urge to go back there and chew her ear off was hard to fight back.

With Jessica's revelation of this other woman, things made bizarre sense. The way Cole was so immediately obsessed with Jessica. The possessive yet terrifying way he looked at her. He had come after a girl who looked almost exactly like the woman he could never have. It had been a game of conquering for Cole. And perhaps revenge.

I wasn't sure what I would do when we found him. The last time I had seen Cole, he had killed me, and then

I had been tortured by my fellow kind for his location.

I wanted to kill him for all the pain he had caused us, but how do you kill someone who is already dead?

I knew one thing though; I would do whatever I had to in order to keep him away from Jessica.

JESSICA

The flight felt like it took forever. The air started tasting stale, the scent of human sweat filling the air. And the noise was driving me mad. The engine noise, the whispers, the sounds coming from headphones plugged into portable devices. By the time we landed, my legs were stiff and cramped. I took a gasping breath as we stepped into the terminal. Fresh air never tasted so sweet after breathing what everyone else had been breathing in and out for hours on end.

We waited impatiently at the baggage claim, watching as suitcases slid down the chute. I noticed a security guard watching us closely. I had to take deep calming breaths to fight back the panic I was feeling. I suppressed the urge to bolt when he started towards us.

I knew there was no real reason why he was going to do what he was going to do. We weren't *doing* anything wrong, but we just *looked* wrong.

"May I ask you where you're traveling from?" he asked as he approached us. I noticed he was having a hard time looking either Alex or Cormack in the face.

"The US," Alex said, never taking his eyes off the man's face.

"All of you?" the guard asked, his voice hinting at the unease he felt.

"Yes," I said shortly.

"Yes," Cormack answered. I noticed how he tried to hide his accent. I didn't blame him. We needed to get rid of this guy as quickly as possible; his accent would probably just bring up more questions.

"Can I see your passports, please?"

My heart pounded as he finally asked the question I knew he would. My palms started sweating as I dug into my carry-on bag.

Alex pulled his out and handed it to the man. I knew what the man should have seen. A much younger and much more human looking version of Alex. The man looked it over, looking between the picture and Alex's face before handing it back.

I thought I might throw up as I handed the guard my "passport."

What the man held was nothing more than a blank, plain white piece of paper folded in quarters. The man looked from it to my face several times, then handed it back. Cormack handed him the same thing, just a plain, folded piece of paper.

"Sorry to have bothered you," the man said as he handed Cormack's paper back. "Enjoy your visit."

We each just nodded as he walked away. We grabbed our bags quickly as they came around the claim belt and started hurriedly toward the rental car counter.

"I *really* hope we don't have to do that again," I breathed. Just one more thing for me to feel guilty about.

"I didn't exactly enjoy doing that either," Alex said as he shouldered my bag. "It creeps me out that I *can* do that."

Alex was the only one out of the three of us that had an actual passport. There had not been enough time to get one for me, and since Cormack had been dead for eighteen years it was obviously going to be impossible to get one for him. Instead we had given the appropriate people something to simply hold while Alex made them think they were seeing a real passport with a real picture.

I hated that Alex had to manipulate someone's mind again, but I also knew it was necessary. It reminded me too much of what Cole had made me see and feel. It also kept the fact that we were going to try and find him front and center in my mind.

X

The airport was quiet and we were the only ones who were at the rental counter. With it being just past midnight, it should have been fairly quiet. I hadn't slept in what felt like days, my nerves and emotions shot, and I swayed as Alex talked to the man and got the papers signed for our car. My legs felt like they were filled with lead as we walked out to the car.

The guys loaded our bags into the trunk, and I climbed into the passenger seat and leaned my forehead against the cool glass.

Alex slid into the driver's seat and started up the car. He then turned his attention to the fancy GPS unit on the dash and started looking up a nearby hotel.

"What are you doing?" I asked as I watched him, my voice sounding like it was being dragged over gravel.

"Aren't we heading straight there?"

"You need to sleep," Alex said without looking at me as he pulled his cell phone out and dialed a number. "I think it would be good for you to get some rest."

"I can sleep in the car," I started to argue, but Alex was already making a reservation.

Not three minutes later Alex had two rooms booked, though Cormack had tried to argue it was pointless to book him a room when he didn't sleep. Ignoring him, Alex backed out and pulled out of the parking garage and onto the street.

"Hey! Hey!" Cormack yelled from the back seat. "Don forget, you're not in America anymore! You're drivin' on the wrong side 'o the road!"

"Oh, right," Alex chuckled as he shook his head. "You would think this wouldn't be so hard since I lived here for a few years."

Cormack swore quietly under his breath and shook his head. "I'm drivin' tomorra'. There's no need for all 'o us to be dead."

I chuckled tiredly and watched the road ahead of us, silently grateful we were going to stop for a few hours so I could get some much needed sleep.

The high-end lobby was empty as we checked in and got our room keys. Again Cormack insisted he didn't need a room, but Alex just ignored him, paid for the room, then handed him the key. I had to agree with Cormack, getting him a room *was* a waste of money, but I wasn't going to complain. I was always happy to be alone with Alex.

The room was just as nice as the lobby had been, but

I noticed little other than the bed. I droppe the floor and collapsed into it. I didn't changing into pajamas, brushing my teeth, or under the covers.

I didn't hear him move across the room o into the bed but Alex was suddenly beside me, his arm wrapped around my waist. I breathed in a si relaxation, his scent flooding my senses.

"Goodnight, Jessica," he whispered into my ear. love you."

"I love you too," I breathed and smiled as he pressed a soft kiss into my temple. Not ten seconds later, I was asleep.

ALEX

It didn't take long for Jessica to fall asleep. I laid there for a while, just watching her face as she slept. I could watch her sleep for hours and did sometimes. I wished I could keep away the nightmares she had though. I knew she still had them even if she tried to pretend she didn't. She didn't like to tell me when she had them. I sensed she felt guilty whenever she did. She was right though, it wasn't fair that she should still have nightmares, even if they were a different kind. She had *lived* a nightmare for nearly sixteen years. That should have been enough.

Curiosity got the best of me after a while, and I forced myself to leave Jessica's side and find our new companion. He wasn't in his room, but as I extended my senses, I realized he was no longer in the building. I went to his open window, climbed out, and scaled the building to the roof.

Cormack was sitting on the far end of the building at the very peak of the roof. He sat with his arms resting on his knees, staring up into the star-peppered sky. He didn't turn to look at me as I walked the roofline toward him, but I knew he heard me as I approached. When I reached him, I sat as well, turning my gaze heavenward.

"I forgot how beautiful they were," Cormack said as he continued to observe the stars.

I didn't say anything as we sat, side by side, two angels on the rooftop.

"I don think ya realize jus how lucky ya really are to be allowed to still be here," he said. I thought I detected a hint of emotion in his voice. If he had been capable, I suspected he might have had tears in his eyes. "You must a made one hell 'o a plea to them, or one hell 'o a sacrifice."

"She's sleeping down below us," I said simply. "And you're wrong. I do realize how lucky I am to be here, to still be able to be with her. I almost lost her, twice. But we're still together."

"She's the reason you're still here?" Cormack asked in shock as he looked me in the face.

"She was dying," I explained. "I traded my life for hers and the council allowed me to come back to her."

Cormack continued to stare wide-eyed and mouthed at me for a moment before he shook his head and looked back up to the stars. "It's really not fair ya know," he said. "I would give anythin' to come back. Do ya know what et's like, to have someone take your life away like that? To be killed en cold blood?"

"Yeah, actually I do," I chuckled. I was surprised at how little Cormack seemed to know. "The one that escaped is the one who killed me. He snapped my neck after he nearly *beat* the life out of me. Over Jessica. Don't you know all this?"

"You never went through a trial," he said as he shook his head. "I just knew they allowed someone to return."

He was quiet for a little after that. I sensed some emotional turmoil going on inside of him. "I envy you, ya know. What you and Jessica have together. I never found that. Always looked for it, but never found it."

"I'm sorry," I said sincerely. Truly I was. I couldn't imagine what life would be like without Jessica. It wouldn't be whole. It would feel pretty empty and pointless.

"Tell me what's happened since I wus taken outa this world," he said after a few minutes of silence. "The world looks so different now."

"When did you die?" I asked. I could tell the following conversation was going to be really strange.

"Et's been eighteen years," he replied with a chuckle. "I can't believe I missed the changing of a millennium. Ya have no idea how strange it es to hear what year it es."

"You're right there," I chuckled. "I can't even imagine."

"So what have I been missin' these last eighteen years?"

I suddenly wished I kept up on current events more and had paid better attention to the news.

JESSICA

Lights flashed and sparkled around us and the music tinkled throughout the carnival. People crowded into the park and vendors shouted from all around us. Garbage lay underfoot, carelessly thrown by people who obviously didn't worry what it was going to do to the environment.

I watched with a smile as he picked up the oversized hammer and drew it up above his head. A moment later, it came crashing down, nearly breaking the booth game. I suppressed a chuckle, knowing it had taken restraint for him *not* to break it. The vendor looked at him in surprise, furrowed his brow and handed him an oversized stuffed rabbit.

"I don't understand why women like these things," he said as he draped an arm across my shoulders and led us down an aisle crowded with people.

"Yeah," I said as I looked at the fuzzy animal that filled my arms. "It is kinda stupid, I guess."

He just chuckled as he flashed his brilliant smile. "Hey, why don't you have him paint your picture?"

There was a young man at the end of the aisle with an easel set up, his brushes on a table beside him, just waiting for customers.

"You don't want to be in it, too?" I asked as I looked at his beautifully captivating face.

"I wouldn't want to taint it," he joked. "I would love to have a picture of you I can look at forever."

I gave Cole a smile as I handed my purse and the rabbit to him and took a seat to pose for the painting.

CHAPTER EIGHTEEN

JESSICA

My gums became raw as I brushed my teeth frantically. I probably hadn't even gotten all the shampoo out of my hair before I had flown out of the shower. How could I worry about how I looked, with so much on the line?

I felt frustrated as I spit into the sink. Emily knew what Cole was. Like *she* had said, he had branded her too, hundreds of times. How could she be so stupid? How could she run straight into the arms of the leader of the condemned?

Yet I already knew the answer. Emily had already explained it to me. Who else would want her, when she had already damned herself? Who better to be with than the leader of the condemned?

"Let's go," I said as I threw my toothbrush into my bag. Alex and Cormack had already loaded all of the other bags into the car.

Alex checked us out of the hotel then joined us outside. Cormack had insisted on driving, true to his threat the night before. Alex didn't seem to mind and to be honest, I didn't mind either. As Cormack had said, there was no need for all of us to be dead.

"So ya jus put an address in this little thing an' it will tell ya how ta get there?" Cormack marveled as we got onto the road and Alex started punching in where we were headed.

"Um, hum," Alex nodded as he entered the information in.

"Amazing," Cormack shook his head and stared out at the road that stretched before us.

Under normal circumstances, I would have enjoyed the scenery around me. I had never traveled outside the country before but had always wanted to. Now that I was getting my chance, I felt distracted and sick. The nightmare I'd had petrified me. Seeing and feeling the things that were happening to Emily unnerved me more than I could ever explain. I didn't want to be feeling those things for Cole again, even if it was just in a dream. It made my skin crawl.

And I didn't for one second forget what had happened after Cole had the woman's portrait painted in the other dreams. I just hoped it wasn't too late.

"So what's the plan of action here?" Cormack asked as the road fell away beneath the tires. I glanced at the clock, surprised we had already been driving for two hours. "How do ya plan on gettin' close enough to grab him an' make him go back?"

"*We* weren't planning on anything of the sorts," Alex said as he stared out the window. "Don't forget, you're the one who's supposed to make him go back. We're just here to get Emily back before something happens to her."

"I know I'm the one to make him go back,"

Cormack said, irritation evident in his voice. "I jus wondered if you had thought of anythin'. Et's not like gettin' that girl back es going to be an easy thing if she's with him."

Cormack was right. Cole most likely was going to put up a fight. The thought terrified me, the last fight I had seen Cole get in over a woman resulted in Alex's death.

"We'll just have to see how things pan out," Alex said. "We don't know what's going on or what to expect."

"That's et?" Cormack asked. "That's all you've got?"

"Yeah, that's all I've got!" Alex barked. I was surprised at Alex. He didn't seem to like Cormack too much. Cole was the only other person I had seen that Alex didn't like. Maybe that was all it was. Cormack was an angel too.

"I could talk to him," I chimed in, wanting to calm the tension that suddenly filled the car. "Distract him while you grab him, Cormack."

"Absolutely not!" Alex shouted at the same time Cormack nodded in agreement with my plan. "You can't be serious about going around that monster again? After everything he did to you?"

"I'm the reason he came out of the world of the dead in the first place. I've got to help make him go back."

Alex shook his head. "No way. We'll figure something else out. The two of us can handle it. There's two of us and only one of him. We'll make him go back."

I detected another emotion brewing under the surface of Alex's skin. Fear. I could imagine how the thought of Cole and me in the same room again terrified him. While this made my heart flutter, I also wanted to say that perhaps they had more to worry about than they realized. I had a feeling being a council member came with a little more than being just any angel, especially an un-judged angel as they both were.

The tension didn't leave the car, and I felt on edge. I hated contention. I supposed that came after listening to my parents fight about me for years. I wanted to do anything to avoid it, but at the moment I couldn't escape.

The GPS chirped that we were 150 kilometers from our destination.

We drove for another good half hour before the thick silence was broken by Alex's cell phone ringing. Puzzlement filled his face as he looked at the caller ID.

"It's Emily," he said quietly as he looked back at me for a brief moment.

"What?!" I nearly screamed, fighting the instant reaction to snatch the phone from Alex.

"Hello?" Alex answered.

"You've got one of those mobile phones?" Cormack said in awe, though I didn't register what he was saying. I was trying too hard to hear what Emily might be saying to Alex.

Alex's face was quickly changing from serious to grave. I could also detect a hint of anger and frustration. As hard as I tried, I couldn't hear what Alex was hearing from Emily.

"Pull over," Alex said quietly, but continued

listening to Emily.

Cormack obeyed and pulled to the side of the quiet country road. Just as he rolled to a stop Alex hung up.

"What is going on Alex?!" I demanded, my voice shaky and frantic. "What did Emily say? Is she okay?"

Alex just stared at the dash and shook his head slowly. "It wasn't Emily."

"It wasn't…" I started to ask before cold, sick realization hit me. Tears sprang to my eyes and I covered my mouth with my hand to hold back the sob. "It was Cole," I said in a choked off cry.

Alex nodded and finally looked at me. "He said Emily is in no immediate danger, but he knows we're coming for her. He wants to see you, Jessica, alone."

"How could he possibly think you'd let me come without you?" I barely managed to speak.

"He's made sure I won't," Alex's voice cracked slightly. "He's found my mother. A few hundred miles away. He said if I don't get there in the next few hours, she'll be dead."

The world seemed to fall silent as I understood what Alex was saying. To make sure Alex would leave my side, he had gone after the one person Alex would do anything to find. Alex had never met his mother, but I knew how much this would mean to him. She was the only family he had left.

"You have to go, Alex," I breathed. "You have to find her."

Alex's lower lip quivered just slightly as his steely gray eyes met mine. I knew if it were possible, there would have been tears there. "I can't," he whispered.

"How can I let you go to meet that monster?"

"You have to, Alex," I said quietly as I leaned forward and placed a hand on his perfectly smooth cheek. "She's your only family."

"You're my family," he whispered.

My insides trembled at his words. I bit my lower lip for a moment to collect myself. "I'll be fine. Cole doesn't know about Cormack."

"I'll protect her," Cormack, who had been silent up until this point, said. "Don' worry about anythin'. She'll be safe with me."

Alex kept my stare for another long moment, his hand coming up to his face to lay on mine. He then turned to Cormack.

"You'd better keep your word," he said, his voice harsh but filled with emotion. "I swear, if anything happens to her, I will hunt you down and rip your wings out myself."

"Alex," I chided. It frightened me to hear him talk like that. It seemed to be happening more and more lately.

Alex continued his hard stare for a second longer. He then opened the door and got out. He barely even slammed it shut before Cormack sped off.

I jerked my head around to catch one last glimpse of Alex, but all I saw was a flash of metallic light.

I gave a quivering sigh as I sat back in my seat. I was glad Alex had not given me a kiss before he left. It would have felt like too final of a goodbye.

After a minute Cormack glanced in the rear-view mirror at me. "He loves you a lot."

"Yeah," I said quietly as I wiped a tear away.

It started raining a few minutes later, making the day feel all the more ominous. The thought that the day couldn't get any worse crossed my mind, but then I realized it could. It could still get so much worse.

When I felt like I had control of my emotions I crawled into the front passenger seat.

"So, now that it's up to just you, what's your plan?" I asked as I stared at the road ahead of us. The female voice coming from the GPS told us to merge onto a highway.

"All I have ta do es get close enough to him to grab him, and et won' be difficult to make him go back," Cormack said.

"What do you mean?" I asked.

"Et's difficult enough keepin' ma self in this world. Et takes constant concentration to keep bein' here. Et's not easy for a dead man to stay in the world 'o the living. I figure if I can only get a hold of the man, I just have to stop thinkin' about stayin' here and it will be done. We'll be back."

"Wait," I asked, panic starting to seep into my veins. "You have to *think* about staying in the world of the living?"

"Oh yeah," Cormack chuckled. "The afterlife is constantly calling. The pull es strong. I don' know how Alex keeps et up. Or how Cole's kept it up for this long. Et's brutal."

I slumped in my seat as I took in Cormack's words. As they did, someone else's words came back to me.

Maybe he knows something you don't. Maybe that's

part of the reason.

Sal had been right.

So this was the real reason Alex wouldn't propose. He was already being pulled back into the afterlife. He really could be sucked back at any moment. That was what he had meant when he insisted all the time that he had no control.

"Why didn't he ever tell me?" I said out loud, not realizing I did.

"What?" Cormack asked, confused.

"That it's so hard to stay. That at any time he might lose it and be pulled back."

By this point I had already said enough and had to explain the entire story to him. I told him about how I knew Alex was going to propose, how nothing had happened after Alex had come back. About how he seemed so stubborn and unreasonable for refusing to ask me again. It all made sense now, and I felt horrible for how I had reacted before.

"The council agreed ta give Alex more time with you," Cormack said as he stared at the road. "They never said how long they'd give him."

I cursed under my breath, suddenly violently resentful toward Emily for being so stupid and eating up the precious time I had left with Alex. If our days were numbered, I wanted to spend every second of them with Alex.

"Please talk about something else," I said with a wavering voice. "Anything else."

He glanced over at me, sadness and another emotion warring in his eyes. It almost looked like jealousy. "I grew up in Scotland, as I'm sure you've already assumed. I was an only child. It was always jus ma mother 'n me. Ma father ran off when ma mother was still carrying me, too young and not ready to be a parent. That was the excuse ma mother made for him anyway.

"Money was a constant struggle for the two of us, and I grew up pathetically poor. I didn't mind most of the time, though. I felt sorry for ma mother. She worked herself ta death, but could never seem to get ahead. I wanted to drop out of high school to help support her, but she wouldn't allow it.

"A few years after I finished school, she fell ill. The doctors weren't sure what was wrong and we couldn't afford to get any further testing. I worked as much as I could and spent the rest of my hours taking care of her as she slowly decayed away. She passed the day after my twenty-fourth birthday.

"While I would miss her terribly, I couldn't be to terribly sad. It was painful ta watch her waste away, eventually forgetting my name and even her own. I didn't want her ta have ta live like that. And besides, she was exalted," he said with a smile.

"Soon after she passed, I decided I was ready for a new life. A fresh start. America seemed like a good place for that. I got all my papers, all that stuff taken care of and moved over. Got a job at a large corporate office working in the mail room. Didn't pay much, but when I needed extra money, I worked a few hours as a bouncer at a club. Never woulda' guessed I woulda' meet my end behind one."

"I'm so sorry, Cormack," I said quietly, watching

his flawless face as he spoke. "You've had a pretty rough life."

"Yeah, *had*," he said with a chuckle. "That's alright though. It wus a good one. I've got no complaints. Except for the being shot part an' it all ending."

I admired Cormack's attitude. He was a good man. Before, when I had thought of him as Adam, I guessed he would be exalted come his own judgment time. I had no doubt now that I was right.

"Cormack?" I said quietly as I looked out at the road ahead of us. "Why haven't you been judged yet? You said it's been eighteen years. That hardly seems fair."

"Little the council does outside of judgment es fair," he said as he looked over at me. "I would think you would know that best."

I could only nod at this. He was right.

"I've never been told why. Given recent events, I can only guess that they wanted to keep somethin' over ma head. They guessed they would need someone like me later.

"An' I've always wondered if there was something left I was supposed to do. Ma life wus cut short, maybe there's somethin' I need to take care of."

I looked over at Cormack as he fell quiet. I hated the council all the more in that moment. Nothing was fair.

The gas station we pulled into was small and nearly empty. I had never seen a station with only two pumps before. While Cormack filled the car, I went inside and asked to use the phone.

It had been nearly two hours since Alex had left and my insides were an emotional storm. I was anxious about having Alex gone, but I knew what finding his mom would do for him. I also felt sick to think what Cole might have done to Alex's only remaining family member. My fingers were barely even able to punch the numbers into the ancient phone. I waited with nervous anticipation as the phone rang. After four rings it went to his voicemail.

I went back outside to find Cormack showing the attendant a map, pointing to where Cole's family's legacy was supposed to be. He didn't seem to trust the "talking box."

"You're only about twenty minutes away, but I don't know what you're expecting to find there. The area's been deserted for as long as I can remember. No one will go near the old Emerson place. Bad things have happened there. People say it has been haunted lately. You'd best just stay away."

My skin crawled at his words. Cole really was back. I'd be seeing him soon.

"I'd stay away from that place if I were you," he said as he started walking back inside.

"Okay," Cormack said as he walked around to the driver's side. "That creeps me out a bit."

"That terrifies me a bit," I said as I slid into the passenger side.

My pulse seemed to pick up another beat with every minute that passed as we got closer and closer to the former Emerson estate. My palms started sweating and I couldn't quite sit still. "You're sure this will be easy, making him go back?" I asked nervously as my hands twisted around each other.

"Once I can get to him, et will be easy. I never said et would be easy getting' to him."

I really, really wished Alex was there with me.

Thirty-three…thirty-four…thirty-five…

Since Alex's disappearance, I had started counting again. The fear was coming back in an all too familiar way.

"I won let him hurt you, Jessica," Cormack said as he placed a hand over mine for just a brief second and gave it a squeeze. "I'd really rather not have Alex rip ma wings out. Don' think that would feel too great."

I gave a nervous chuckle, grateful to Cormack for trying to lighten the mood.

The voice from the GPS announced we had arrived at our destination as we pulled off the decaying main street and onto what was little more than a path of gravel that used to be a cobblestone road. Mature trees lined what had once been the road leading onto the property. Through them I could see several smaller buildings I could only guess were servants' quarters and out-buildings, a barn, a carriage house, a shed.

I thought my heart was going to hammer out of my chest as we pulled to a stop in front of the decayed mansion.

CHAPTER NINETEEN

JESSICA

The building before us was massive. Different wings spread out over the property with balconies supported by pillars, arched windows were scattered across the face. I had never seen a bigger house. Or one so un-structurally sound looking. The middle of the roof sagged; a section of the massive front porch had caved in. It looked as if every window had been broken in, shards of glass shining in the gray light. I could only imagine how the place looked in its days of glory.

Cole had hinted that his family had been wealthy. I felt I had greatly underestimated *how* wealthy they had been.

I don't know if I can do this, I thought to myself. I was fighting off a fully-fledged panic attack.

"You ready?" Cormack asked as he unbuckled his totally unnecessary seatbelt.

"Um hum," I lied as I undid mine and opened the door.

The air around us seemed unnaturally silent as we walked across the soggy grass up to the front door. Every nerve in my body was screaming at me to turn and run. Fear that Cole could be watching us from a busted out window saturated my system. I felt sick. I felt like I might pass out.

Without even realizing what I was doing, I grabbed Cormack's hand in mine. Had he been human, my grip would have broken every bone in his hand.

The front door was broken in and it hung skewed on the hinges. The grand entrance showed obvious signs of squatters, broken bottles, newspapers, and stray socks lay scattered across the cracked and dusted floor. A mirror hung on one wall and it had been broken, a spider web of seven years bad luck.

My body shook violently with fear and the numbers rattled off in my head, faster than I would have been able to say out loud. I looked at Cormack. It was obvious he was trying to look brave and unnerved, but I saw his underlying emotions. Fear and nervousness. It terrified me to think *why* Cormack would be afraid. *He* was already dead. What could Cole do to him?

He met my eyes briefly and we both seemed to understand what the other was thinking. It was me Cole wanted to see.

"Cole?" I said aloud, my voice seeming to fall flat in the vast expanses of the mansion. "I'm here."

We both listened with expectancy, straining to pick up on the faintest of noises. Our ears fell only on silence.

I pulled Cormack down a hallway that looked as if it stretched on and on for miles. We checked every door. With each one, I felt afraid my heart might explode with my fear as it was opened, only to reveal an empty room. I knew that if Cole was here, he would have heard us the moment we walked through the door. The floor gave us away as it creaked and moaned under our weight.

Finding nothing down the hall, we went up a flight of stairs and continued checking doors. At one point we had to turn around and go back down when we found a section of the house that had given way, the hallway dropping down into another room below.

I didn't like this game of hide-and-seek. The shadows seemed to move and dance, but neither I nor Cormack saw or heard anything actually move. I wasn't sure how much more of it my nerves could take.

The bottom floor of the house was completely empty. We moved onto the last section of the house, the upper south wing. It was behind the fourth door we found her.

Emily was standing at the window, looking outside toward the rear of the house, her back turned to us. She didn't turn to look at us when the door noisily opened.

"Emily?" I whispered hoarsely.

When she still did not turn around, I stepped hesitantly into the room, Cormack followed me. My eyes darted nervously around, watching for any signs that Cole was in the room with her.

"Emily," I whispered as I got closer to her. "We've got to get out of here. Don't you realize what is going on?"

I placed a hand on her shoulder and Emily whipped her head around to look at me. I nearly didn't recognize the woman who looked into my face.

Emily's normally tan skin was pale and lifeless looking, her eyes shallow and dark. The skin of her lips was dried and cracked. But it was her eyes that frightened me most. They were bloodshot and fierce, hatred spewing out of them. They were the eyes of a crazed woman.

"You're too late, Jessica," she said with malice in her voice. "Cole will be mine forever now. I've already taken that step. You can't have him now."

I didn't understand what she was talking about.

"Jessica," Cormack whispered as he came to my side and my eyes followed his.

I hadn't noticed the knife in Emily's hand. Or the blood that dripped from it and her wrists onto the floor.

"You've got your own beautiful man, you can't have mine. He's mine, no matter what he says," Emily said as she turned her body toward me, the knife held tightly in her fist. Her eyes looked wrong, unfocused and confused. "We're going to be together forever in the afterlife."

"Something's wrong with her," Cormack said.

"He's manipulated her," I said quietly, very aware of the sharp point of that knife. "Cole made me think things that weren't real."

"He's done nothing to me!" Emily shrieked, but her tone didn't sound so sure. "We're going to be together. I'll finally have what you and Alex have." Her tone was losing confidence with every word she spoke, her voice breaking.

Cormack took a step forward, obviously not afraid of the damage the knife could do. He held Emily's gaze steadily as he approached her. She looked at him doubtfully, but did not stop him as he brought his hand up to her temple.

Emily closed her eyes as he did, her brow furrowing as they stood connected for several seconds. She suddenly took several gasping breaths, making me jump violently. When she opened her eyes again, they looked clear and focused. Tears streamed down her face as she looked at me.

"He…I'm so sorry…," she started to say, but her eyes suddenly rolled back into hear head. Her body went instantly limp, but Cormack caught her before she hit the floor.

"Well, well," a chillingly familiar accented voice said from the doorway. "They sent the conveyor to drag me back. Did they promise you your own final judgment in return for your services?"

The world seemed very quiet as I turned where I stood to where I had heard the voice come from. Cole stood in the doorway, wearing only a pair of white cotton pants, his menacing wings in full view as they brushed the floor.

I didn't even hear it as Cormack's shirt shredded to pieces and his own wings burst forth.

"Two things can happen right now. The first is that he stays and your friend here bleeds to death for no reason. I don't want her and have promised her nothing, despite what she has led herself to believe.

"Two, he leaves and gets her to a hospital, and you and I can have a little chat."

Strange feelings flooded through me as I met Cole's eyes. I remembered all the feelings of desire for him that coursed through me as I lay dying. The way I craved for him to touch me, the way the sound of his voice made me feel alive. I knew they weren't real, but they had *felt* real.

"Cormack, you have to go," I said quietly, my eyes never leaving Cole's flawless face.

"I promised Alex, though," he hissed as he readjusted his hold on Emily's body.

"Ah, Alex," Cole said with a chuckle. "Now there is quite a problem. Taken care of for the moment, but I'm sure it won't be long before he causes me trouble again."

My blood boiled as Cole spoke of the man I loved more than my own life. Before I even thought about what I was doing, I rushed at him. "You will *not* speak of him!" I screamed and slapped my hands at his chest and shoved with as much force as I possessed.

It made me sick that the haunting, familiar feeling of longing and desire flooded through me. But at the same time, it felt as if I had just put my finger into an outlet, a jolt of *something* radiated from where my hands connected with Cole's skin. I jerked back, feeling like my brain had been slapped. *What was that?*

But the most startling thing was Cole's reaction. I was in no way strong enough to cause Cole pain, but as I struck him, he jerked away from me, a terrifying hiss escaping his lips. A perfect imprint of my hands remained on his chest, his skin looking gray and decayed.

"Alex's plea has worked well," Cole said, his voice sounding light but his eyes burning with malice as he looked up from his chest at me. "It seems I cannot touch you."

My brain struggled to catch up with what had just happened. Cole couldn't touch me. He couldn't hurt me. While I was still terrified of him, he couldn't harm me.

"Everything's fine, Cormack," I said as I looked back at him for a brief moment. "Get Emily to a hospital before she bleeds to death. I didn't come all this way after her for nothing."

"Jessica, I can't," he started to argue.

"Now!" I screamed at him, my nerves starting to crack. "Get her out of here!"

He gave me a serious look, going back and forth between me and Cole. I thought I heard a low growl escape his chest before he balled Emily up in his arms and leapt straight out the window.

Now alone, I turned my attention back to Cole. I wanted to run, I wanted to scream. I wanted to beat Cole until he bled and begged me to stop. But I couldn't do any of those things right now. I could only stare back into those cold, black eyes.

"It is a pity really. She is quite a beautiful creature. It would be a waste if she were to die," Cole said as he never broke his probing stare. "She was not the one I wanted and still want, though."

"How can you possibly still be hopeful?" I asked, my voice surprisingly calm. "After everything that has happened?"

"Your beloved Alex said once that I had no idea what real love is. He was wrong. I think you know that."

I didn't want to admit it, but Cole was right. I did know that Cole was capable of real love. The way he loved though had gotten twisted into obsession and had led to dozens of women's murders.

"But you don't love me," I whispered. "I'm not her."

"No, you're not," Cole said, the corner of his lip twitching, itching to crack a smile.

I had been so focused on the more-than-man before me, I did not notice at first how the walls were patching themselves together, how the glass grew in the window frames, how the dusted floor became polished again. When our eye contact finally broke, my mind blanked momentarily in surprise at the difference there was from just a few moments ago.

The room we were in was no longer in ruin. It was instead a lavishly decorated bedroom, a massive four poster bed sitting in the middle. A small crystal chandelier hung from the ceiling. Paintings and tapestries hung from the walls.

I marveled at the eighteenth century décor around me. It was a few moments before I realized what I was seeing meant.

"Get out of my head!" I screamed, the force of it surprising me.

"I may not be able to touch you, but I can still make you see what I wish," Cole said as he took a step toward me, that smile tugging on his lips again. "Will you walk with me Jessica? See my home as it once was? The way it was when I should have inherited it?"

My initial instinct was to scream at him again and

tell him to go back to hell. The feeling of being on a heavy drug seeped into my system, bringing with it all sorts of horrid memories. But I didn't think Cole could harm me. I wouldn't let him get that deep into my mind. I wouldn't allow him to make me want to hurt myself again. And besides, I needed to get on his good side, if he had one, and convince him to go back to the world of the dead where he belonged.

In answer to his request, I stepped out into the hallway with him. I tried to ignore the satisfied smile on Cole's face.

"I told you once of my family's wealth," Cole said as he led me down the hall. "You have no idea. In the late seventeen hundreds, my family was one of the most influential this side of England. Second only to the Anthonys."

I understood now why the woman from Cole's letters had agreed to marry James Anthony. His family was still worth more than Cole's.

"All of this should have been mine. My father was well past his expiration date, and I was the only child. My mother had internal problems; she couldn't have any more children. I was robbed of all of this."

We wandered into a library. Cherry wood shelves lined the walls, from floor to ceiling. Books were crammed onto them, their spines looking old and worn. I recognized some of the titles, knowing they most have been first edition copies, and very valuable in today's world. Other books were written in languages I didn't even recognize.

From the library, we took a set of stairs to the

ground floor. A few doors down, Cole opened one.

This room looked like a mini version of the library. Shelves and books lined the walls but a massive desk dominated the middle of the room. Dark tapestries gave the room a sinister but sophisticated look.

"This was my father's office," Cole said as he approached the desk, running his fingers over a large leather volume. "This is where he laid out his plans and built his empire. I spent many hours in this room, learning of his ways that I would never be given the chance to use."

I wasn't sure I wanted to know about what Cole kept hinting at. Everything about Cole was terrifying; I didn't need any more added to it.

We wandered down the hall further and entered a massive kitchen.

"I avoided this room like the plague," Cole reminisced. "I could not cook to save my life. I never had a desire, however. That was what the servants were for. It was in this room that I made love for the first time, though. I can't say it is all bad memories coming from this kitchen."

My skin crawled as Cole shared this with me. Too much information.

He then led me to a grand ballroom, its wooden floors stretching on and on. The walls were a bright white, the light streaming in through the windows dancing off the massive chandelier dangling from the ceiling. Our footsteps echoed softly off the walls.

"The king and queen were entertained in these walls. My father was close friends with the king himself."

I didn't want to think about all the women Cole had probably met and seduced within these walls.

He then led me down another hall and up a flight of stairs. We were now close to where the hallway had collapsed into the first floor. Just before we got to where I knew the spot was, Cole opened a door and indicated for me to enter.

"And this was my room," he said quietly, his voice too close behind me for comfort.

The room we entered was as grandiose as any other we had been in. Everything was beautiful and perfect. Another massive bed dominated the room, covered in a deep red quilt. The rest of the room was decorated to match.

I felt my blood pool in my feet, though, when several frames on one wall caught my attention. At first I thought it had been a framed mirror, my own reflection looking back at me. Then I realized: this was the other woman. But it was what was below her painting that horrified me.

More than a dozen beautiful women stared back at me, peaceful smiles on their faces. I recognized those faces. The women Cole had choked in my nightmares. The last one in the line was all too familiar. It was Emily.

I threw up on the floor, right then and there.

"Get out!" I screamed as I spit on the floor, trying to get the taste of bile out of my mouth. "Get out right now!"

My brain felt like it had been invaded by a heavy

fog, swirling around so that I couldn't think straight. I wanted it out. It felt as if the heaviest blanket that existed had been draped over me, and it was suffocating me from the inside out.

"Get out of my head!" I shrieked.

It was almost as if I watched the clouds roll back, retreating from the corners of my brain. Cole pulled out. I took a gasping breath as I collapsed onto my hands and knees. They both shook as I forced myself back up to my feet.

When I looked up again the room was back in ruin and decay. The paintings still hung on the wall, all of them but Emily's looking dusty and cracked.

"They all paid for the pain Jane caused me," Cole's voice said malevolently from behind me.

I turned to look at the dark angel behind me and nearly screamed when I saw him.

Apparently Cole had been manipulating my thoughts from the moment I first laid eyes on him when Cormack and I had arrived.

Cole's eyes were blacker than I thought it was possible for the color to be. The veins around his eyes swelled, but instead of looking red or bluish from blood, they looked black, like ink ran through Cole's veins. The rest of Cole's body was terrifying. All of his skin looked as if it had shrunk just slightly, clinging too tight and stretched on his skin. His once glorious and perfect wings were now a mockery of what they had been. His feathers looked skewed and thin. It looked as if he had lost nearly half of them.

"And now you see me as I truly have become," he

said evenly, his eyes burning with intensity.

Cole finally looked like the monster he was.

"So that was her name? Jane?" Maybe it was a defense mechanism, my need to change the subject to something slightly less terrifying. I was afraid I might pass out if I didn't. I would have thrown up if I hadn't already just done that. My eyes dropped from Cole, resting on the floor, just in front of his feet.

Cole stepped around me and approached the painting of her. "Yes, Jane was her name. My Dearest. We were in a relationship for six years, if you can call what we had a relationship."

"What happened?" I asked hesitantly as I looked at the woman who was so hauntingly similar to myself. "Did you ever see her again after the last of the letters?"

"Once," Cole said as he stroked a finger down the frame of the painting. "I begged her to allow me to see my son. She tried to deny that he was mine, but she knew. He looked nothing like James. He had my eyes, my hair, my build. I think most people suspected he was my son, even Jane's father.

"She met me in the next town over, where we would be less recognized. William was five years old. It was like looking at a painting of myself when I was younger. Jane, she could hardly look at me. She knew what she had done, how she had forsaken me. After that brief meeting, I never saw her or my son again."

"It was wrong of her to keep him away from you," I said, actually feeling sorry for Cole.

"I sent him a gift, every year on his birthday. I have no idea if he ever received them, if Jane ever allowed them to get to William."

We were silent for a few moments, both staring at her portrait.

"Why did you leave me the letters, Cole?" I finally asked, my voice very small.

He was quiet for a while, I wondered for a brief moment if he had even heard me. Finally he turned to me, his eyes looking empty. "I see two people when I look at you, Jessica. On the one hand I see you, the woman who's lived through hell her entire life, but is still sane, still able to cope and function. But on the other hand, how can I not see Jane?

"It's illogical and obviously ridiculous, but I wanted to wake something up in her. To make her remember why she loved me, the way I made her feel. And maybe I thought I could draw that out in you." He turned and looked back at her face, the skin he had known so well for so long. The woman he had longed for for centuries.

I couldn't say anything to his reasoning. I didn't know what to say.

As if looking at her portrait was too much for him, Cole turned from it and walked out the door and into the hallway. I followed him as he walked out into the grand but crumbled entrance and walked outside.

He said nothing as he made his way through the overgrown grass, across a lawn area. His pants clung to his legs as the dampened earth tried to entrap him. The air was heavy with moisture, the rain recently ended. He slowed as we got to a stone wall and ducked through a doorway, the wooden door decayed and rotted away.

"Of course, that was my first thought when I saw

you during the trial. You looked too similar; you could have been Jane's twin. My emotions were so confused. On the one hand, when I looked at you I saw her and the feelings I had for Jane surfaced. Yet on the other, I had to be rational and think it through. You looked so similar, you had to be related. Jane had no other children, just William. If you were related to Jane, you were related to me."

The garden we entered into was a jungle by now, after centuries of being neglected. Trees sprouted up in random places, the grass grew long and wild. The only evidence that this had once been a tame piece of land was the crumbling stones that surrounded us.

"I cannot explain to you the relief I felt when I discovered that you were not related to my son. Nor can I explain the hope, the irrational desire that surged in me. I had hoped that I could make you fall for me. You should have. Any normal woman would have, just look at me."

I did. While Cole was terrifying now, he was still beautiful in a morbid, unworldly way. Yes, any woman should have fallen in love with him. At least in lust.

"I had already fallen for Alex," I said quietly, still not looking at Cole fully.

A terrifying hiss came up Cole's throat. I backed away two steps before I even thought about it.

"And yet again, I couldn't have the woman I wanted. Lost to me to another man," Cole said, his voice filled with venom. He paced the perimeter of the garden, his fists balled angrily. "Furious does not even begin to explain how I felt when Alex did what he did, when he stole you from me in the moment you were about to become mine.

"I wanted revenge but couldn't do a thing to you. I couldn't touch you. Your family and disturbed friend were protected.

"I watched you. I couldn't make myself stay away. I craved being around you like nothing I had ever felt before. It hurt to see you in so much pain. I wanted to take it away, to make you feel the things I knew I could make you feel.

"And yet I wanted you to hurt. The pain Alex was causing you. I wanted you to feel the pain I have felt for the last two and a half centuries. I wanted you to feel pain. I wanted to rip your throat out, to strangle you, to hurt you in every way I could imagine possible."

Cole paced the perimeter of the garden wall like a caged, rabid animal. I swallowed hard, my eyes unable to meet his. If I had ever questioned what terror felt like, I understood *exactly* what it felt like right then.

"Then I came here I realized it wasn't you exactly I wanted revenge upon. It was the woman who would not take me as I was. I was and am Cole Emerson, and she still wouldn't have me!"

It was sick and wrong, but I realized why Cole did what he did to those women. He was taking his revenge out on them. He wanted to kill Jane for what she did to him, but couldn't bring himself to do it. He loved her too much. So he took it out on the other women. The ones who meant nothing to him. And Emily had run straight to him just after Cole had yet again had a woman taken from him.

"Were you planning to kill Emily? Like you did with those other women?" I asked quietly, my voice slightly shaky.

"Yes," Cole answered coldly. "She would have met the same end as the others."

I felt sick. The walls around us started to spin a little. "What is wrong with you? How can you have no remorse for what you have done? For what you were going to do?"

"Unlike you, Jessica, I lack much of a conscience. You could say I am the most selfish man you will ever meet. I get what I want. There will be consequences if not."

"No wonder Jane wouldn't have you," I spat back.

Cole's eyes flashed with anger, and he was across the garden in a movement that was faster than I could see. I barely even saw it as he raised his hand and struck at me. A sound like the crack of thunder reverberated off the stone walls, and Cole was thrown back. I jumped back, not because Cole had actually touched me, but for the shock that blasted between us.

Cole lay on the ground a good fifteen feet from me, his eyes burning, but a small smile tugging at the corner of his mouth.

"How could Emily have been so stupid," I said, my tone low but harsh. "How could she not see you for what you are?"

Cole didn't make a move to stand up, just propped his bare back against the wall. His wings folded at his side. "I couldn't believe it at first either. I've seen her brand. I know she went through the same thing you did, for different reasons. I was the one who burned the mark into her skin. Yet there she was, standing before me, begging me to take her as my own.

"She wanted the offer I gave to you. She would give herself to me. She wanted me; she also wanted that position on the council. She claimed affection for me."

My skin crawled again, as it had hardly stopped doing since I had seen Cole again. I couldn't even imagine wanting to do what Emily was willing to do with a creature that looked like Cole.

"She of course didn't see me as I truly am," Cole said with a smirk on his face.

"You're despicable," I hissed as I turned and walked out of the garden.

I didn't know where I was going and I didn't care. I just needed to be moving. I needed out of the enclosed space that had brought forth so many wretched truths.

A demented chuckle sounded in the back of my mind, my brand prickling.

The sun was dropping dangerously low in the horizon as I walked across an open field. I didn't care that I wouldn't be able to find my way back to the decaying mansion once the light was gone. I wouldn't be sleeping tonight. Even if I did feel tired, there was no way I was going to sleep in that vestige of a home or with a deranged angel loose to do as he pleased while I slept.

I found an old wagon, sitting lonely out in the middle of a field. I crawled up onto the front driver's seat and just sat and watched as the sun set, the stars flickered into view, and the moon phased into the sky. A warm breeze picked up, ruffling my unruly hair. The air smelled sweet, like grass and wheat. It helped to calm my senses just a bit.

The events of the last few hours replayed in my mind, and I wondered what had happened to everyone. We had set out as a group of three, on this insane mission to make the leader of the condemned return to hell. And now here the remnants were, only myself left to make Cole go somewhere he obviously didn't want to go.

Thoughts of Alex dominated my mind. I missed him already, felt pained with how badly I wanted him here with me again. I hoped he had found his mother in time, though. He needed to know her. I only hoped she had cleaned up her life since the last time she had seen her son, when he was only a few weeks old.

As I recalled seeing Emily standing at the window, blood dripping to the floor from her wrists, I felt sick. I still couldn't understand her actions, the ones that were actually her own. I still hoped she would be okay, though. I didn't want to lose my best friend. She was the only one who understood my twisted past. I had to trust that Cormack had gotten her to help before it was too late.

The conversation Cole and I had about Jane came back to me. He had said how Jane had forsaken him. Now he had forsaken Emily. That was all Emily wanted, was a man who would love her as intensely as Alex loved me. Cole had wanted a woman who was now long dead and would never have him. I wanted Alex to marry me, but he refused. And Alex was being pulled into the world of the dead. We were all forsaken.

I suddenly felt very alone and in despair.

CHAPTER TWENTY

ALEX

My insides were a knotted mess as I ran up to the deserted building. I wanted to throw up, thinking maybe that would help clear out the sick feeling that was seeping into every corner of my body. If only my stomach hadn't been empty for the last six months.

The building was falling apart and looked like it was infested with all kinds of disgusting rodents and diseases. A section of the roof was caved in, and I could see mold growing inside one of the windows. It looked exactly like the kind of building drugs would have been made in.

I checked the front door and found it bolted shut. Checking to make sure no one was around to see, I punched a clean hole through the metal surface and unlocked it from the inside. It couldn't have squealed louder as I pushed it open. If there was anyone else in the building I had given them plenty of warning to clear out if they didn't want to be found.

The smell hit me like a punch in the gut when I walked in and would have been enough to make a normal person puke right then and there. A mix of mold, human waste, and what I assumed was drugs. I couldn't be sure. Somehow I had managed to stay away from that stuff so I couldn't tell.

The room I walked into was devoid of life other than the mouse I saw scamper under a mildewed blanket. I could hear the sound of water dripping inside a wall. Extending my senses, I heard what I was looking for.

Less than two seconds later, I was up the stairs and into what at one point had probably been a bedroom. Lying sprawled on the floor was a woman and next to her was a crusty-looking syringe.

"Caroline!" I shouted as I gathered her up in my arms and shook her. Her eyes opened slightly, but wouldn't focus on anything. They just rolled around in her head.

"Caroline, you stay with me!" I shouted as I picked her tiny frame up in my arms. I was afraid she would snap at just the movement of being picked up. She was all skin and bones.

She smelled heavily of cigarette smoke and faintly of vomit. She looked like she hadn't bathed in a few weeks. Her clothes were torn and crusted.

"Caroline, you've got to stay with me!" I screamed. Panic surged through me as her breathing became more and more faint. The sound of her heart beating started coming more infrequently. She was dying, fast.

I didn't even care if anyone saw me moving the way I did. While I managed to keep the wings contained, I was moving faster than should have been possible. I didn't care, I had to get this woman to the hospital or she was going to be dead in just a few minutes. The deserted parts of town gave way into habitation as my feet barely pounded the pavement.

"Someone help me!" I yelled as I burst through the doors of the emergency room. A male nurse jumped two feet in the air at my shouts. A lot of the stares I was getting used to, and one hundred twenty-four seconds later, Caroline was being wheeled into a room.

I collapsed into a chair in the waiting room and hung my head. My entire frame trembled slightly, my nerves trying to go a million directions all at once. I was going to crack any second.

I didn't know what I expected to find when I went to save Caroline. Cole had only indicated that if I didn't get to her within an hour she would be joining our world and coming to his side. As evil as Cole was, I knew he hadn't done this to her. She'd done this to herself. My grandparents had hinted at an addiction, had never had anything good to say about her. So why had I had any hopes of finding a woman who would be fit to be my mother? I should have known better than to hope. I'd gone my whole life without a mother, why would I hope to gain one now?

A war raged within me as I watched the sun go down outside. Jessica and Cormack would have reached Cole and Emily by this point. What was happening? Was Jessica safe? Was Emily? It was driving me mad that I had no way of reaching anyone. I'd buy Jessica a cell phone first thing when we got home.

I wouldn't let the thoughts of *if* we got home surface.

The thought of Jessica in the same room as Cole again made my blood boil. I didn't even realize I crushed the arm of the chair I was sitting in.

"Mr. Wright?" a woman asked as she came into the waiting room. *Who else would I be?* I thought to myself. *There's no one else in here.* Instead of snapping at the woman, I just nodded.

"You can go back and see your mother now," she said as she indicated for me to follow her.

My emotions twisted all the more, having someone else call that woman my mother. No one had ever talked about my mother in reference of going to see her.

The nurse took me to a room and left me alone there. I paused in the door. I could just leave right now. She was under medical supervision and she should survive. Letting myself hope further that she would become a woman I would be proud to call my mother was obviously stupid. I could spare myself a lot of heartache if I just left right now and didn't let this mess of a human into my life. I was already dealing with enough right now.

I took a deep breath and stepped over the threshold. I closed the door behind me.

She seemed to be asleep, but I wasn't positive as I walked to her side and just stared at her face. She was still filthy, her eyes looking like they were sinking into her head. Her skin looked leathered and pocked. Her hair seemed to be thinning and looked brittle.

Looking in this woman's face, I felt ashamed. I suddenly wasn't sure I wanted her to wake up and find me here. I wasn't sure I wanted to meet her. What good was it going to do? She hadn't wanted to be a part of my life for these past twenty-three years, why should I force her to be a part of it now?

My stomach jumped into my throat as her eyes fluttered open, piercing blue orbs looking up at me that confirmed who she was. They were exactly like mine had been.

Her brow furrowed as she stared at my face, her eyes probing and searching. “Alex?” she whispered finally.

I couldn’t say anything, only nodded. I wasn’t surprised she recognized who I was. I’d been told hundreds of times how much I looked like my father.

Her face hardened, the furrows in her face no longer confused, but angry looking. “What are you doing here? How did you find me?”

I was taken aback at her abruptness. I hadn’t expected harsh words to come from the woman who I had just saved from crossing into the land of the dead. “I…” I stammered. “You were nearly dead. I brought you to the hospital.”

“How did you find me?” she said again, her voice a little less harsh this time.

“Um, I can’t really say how,” I struggled to answer. “What does it matter?”

Surprisingly this seemed to be a good enough answer for her. I supposed to a drug addict it was. “Yeah, well, maybe you should have just left me there.”

“I couldn’t just let you die,” I said quietly as I backed up two steps and took a seat in a chair. “You’re not getting off that easily.”

We both just sat there, glaring at each other through the dim light. Neither of us knew what words to say. What did you say to the son you never wanted, but who had just saved your life, even if you didn't care about it? What do you say to the woman who gave birth to you, and then abandoned you and your father for more than twenty years?

CHAPTER TWENTY-ONE

JESSICA

I did not leave the wagon all night, and by the time the sun started to work its way back into the sky I felt stiff, but determined. I wasn't going to let Cole bully me or scare me away. One way or another, he was going to go back to the world of the dead.

The grass in the fields came up above my waist as I walked back toward the house. The sun shone brightly and danced off Cole's wings as he walked toward me. They looked more metallic than white in the light, distorted versions of what they should have been. They looked broken and twisted. Yet still menacing. As Cole stopped just five feet from me, a feather floated softly to the ground.

"I want to make a deal," I said, my tone confident, reflective of how I actually felt inside for once. "I will listen to whatever you have to say, go with you wherever you want me to go. But you have to make me a promise."

"And what might that be?" he asked, his voice surprisingly not mocking as I expected it to be.

"That you'll go back to where you belong."

Cole just stared at me with those black orbs for

several long moments. I tried to interpret the emotions I saw running through them. Resignation, despair, understanding, frustration. I couldn't quite tell.

"We'll see how things play out," Cole answered, not promising anything.

"Fine," I agreed. At least he hadn't said no.

"Come with me," he said as he turned and started walking.

Silence fell on us as we walked through the swaying grasses. I trailed behind Cole, watching him as he moved. How was it possible for a creature to be so beautiful and terrifying at the same time? Even though I had watched Alex almost nonstop for the last few months, I still stared in wonder as I watched Cole move. But the wings were wretched to look at. There were wide gaps between many of the feathers, evidence of how many of them he had lost. Even as we walked through the fields, another fell softly to the ground. I bent briefly to pick it up.

We approached a barn, its walls tilting and part of the roof rotted away. Cole walked up to an ancient-looking tree just ten feet from it. Many of its branches were touching the roof of the barn, threatening to push it over.

Cole looked up at the tree as he laid a hand on its rough surface. He walked around it once, looking closely at its surface. He finally stopped at a certain spot. He traced his fingers over it tenderly.

I walked to his side to see what he was looking at. At about Cole's eye level there was something carved into the bark.

C & J
Forever

"Cole and Jane," I said softly as I looked at the cruel letters.

"Forever," Cole said so quietly I could barely even hear it. "I could never have Jane, even in the afterlife. She'd done enough to be granted blue eyes, despite all the transgressions she'd committed with me. Forever indeed."

I recalled the letters between Cole and Jane. Jane had spoken of a night they had spent together in the barn. I had little doubt this was that barn. They had marked their special place with their initials.

"It seems ironic," Cole said as he backed away from the tree a few steps. "That this was the place my life both began and ended."

My brow furrowed as I looked at him, wondering what he meant.

"From what my mother tells me, I was conceived under this very tree. My father was just about to inherit the Emerson estate. They married just months after that. I was born not long after.

"It was also from this tree that my father had me hanged."

I felt all the color drain from my face.

"It took them a long time to figure out what was happening. Beautiful women would come home with me, but they never left. I was careful not to let anyone but perhaps a servant see them come in. They were too afraid of me to say anything. But eventually, my father saw some things he was never meant to see. To say he was enraged would be a grave understatement.

"He came at me with an iron rod. He must have broken half the bones in my face. After he beat me unconscious, he had a few of his men carry me to this tree. They synched a noose around my neck and sat me up on a horse. They waited until I woke up.

"The old man looked into my face and said 'Congratulations, you've killed the Emerson legacy. You are no son of mine.' He then slapped the horse, leaving me dangling in the air.

"I was twenty-seven the day I died."

I wasn't sure what to feel as I followed Cole around to the back side of the barn. Cole had met a terrible end, but I wasn't sure if I felt he deserved what happened to him.

Another field stretched out behind the barn. Cole walked to a place only about ten feet away from the west wall.

"He buried me in a three foot deep hole here," Cole said disgustedly as he looked at a nondescript spot on the ground. "He didn't even have the decency to put a marker on his only son's grave."

Without saying anything else, Cole leaned his back against the barn wall and slid to the ground. His head hung low, his forearms resting on his knees, his hands dangling between them. For once, I felt like I was seeing something different in Cole than I had ever seen before. Not the monster, not the man who thought he could have anything he wanted. But the man who was beaten down, the man nobody loved.

I started searching through the grass. I grabbed every rock that was of any significant size, piling it up in one certain spot, roughly where Cole said his body had been buried. With each stone I placed, I felt Cole's mood shift. Lighten wasn't the right word, but it was the closest I could think of.

He watched me without saying a word. I felt his eyes burn with intensity as he did. It was different from all the other looks I had gotten from Cole before. They had always been full of craving, lust, desire. This look was curiosity and perhaps, admiration? Whatever it was, it confused me.

After I had the grave marker made, I placed a few wildflowers on top of it. It felt weird. Placing flowers on the grave of the being that was watching me.

Slowly, I walked to Cole's side and sat on the ground beside him. Neither of us spoke for several long minutes, just stared out across the open field at nothing. The warm summer breeze picked up, sending Cole's unidentifiable scent my way. So similar yet so different from Alex's. I heard the grass rustle as the air blew across it. It smelled like earth and decaying wood, here so close to the ground. It was comforting.

"I'm dying, Jessica," Cole finally spoke as he stared out over what should have been his. "Well, not dying. I can't exactly die since I'm already dead. Decaying, I guess you could say. Fading."

I hadn't really thought of it that way, but it made sense. Cole didn't exactly look his best.

"I'm not human anymore, Jessica. I don't belong in

this world. I'm fighting to stay in the world of the living with every fiber of my being. I'm slowly being pulled back, though. I can't fight what I am. I can't even hide the damn wings anymore."

Cole leaned forward, his head sinking low. As he did so, his hair fell away from his neck, revealing his shadowed brand. I had seen it once before, one light, barely visible X and another more defined one with it. It was like he had jerked away when they branded him, as if he had fought with them. It had been a nearly white color before. It was now almost a blood red and almost looked infected.

Without thinking, I raised a hand to it and very lightly touched a finger to it. I had forgotten what contact between the two of us did until there was a decaying mark of my finger on the back of his neck to match the handprints on his chest. Cole didn't even flinch away, even though I knew the pain it must have caused him.

"This is what's going to happen to Alex, isn't it?" I asked. It felt as if there was a large lump in my throat and a huge rock in the pit of my stomach.

"Yes," Cole said softly as he turned his black eyes to meet mine. I was surprised to see no anger in them as I mentioned Alex. No jealously. "He won't be able to fight it much longer. Eventually he's going to be pulled back."

"But the council agreed to let him come back," I started to argue, feeling desperate. Even as I tried to ration, I knew the truth, I knew what was going on. I understood now.

"He's not of this world Jessica. Yes, they agreed to let him come back to you, they never said for how long. Eventually it's going to become too much for him. Even as we speak now, *I* can hardly fight the pull."

I struggled to keep my breathing steady. I closed my eyes and leaned my head against the barn wall. A tear rolled down my cheek. I should have known a thing that was too good to be true when I saw it. Of course Alex couldn't stay. He wasn't human, he wasn't alive.

But how much time did he have left?

"Please tell me you didn't kill Alex's mother," I said through my silent tears, trying to distract myself.

"I didn't kill Alex's mother," Cole said as he looked back out over the field. "*I* didn't do anything to her. She did it to herself. I just found her, recognized that if someone didn't help her soon, she was going to be dead."

A few more stray tears rolled down my face as I closed my eyes for a moment. Apparently Caroline hadn't changed at all. Alex wasn't going to be finding a woman who was fit to be called a mother. She was still the same drug addicted woman that had abandoned him twenty-three years ago.

As I shifted on the ground, I heard the sound of paper crinkling. I pulled the paper from my back pocket and unfolded it. It was Cole's letter to me.

"What did you mean by this?" I asked. As I did, my eyes scanned his words again.

Goodbye, Jessica. Eventually we all have to face our demons. I've gone to face mine. Perhaps someday I can help you face yours.

Cole stood in one invisible movement. He glanced down and started to extend his hand to me, then realized what that would do to him and withdrew it to his side. "Come with me."

I stood on shaky legs and followed Cole around to the front of the barn again. The entire building rattled as he swung a door open. For a moment he watched it, gauging as I was to see if it was going to come down. When it finally stopped moaning and creaking, he motioned for me to follow him in.

The smell of rotting wood intensified as we stepped inside. My eyes took a moment to adjust to the dim light. This appeared to be some kind of maintenance shed, filled with ancient looking tools and pieces of equipment I could barely identify. It seemed strange that the estate had just been abandoned, everything left basically untouched.

We walked to the center of the building and Cole stopped. He turned to look at me, his eyes probing, searching. He didn't say anything for a moment as he looked for something within me that I didn't know the answer to.

"Do you trust me?" he asked, never breaking his stare.

"No," I said without hesitation.

That half smile crept back onto his face. "I guess that is warranted," he chuckled slightly. He took a step closer to me, his face growing serious. "Will you do something I ask, if I promise no harm will come to you because of it?"

I didn't answer him right away, carefully considering his words. I didn't trust Cole, but I believed he would keep his word. I saw it in his eyes. "You promise?" I asked, my tone doubtful.

"I promise," he said as he looked intensely at me.

"What?" I asked him, now having his word.

"Just close your eyes. Don't look. And don't move."

His request frightened me. I didn't want to comply with what he asked of me. But I had agreed. I closed my eyes.

Cole didn't make any sound, but I sensed him as he moved to the north wall of the barn. My palms started sweating, and I wiped them on my pants nervously.

Four seconds later, a pain like I had never known pierced me in the right side of my chest.

My eyes flashed open, going immediately to the source of the unbearable pain. Sticking out of my chest was the handle of a very large, very rusty blade. My mind couldn't even process the fact that no blood was seeping from my damaged body.

I looked up at Cole as he moved toward me, and I dropped to my knees. I waited for my vision to blur, to start feeling lightheaded as I should have felt. Instead, the only thing I felt was the pain.

Cole's face was intent as he slowly knelt before me. I was surprised to see that his face also looked pained, as if what he had just done to me caused *him* pain. He locked eyes with me, a million other emotions rolling through his. "This is going to hurt," he said, his voice sounding regretful.

Cole was right. A bloodcurdling scream ripped from my throat as Cole yanked the blade out of my chest. There wasn't even any blood on the knife as he dropped it at his side. His eyes never left the gaping hole in my torso. My eyes fell back on my chest and grew wide. There was a long, slender hole there, the edges rough and torn from being slashed open. But it was shrinking. Fast. My skin netted itself back together, the wound healing on its own. The pain ebbed away, until I couldn't even remember what it had felt like, having a knife embedded in my body. Within ten seconds, the hole had completely closed, and I felt perfectly normal again.

Except for being totally freaked out.

"What…?" I gasped in terror. I couldn't take my eyes from the small white scar on my skin.

"That should have killed you," Cole said softly, traces of awe in his tone.

Anger boiled in my blood as I looked back up at Cole, his face only two feet away from my own. Before I even thought about what I was doing, I slapped my hand across his face, leaving another decayed looking gray mark. "What is *wrong* with you?!"

"I'm sorry," Cole said, his expression looking shocked, though I didn't think it was from me slapping him. "I had to test my theory."

"What theory?" I growled. To say I was livid at what Cole had just done was a massive understatement. "You promised me you would do nothing that would hurt me."

"I promised no harm would come to you," Cole said softly. "Are you harmed?"

I was about to scream back at Cole, but had to think about his question. He was right, I wasn't harmed. Horrified, but not harmed, despite the hole that had been ripped in my shirt and the thin white line on my skin.

"What theory?" I asked again through clenched teeth.

"Don't you feel any different than you did six months ago?" Cole asked, his tone sounding slightly excited.

"Of course I do," I spat. "I was two inches from death five months ago! No thanks to you!"

"You were less than two inches," Cole said as he stood up. He motioned for me to follow him. He started walking back toward the mansion. "You were at death. You couldn't have come any closer to death and still come back."

"What are you talking about?" I called after him, trying to keep up with his swift pace. "What does this have to do with you lobbing a knife into my chest?"

We entered the house through a back door. Cole didn't answer my question as he walked down a hall and entered a room. He stopped just inside and placed me before a floor to ceiling mirror, being careful to only touch me through my clothes.

"Don't you notice how you don't look a day older than you did the day I killed Alex?" Cole said quietly, his lips too close to my ear for comfort.

"It's only been six months," I said lamely. "I'm not likely to notice any difference in that short of time."

Cole's shoulders fell slightly and his face looked a little frustrated. "I suppose even your eyes can't see that much detail. Don't you *feel* different? Or perhaps the better question is don't you feel *exactly* the same?"

"What are you trying to get at, Cole?" I asked, feeling my insides start to quiver. I didn't think I really wanted to hear the answer to that question.

"You haven't changed a bit from the day Alex made the exchange, his life for yours. You haven't changed at all since you were more dead than alive."

Irritation joined my fear. "Just tell me what is going on, Cole! What are you saying has happened to me?!"

"I think, Jessica," he hesitated, trying to think how to word this just right. "I think you may just be indestructible now, immortal if you will."

As the word sank in I burst into laughter. "You're insane! You can't be serious? Immortal? I'm going to live forever? Uh huh, I believe that one!"

Cole took two steps back from me and sat on a creaky chair. "I'm not making a joke, Jessica. You should have died there in the barn. I know how to throw a blade, it should have killed you instantly."

My face slowly grew serious as I recalled what had just happened. Cole was right, I should have died. There was no question about that. But everything else he was saying was ridiculous.

"As I said, I have a theory," he said seriously, seeing that he had my attention now. "I don't think even you realize how close to death you were when I nearly had you. I fought panic for days before the events that occurred to save your life. I thought at any moment, you were going to slip away, before I had talked you into joining me. I knew you might go at any moment. You were changing into what I am, becoming more and more like me with every passing moment.

"You're mostly angel now, Jessica, and yet still human. If only just barely still human."

He didn't say anything for a moment as that sank in. I couldn't take what he was saying seriously, it was just preposterous.

"Most of your human self died during those days you spent in my basement. You were becoming so close to what I am. I would guess you're roughly eighty percent angel. When Alex made his sacrifice, he stopped you from totally dying, but too much of you had already died. It couldn't come back. You became stuck in this strange limbo between the world of the dead and the land of the living. And then Alex traded his life for yours. That is part of my theory as well.

"As long as Alex is dead, you will never die. They traded his life for yours. While they still have Alex's life, as long as he remains dead, they can never have the rest of your mortal life. That small percent that was left.

"As I said, you haven't changed at all since I last saw you. You're frozen where you are. I don't think you will age for the rest of your days. And those are going to be endless. Angels can't die. We're already dead."

My head spun from everything Cole was saying. Nothing and everything he said made sense. His logic was impossible. It couldn't be true.

The memory of accidently flinging myself off the

cliff hit me. Half the bones in my body should have been broken, and yet I had walked away without a scratch. The accident with Austin. I should have been killed. And then there was the entire matter of how I had physically changed so much, how my face didn't even seem like my own. I moved nearly as fast as Cole and Alex did. I didn't even bleed anymore.

I leaned my back against the mirror and didn't realize my legs were giving out on me until my rear hit the ground. All my insides seemed to suddenly disappear, I felt hollow. My own body felt alien suddenly. Everything in my world came to a standstill, and I saw nothing as I stared at the floor, didn't even hear the words Cole said to me. I didn't even notice how after a few minutes Cole walked out of the room and left me alone.

I could only even consider, not accept, but consider one word that described what Cole said had happened to me. I was stuck. I couldn't move forward, I couldn't move on into the afterlife. How I was now was how I was always going to be. I was held forever where I was. And Alex was soon going to be pulled away from me. Forever. And I'd never be able to go with him.

CHAPTER TWENTY-TWO

ALEX

"No," I hissed. "No. No!"

Yet again, I had just walked in a big circle. Here I was, back at the parked car.

Just a few hours after Caroline had woken up, I was shocked to see Emily being wheeled into another room. As I looked down the hall, I saw Cormack following the stretcher. I nearly lost it when he told me what had happened. Had his wings been out, I would have ripped them out right then and there.

With someone there to keep an eye on Caroline, I left her in Cormack's charge. I drove like a maniac back to the address I had. As soon as I got within five miles, the GPS shorted out and the screen went blank. I drove on every street that seemed like it might go in the right direction and before I knew it, I was right back at the hospital. I couldn't even remember getting back into the city.

I drove all night trying to get to the estate and always ended up back right where I had started. Trusting the nursing staff to watch Emily and Caroline, Cormack had come with me to guide me there, but even with him, we could not find the way.

Someone was messing with our heads and keeping us away.

In desperation, I had parked the car as soon as the GSP started to go out and started walking. And here I was again, back at the car.

In my frustration, I bent and picked up a rock and hurtled it into the dimming light as a scream ripped from my chest. My hands knotted in my hair as another scream was released into the sky.

Not knowing what else to do, I climbed into the car. I simply stared out over the open fields before me, trying to will Cole's influence out of my head.

I would *never* mess with anyone's head again.

The drive back to the hospital was numbing and helped to calm me down. By this point, both Emily and Caroline had been moved into normal rooms. I found Caroline sleeping, her body hooked up to all kinds of monitors and tubes. Her heart had stopped during the night after I had brought her in. The doctor said it was due to all the drugs that were still leftover in her system. He had also told me her recovery wasn't going to be easy since she would also begin symptoms of withdrawal soon.

I walked down the hall and found Emily's door cracked open. I could see Cormack sitting close to Emily's bed on a stool. He held one of Emily's hands in his own.

"I'm going ta get ya out of here soon," I heard Cormack say quietly.

"I don't think they're going to let me out for a while," she said, her eyes never leaving his face.

"They're going to want to take me to the psych ward. I did kind of try to kill myself."

"Do you want ta leave?" Cormack asked.

"Of course. I don't want to waste any time."

"I'll get you out of here then," he said with a smile.

I turned and walked back down the hall toward Caroline's room. I'd seen the way Cormack had been watching Emily as they worked on her. You would have guessed they'd known each other for years, not mere minutes. I didn't really believe in love at first sight, but there was something powerful going on between those two.

Seeing the two of them together just made it all the worse that I didn't know what was happening with Jessica.

Cormack got Emily released. She was right, the doctor wanted to admit her to the psych ward, but suddenly in the middle of explaining that, he said she could leave that afternoon. I didn't miss the way Cormack's eyes were so concentrated on the doctor.

Emily insisted that she couldn't go home when she didn't know if Jessica was alright. She felt so guilty about what she had done, it made *me* feel guilty. She kept a constant stream of apologies going. When I couldn't stand to hear it anymore, I told Cormack to take her back to the hotel they had checked into.

Once the two of them had left, I waited in Caroline's room. It made my stomach knot to see the way they looked at each other in such a hesitant but natural way. Emily would slide her hand into Cormack's, her eyes looking at his face, gauging his reactions to her cautious forwardness. Emily finally had her angel and Cormack had found the woman he had searched for before he had been murdered.

With the two of them gone, there was no one else to watch Caroline. I had to give up my futile search for Jessica to keep an eye on her. I wasn't about to let her run away from me again.

I had been out in the hall talking to Emily on my cell for a few minutes, again listening to her apologize for what she had done. When I finally managed to get off the phone and came back into the room, Caroline was awake and to my surprise, mostly dressed in her regular, though disgusting, clothes. She was dragging a brush through her hair when I walked in.

"What's going on, Caroline?" I asked as I closed the door behind me.

"The doctor said I can leave now," she said, her voice sounding terrible.

"Where are you going once you get out?" I asked as I folded my arms across my chest.

"What does it matter to you?" she said harshly, though she wouldn't look me in the eye. I noticed how she was sweating and her hands trembled.

"You abandoned me for over twenty years," I said through my teeth. "I'm not about to let you get off so easy again."

"Well it seems like you've managed on your own just fine," she croaked as she stood.

"You think it was easy for me?!" I shouted. She took a step back and sat back down on the bed. "You think it was easy being the kid with no mother? You think it was easy watching all the other kids at school have their moms drop them off, to see their moms making cupcakes and bring them into the class? All the other kids had their moms pick out their graduation clothes, had them give them advice about girls. I needed a mother, and you weren't there!"

"I couldn't be your mother!" she shrieked back. "I wasn't fit to be anyone's mother! But then your father knocked me up and I didn't know what to do. I, I wanted to…" she trailed off.

"You wanted to what, Caroline?" I asked in a low voice, suddenly unable to look her in the eye. "You wanted to get rid of me?"

"Yes!" she said, her voice cracking. "I didn't know what to do with a baby. I couldn't stop using the drugs when you were growing inside me. I'm not a good person, Alex. I've never claimed to be one."

"People can change," I said quietly, feeling nothing but hopelessness.

"Not me," she said as she shook her head and looked down at her hands in her lap. "I am the way I am. I've accepted that. My lifestyle is going to kill me someday. You just pushed the date back a little."

"I needed you," I said as I finally looked up into her crystal clear blue eyes. "You should have been there for me."

"Yeah, well, at least you have your father," she said as her eyes shifted away from mine.

"Dad died when I was seven," I said hollowly.

Caroline didn't say anything for quite a while, just

stared at the floor. "I barely even remember him, you know. It was a long time ago. There's a lot that I don't remember from back in those days."

My insides felt like they had been gutted out and dumped in the garbage. Everything that was happening right now was wrong, but I didn't know how to change it.

"Come on," I said as I motioned for her to stand and backed away. "If the doctor said you could leave you're coming with me."

"Alex, I…"

"I'm not giving you a choice, Caroline!" I bellowed as I turned back toward her. She jumped away, her eyes wide with fear. "I'm not letting you go back into those rat infested houses to go shoot up again and kill yourself. You're coming with me whether you like it or not!"

She gave the tinniest of nods and followed me out.

We got discharged from the hospital and neither of us spoke as we drove to the hotel Emily and Cormack were staying at.

X

Twice that night, I caught Caroline trying to sneak out of the room. It was awkward sharing the room with Emily and Cormack, but I needed someone to help watch the drug addict.

Their relationship or whatever it was that had evolved between the two of the confused me. Emily was forward and Cormack was just as open to everything she gave to him. But they were both so hesitant. I wondered if they too were constantly thinking about the fact that he wasn't supposed to be here.

"Who is she?" Caroline asked as she sat in a chair by the window and looked at me. We were alone, Emily and Cormack out for a walk.

I turned my head to her, her frame strangely aglow from the light coming in behind her. "What?"

"Who's the girl? The one we're just waiting around for? I know there is one, it's written all over your face."

"Jessica," I said. My body felt relief just at saying her name. At the same time my hands shook.

"Is she good for you?" she asked as her eyes probed my face through the dimming light.

"She's my whole…" I paused, about to say life but I didn't have even that anymore. "Everything."

"How long have you been together?"

"Seven months."

"I was four months pregnant with you when I had known your father for that long," she said with a crooked and gross-looking smile. I only looked away and gave a nod of acknowledgment.

"She's the one, isn't she?" Caroline asked, her voice suddenly serious. It shook from the effort it took to keep it even.

My emotions swirled as I gave a nod. If I'd been capable, I would have had tears springing to my eyes. *Was she okay?*

"You pop the question yet?"

I pursed my lips together and shook my head, my eyes glued on the floor.

"Why not?"

I didn't answer right away, going over all the reasons why in my head. "Because some things have happened to me in the last few months. I might not be here tomorrow, or the next day."

"You get in with a bad crowd?" she asked as she narrowed her eyes at me. She scratched at the crease in her arm furiously.

"In a way, I guess," I said with a lifeless half smile. "But that's not what I meant."

Caroline was contemplative for a minute as she stared at me. "The lifestyle I live is not good in any way, shape, or form. But I have learned one thing from it. Live in the moment, in the here and now. Enjoy the high while you're on it. Sometimes the high is better than the reality.

"You love this girl, I can tell. She's your drug. Damn what might happen tomorrow. If she loves you as much as you love her, it won't matter if you've only got a year or twelve hours."

Despite the drug analogy, what Caroline had said struck me hard. My reasoning that I wouldn't leave Jessica just after we were married seemed to crumble.

But could I do that to her? Could I risk that I might not be able to fight it any longer and be pulled away from her to leave her alone forever?

"What little you might have may not be enough, but make it enough to last forever, Kid."

CHAPTER TWENTY-THREE

JESSICA

The sun reached the highest point in the sky and started drifting westward, though I didn't notice. I sat in a numb, shocked state, not thinking, not feeling anything. My life had already been too filled with the impossible; I couldn't handle one more thing. One more huge, massive, way-beyond-life-altering thing.

Darkness had started to set again before I started to come to my senses enough to realize Cole had come back and was sitting on the floor in front of me. His expression was perplexed as he looked at me, his eyes unwavering. It looked as if he had decayed further. His skin looked all the tighter, the black spider-webs around his eyes becoming more pronounced. There were even fewer feathers left on his wings now.

"You've got to be wrong," I said quietly. "I can't…" I trailed off, my voice quivering. And yet I recalled all the impossible things that had happened to me recently and knew he was right.

Cole's expression hardened slightly, though his eyes remained concerned looking. "Suck it up," he said quietly, his voice firm. "Quit feeling sorry for yourself."

I felt like Cole had just slapped me across the face. His words jarred my brain back into thinking and feeling again. "Excuse me?!" I said harshly, my eyes narrowing at him.

Most eyes wouldn't have caught the way Cole's tense form seemed to relax a bit, but my apparently more-angel-than-human eyes did.

"There are worse things that could happen to you," Cole said as he sat forward, resting his forearms on his knees. "I don't recommend dying. Being hung from a tree by your father isn't the best experience. I should think you don't recall your own slide towards death too fondly either."

"I don't want this," I said quietly as I shook my head. "I just want to be a normal person."

"Don't you realize what most people would do to have what you've been unwittingly given? What I would do to have it? You've got something that mankind has been searching for, for thousands of years!"

"I still don't want it," I whispered.

"Quit feeling sorry for yourself!" Cole roared as he stood up. "Do something about it! Don't just mope around! Use their mistake against them! They've got claim on something that you want right now. Take it back. Fight!"

I felt my heart start to pound as I understood Cole's words. He was right. I had an advantageous position. They screwed up, and I knew they weren't going to be happy about the outcome.

I wasn't happy with what they were trying to do to Alex.

"You don't love him near as much as you claim to if you aren't willing to use this against them," Cole said in a low tone as he looked down at me. "They can't claim you. If you can't be judged, *what are you willing to do to save him*?"

Adrenaline surged in my system and my pulse raced as Cole's words sank in. What did I have to be afraid of? What did I have to lose?

Death and judgment were no longer a factor in my life.

I climbed to my feet, standing face to face with Cole. He towered above me but for the first time, I didn't feel inferior to him.

"You know," I said. "You could have been a great man. I wonder what you could have become if you hadn't made the mistakes you did.

"Thank you, Cole."

He didn't say anything for a while as his black eyes searched mine. He just stared at me, his mouth a straight line. "How can you still see any good in me?" he asked. "After everything I've done to you?"

"Sometimes you just have to try and see things in a positive light. I know there is a good man buried inside there somewhere."

"He's in there pretty deep, if there is one," Cole said quietly.

"You'd better start digging," I whispered.

As we spoke, Cole had slowly leaned in closer. His eyes seemed excited, his demeanor was lighter. He seemed, almost, happy. Or even relieved.

"You don't have to hold onto her forever," I said quietly, his face now only a foot away from mine. "You don't have to stay angry. They say forgiveness is divine."

As I stared back into Cole's black eyes I could tell that this was over. I had won. At least in this battle.

Cole reached a hand up and tucked a lock of hair behind my ear. I heard his flesh sizzle and saw it change into the ugly gray hue as he did so. He didn't flinch though, just continued to look into my eyes. "Thank you, Jessica. I truly am sorry for all the pain I have caused you. It may not seem like it, but I really do have real feelings for you." I felt the shock as Cole leaned his forehead against mine and he placed his hands on the sides of my arms. "*If* you ever do find a way to make it back into my world, my offer will always be on the table."

Maybe it was just relief that I knew what was coming, maybe it was just the shock of seeing such a sincere side to Cole, but I didn't pull away as he tipped his lips forward and pressed them to mine. The shock that came with touching Cole now coursed through my system, sped along by adrenaline. It was tender and sincere, brief. Yet incredibly intense.

When Cole pulled away and I opened my eyes, a single tear escaped. All the veins in Cole's body bulged, his skin turning frighteningly black. His image seemed to fade and re-solidify. I wasn't sure if it was just that he couldn't fight the pull anymore, but I suspected it was just because Cole had finally stopped fighting. He was ready to go back where he belonged.

Cole took two steps back from me. One side of his mouth curled up into a little smile. "Don't give up Jessica," he said. "You've got to fight for what you want. I've finally faced my demons. I'll continue to try and help you face yours."

"Thank you, Cole," I said quietly as a few more tears rolled down my face.

"Goodbye, Jessica."

Cole's form started to decay away, the same way it had when he touched me. The air around us seemed to quiver and swell. Within a few moments, he had grown transparent and was gone. The air fell still.

My knees nearly gave out as relief washed over me. It was finally over now. Cole had gone back to where he belonged. I didn't have to worry about him any longer, didn't have to feel like I had to be on my guard. Cole would never watch me from the shadows again, a constant fear in the back of my mind. My emotions surged in waves as I stumbled to and out the front door.

Running wasn't something I enjoyed doing, but I ran faster than I could ever recall doing as I got out of Cole's home. My feet pounded the gravel and grass as I ran back to the main road. They couldn't carry me fast enough as I sprinted through the fading light.

The closest house I found was just short of two miles away. I rapped on the door as I tried to catch my breath. An old woman with nearly purple hair answered the door.

"May I please use your phone?" I gasped before she could even say anything.

"Are you alright, my dear?" she asked with a concerned expression letting me inside.

"Yes, thank you," I said as I stepped through the door and she closed it. "I just need to call for a ride."

"Phone is back through this way," she said as she walked back toward a tiny kitchen.

I had to try three times before I dialed the number right. My fingers didn't seem to want to function correctly.

"Hello?"

"Alex!" I nearly cried out. Tears sprang to my eyes again at just the sound of his voice.

"Jessica?!" He sounded panicked on the other end. "Where are you? I'm headed out to the car right now!"

I asked the woman for her address then relayed it back to him.

"I'll be right there!" he said, his voice pitched. "And Jessica, I love you."

"I love you, too," my voice cracked.

I hung up the phone. I thanked the woman and went outside to wait on the edge of the road.

My emotions raged the entire time I waited. I wanted to break down and cry. I wanted to crawl up in my bed and just disappear for a month. And yet Cole's words rang in my head. I needed to suck it up and fight back.

There had never been a longer twenty minutes then those I had to wait for Alex to come get me. It was totally dark by the time I saw headlights turn down the quiet street and screech to a stop in front of me. Before I even stood up from my spot on the grass, Alex was already out of the car and had scooped me into his arms.

"Jessica," Alex whispered and his voice cracked.

My lips found his and they trembled. My entire body shook and I would have collapsed to the ground had Alex not been holding me so tightly.

"I'm so sorry, Jessica," he said as he buried his face in my neck. "I didn't know what was happening, I thought you might be…"

"Shh," I said as I ran a hand over his back. "I'm alright. It's over now."

Alex pulled back to look me in the face. "He's really gone?"

I nodded. "It's over."

He kept looking at me for a long moment before he released me and led me back to the rental car. He opened my door then got in himself. Putting the car into drive, he peeled away from the curb and hurtled down the road. I couldn't blame him. I wanted to get as far away from this place as possible.

Alex took my hand and kept glancing at me. I could see the questions tumbling through his head, unable to find one to start off with.

"I'm fine, Alex," I finally said for him. I had no intention of telling him that not long before I had had a six inch long blade sticking out of my chest. "Cole and I just talked for a while. We both had some things to say that each other needed to hear."

"You just talked?" Alex said doubtfully. "For a week?"

"A week?" I said, shocked. "What are you talking about? I was only there for two days."

Alex's brow furrowed. "You've been gone a week. Trust me, I didn't lose track. I can tell you how many *seconds* you've been gone."

I shook my head. It didn't make sense. How could

I not notice an entire week go by? How could I mistake a week for two days?

I could if someone had never gotten out of my head completely.

"Cole," I hissed.

As if this were explanation enough, Alex moved on.

"He was messing with my head too. I tried coming to you," he said. "I couldn't find the property. The GPS kept shorting out. Even Cormack couldn't find his way back."

"He kept you out," I stated the obvious.

Alex only nodded.

"Is everyone okay?" I asked, wanting to change the subject. My feelings regarding Cole were too all over the place at the moment to talk about him any longer.

"For the most part," he said as he pulled into the parking lot of a small but well-kept hotel.

We walked up to the second floor and Alex opened a door. As soon as we got inside I was attacked by Emily.

"I'm so sorry, Jessica!" she started sobbing as she pulled me tighter into her. "I don't know what got into me! I should have known better!"

I patted her back, accepting her embrace. Happiness flooded through me. I was so relieved to see her. "It's alright. Are you okay now?"

Emily took a step back, wiping her eyes. I noticed the bandages that were still wrapped around her wrists. "Yeah, they stitched me up. I needed a transfusion, but I'm okay now." To my surprise she took another step back, joining Cormack at his side. "You guys got to me just in time."

I didn't miss the way Cormack beamed down at Emily. I couldn't help but smile back.

Another person was sitting quietly in one corner of the room. She had dirty blonde hair and the most frightening-looking complexion I had ever seen on a person. Her shockingly blue eyes made it obvious who she was though.

"Jessica, I'd like you to meet my mother," Alex said softly. "Caroline."

I took a few hesitant steps forward. She extended her hand, but I simply wrapped my arms around her. "I'm so glad to meet you."

Caroline seemed hesitant and uncomfortable as she patted my back twice then pulled away. I noticed how she would hardly look anyone in the eye. "It's nice to meet you, too," she said in the husky voice of a heavy smoker.

I smiled at her, feeling slightly sorry for her, and joined Alex again.

"I suggest everyone gets some sleep," Alex said as he looked around at us all. "We're all going home tomorrow."

X

We all crowded into a row of seats on the plane and everyone listened with rapture as I told them what had happened in what I had thought was two days. It was harder than I thought it would be, telling them of Cole's final hours. I should have been relieved, and I was. But what surprised me was that I felt a little sad. It was unreasonable and ridiculous, but for some reason I felt an odd little twinge in my chest recalling the last few minutes Cole and I spent together.

Everyone was relieved when we got home finally, especially Sal and Amber. Well, everyone except for maybe Caroline. Alex had insisted that she come home with us, but I could tell she was uncomfortable. I hoped that in the coming days and weeks she could learn to bond with her son and perhaps start to form some kind of relationship with him.

As I suspected, it quickly became obvious that something had happened between Cormack and Emily in the time I was with Cole. She finally had her angel. But it seemed there were no perfect happy endings when it came to angels.

Two days after we got home, Emily showed up on my doorstep at five in the morning. She was puffy eyed and her nose was running, but to my surprise there was a slight smile on her face.

I didn't even have to ask what had happened as I ushered her in and we sat on one of the leather couches.

"He's gone," she said, her voice sounding small. "He wanted to stop fighting. He was ready to move on."

"I'm so sorry, Emily," I said as I wrapped my arms around her.

"Thanks," she said as she sniffed. As she pulled away she wiped her nose with a tissue.

"Are you going to be alright?" I asked, my expression concerned. "Don't you dare lie to me."

To my surprise Emily gave a little smile. "Actually,

I am," she said as she nodded her head. "It's harder than I could have possibly imagined, seeing him go. But…he gave me hope. He told me to never stop fighting. He said it's worth it to reverse what I've done.

"I'm going to have to work really hard," she said with a sniffling chuckle.

A smile spread on my face and I felt my heart flutter. "There's always hope. You can't give up."

"I'm not going to," she said with a quivering voice through the smile on her face.

"Things will work out," I said, not only to her but to myself. "They have to."

She nodded with a smile. She then stood. "I've got to get going. The university called me yesterday. The other teacher they picked fell through. They offered me the job."

"That's great!"

She opened the door but hesitated for a moment. "Things really are going to be okay," she said as she looked back at me.

I could only nod and wave goodbye as she stepped out.

If I hadn't have been so tired of feeling so weak and like such a wimp, I probably would have started crying. But I was sick of feeling like I was just succumbing to all my fears and uncertainties. I wasn't going to let things be out of my control anymore. It was time for me to take charge for once.

I walked back down the stairs to look for Alex. I found him standing out on the deck, looking over the water. The sun had started to rise, its morning glory sparkling on the water. His wings trailed softly to the ground, the sunlight starting to dance on the metallic surface. I wrapped my arms around Alex from the side, inhaling his wonderful smell. I closed my eyes in shear happiness.

He turned and wrapped his arms around me. He was silent as he stared down at me, his gray eyes burning with intensity. I saw a million words running through them, unable to find exactly the ones to express the things he had to say.

I reached up to my tiptoes and lightly pressed my lips to his. They tingled as I pulled away.

Alex held my eyes again and my heart suddenly started racing for a reason I didn't understand. He stepped away from me slightly, and very slowly, dropped to one knee.

A single, pure white and perfect feather softly floated to the ground. My heart nearly beat out of my chest.

"Jessica, will you marry me?"

ACKWNOLEDGMENTS

I owe some huge thank yous to a lot of people. First, to my family for always being supportive. I love you all and you all inspire me. A huge thank you to Jenni Merritt for always being there for me when I need to rant about writing and for her never-ending support. And a huge thank you to her for helping me with the cover for *Forsaken*. Thank you to *The Teen Book Scene* and the entire blogging community for so much help and support in getting the Fall of Angels series out there. You have been awesome. And lastly, to you. Thank *you* so much for your support! It means the world to me.

Keary Taylor grew up along the foothills of the Rocky Mountains where she started creating imaginary worlds and daring characters who always fell in love. She now resides on a tiny island in the Pacific Northwest with her husband and their two young children. She continues to have an overactive imagination that frequently keeps her up at night. She is the author of THE FALL OF ANGELS trilogy, THE EDEN TRILOGY, and WHAT I DIDN'T SAY.

To learn more about Keary and her writing process, please visit **www.KearyTaylor.com**

THE FALL OF ANGELS TRILOGY

Branded

Forsaken

Vindicated

Afterlife: the Novelette Companion to Vindicated

ALSO BY KEARY TAYLOR

THE EDEN TRILOGY

The Bane

The Human

The Eve

The Raid (an Eden short story)

The Ashes (an Eden prequel)

What I Didn't Say

THE McCAIN SAGA

Ever After Drake

Moments of Julian

Depths of Lake

Playing it Kale